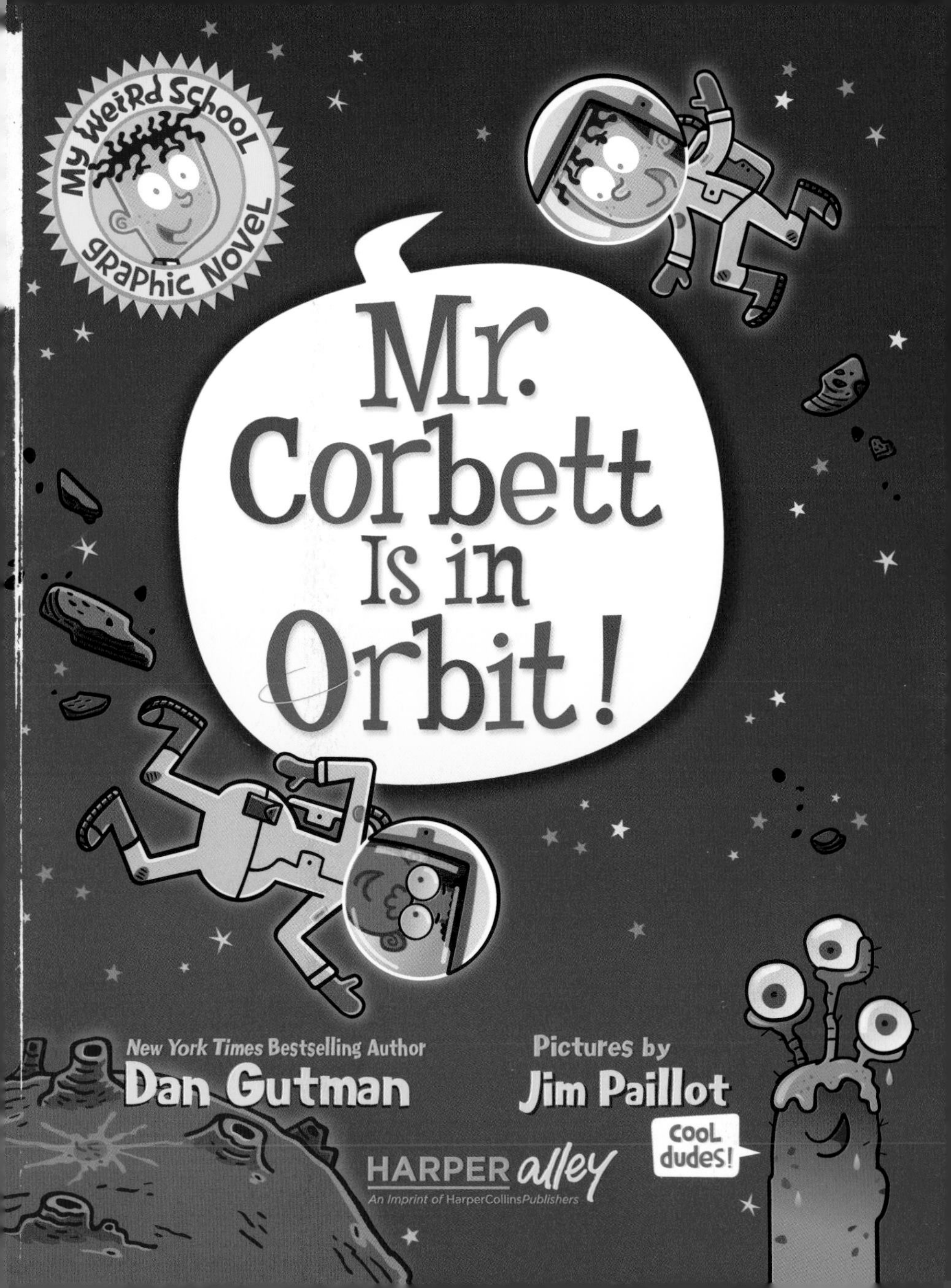
My Weird School graphic Novel
Mr. Corbett Is in Orbit!
New York Times Bestselling Author
Dan Gutman
Pictures by
Jim Paillot
Cool dudes!
HARPER alley
An Imprint of HarperCollinsPublishers

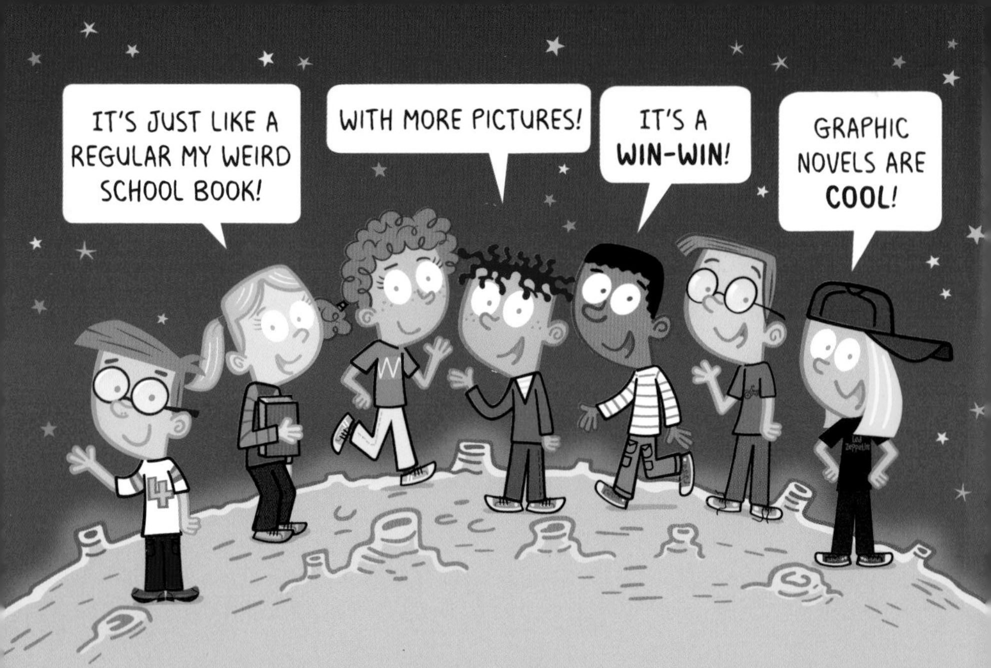
IT'S JUST LIKE A REGULAR MY WEIRD SCHOOL BOOK!
WITH MORE PICTURES!
IT'S A **WIN-WIN!**
GRAPHIC NOVELS ARE **COOL!**

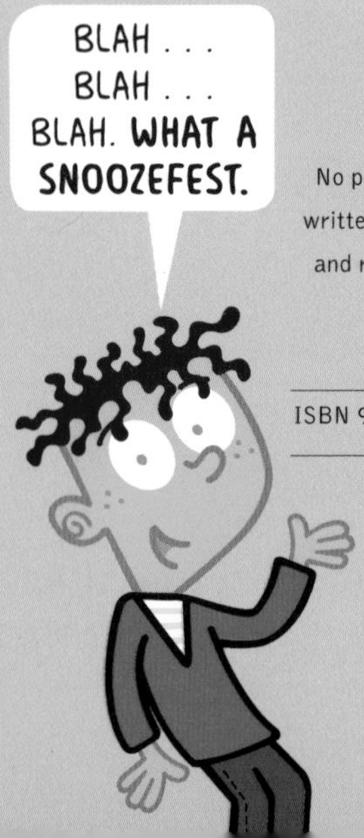
BLAH . . . BLAH . . . BLAH. **WHAT A SNOOZEFEST.**

My Weird School Graphic Novel: Mr. Corbett Is in Orbit!

 For information address HarperCollins Children's Books, a division of HarperCollins Publishers, 195 Broadway, New York, NY 10007.

www.harpercollinschildrens.com

ISBN 978-0-06-294761-1 (pbk. bdg.) — ISBN 978-0-06-294762-8 (hardcover bdg.)

Typography by Martha Maynard

20 21 22 23 24 EP 10 9 8 7 6 5 4 3 2 1

❖

First Edition

Warning!

THIS BOOK CONTAINS SCENES OF GRAPHIC VIOLINS. READING IT MAY CAUSE SIDE EFFECTS SUCH AS DIZZINESS, RUNNY NOSE, HEARTBURN, SWELLING, AND ITCHY LIPS. READ ONLY AS DIRECTED. KEEP OUT OF REACH OF CHILDREN. AVOID CONTACT WITH EYES. IF SWALLOWED, GET MEDICAL HELP RIGHT AWAY. IF RASH DEVELOPS, DISCONTINUE USE. STORE AT ROOM TEMPERATURE.

YOU CAN'T SAY WE DIDN'T WARN YOU. WELL, YOU CAN SAY IT, BUT YOU'LL BE LYING. IF YOU WANT TO READ A HEARTWARMING GRAPHIC NOVEL ABOUT CUTE PUPPIES, YOU PICKED THE WRONG BOOK.

To all the kids who have read My Weird School, and all the parents, teachers, and librarians who have shared the books with their sons, daughters, and students

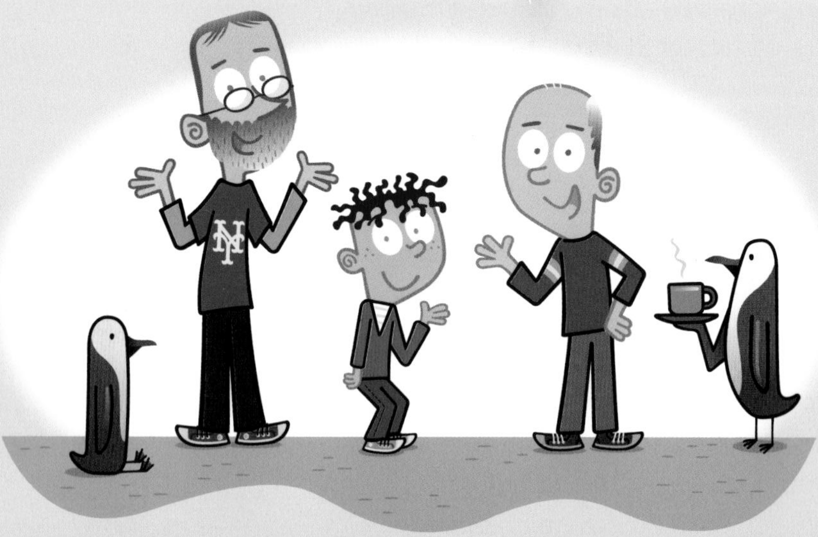

Table of Contents*

*I DON'T SEE ANY **TABLE**. WHAT DO **TABLES** HAVE TO DO WITH ANYTHING?

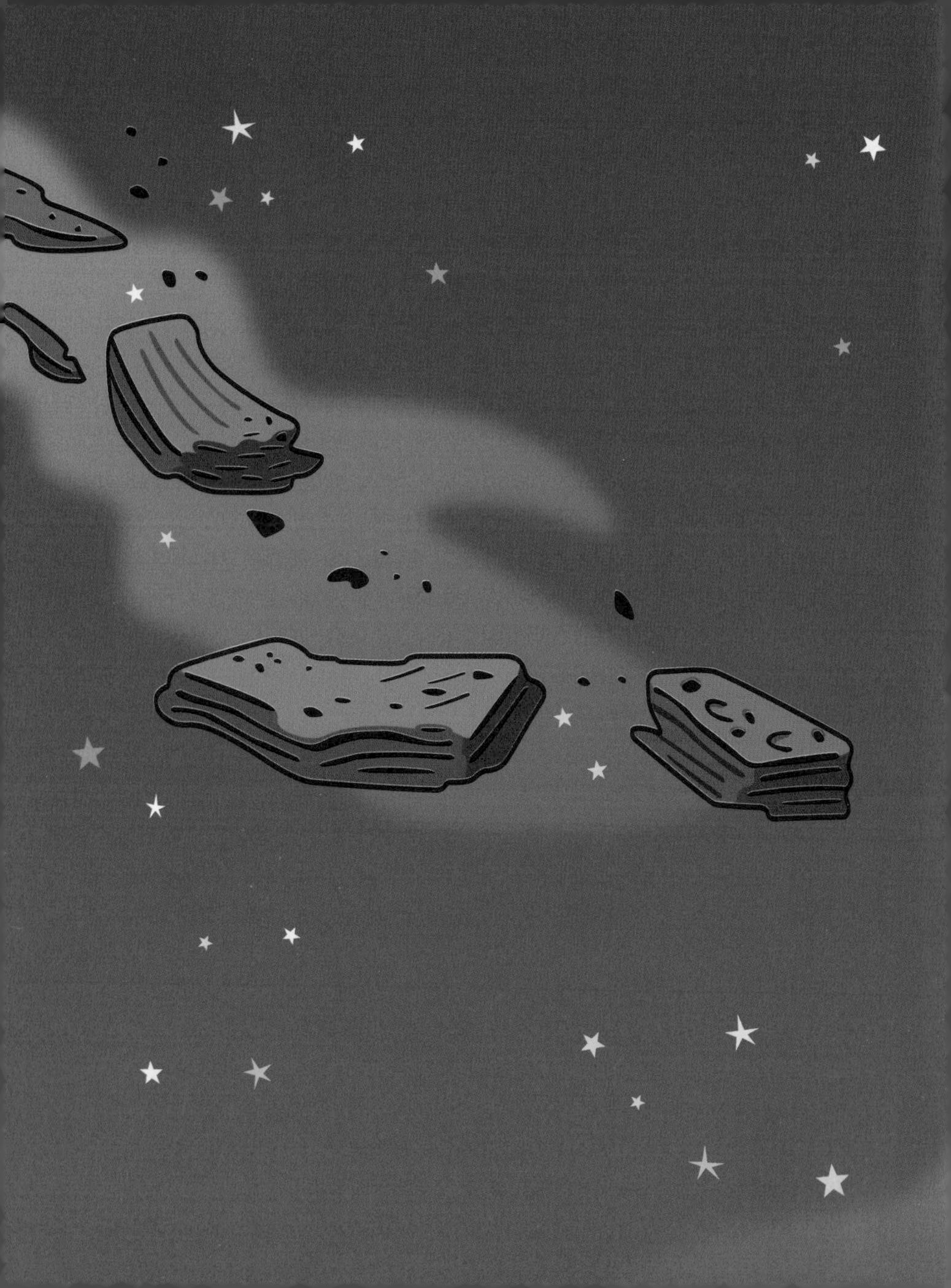

CHAPTER 1

The Beginning

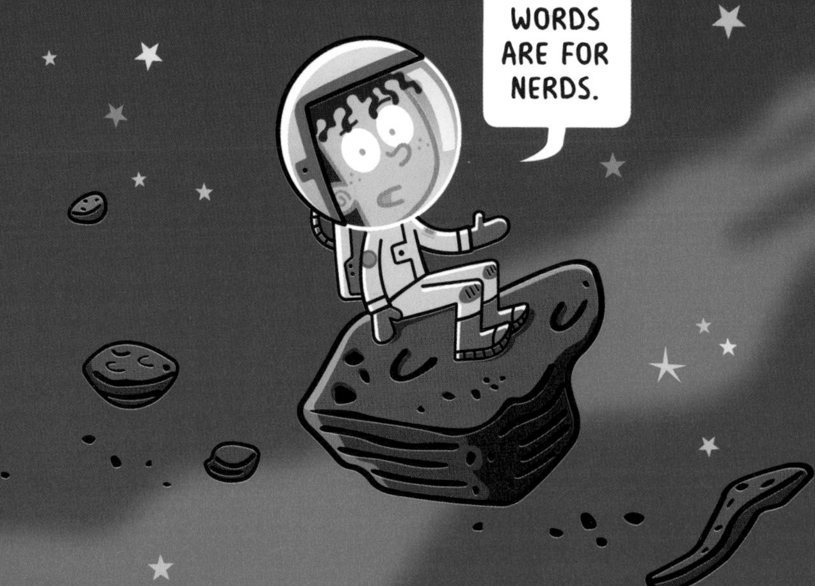
WORDS ARE FOR NERDS.

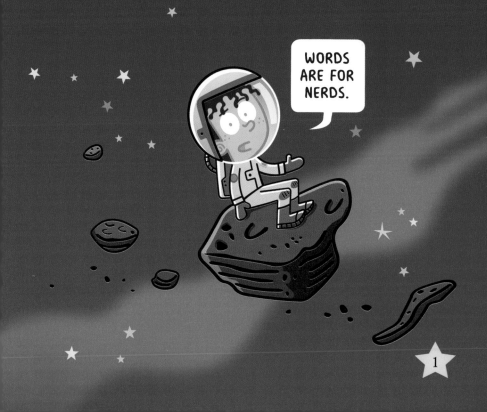

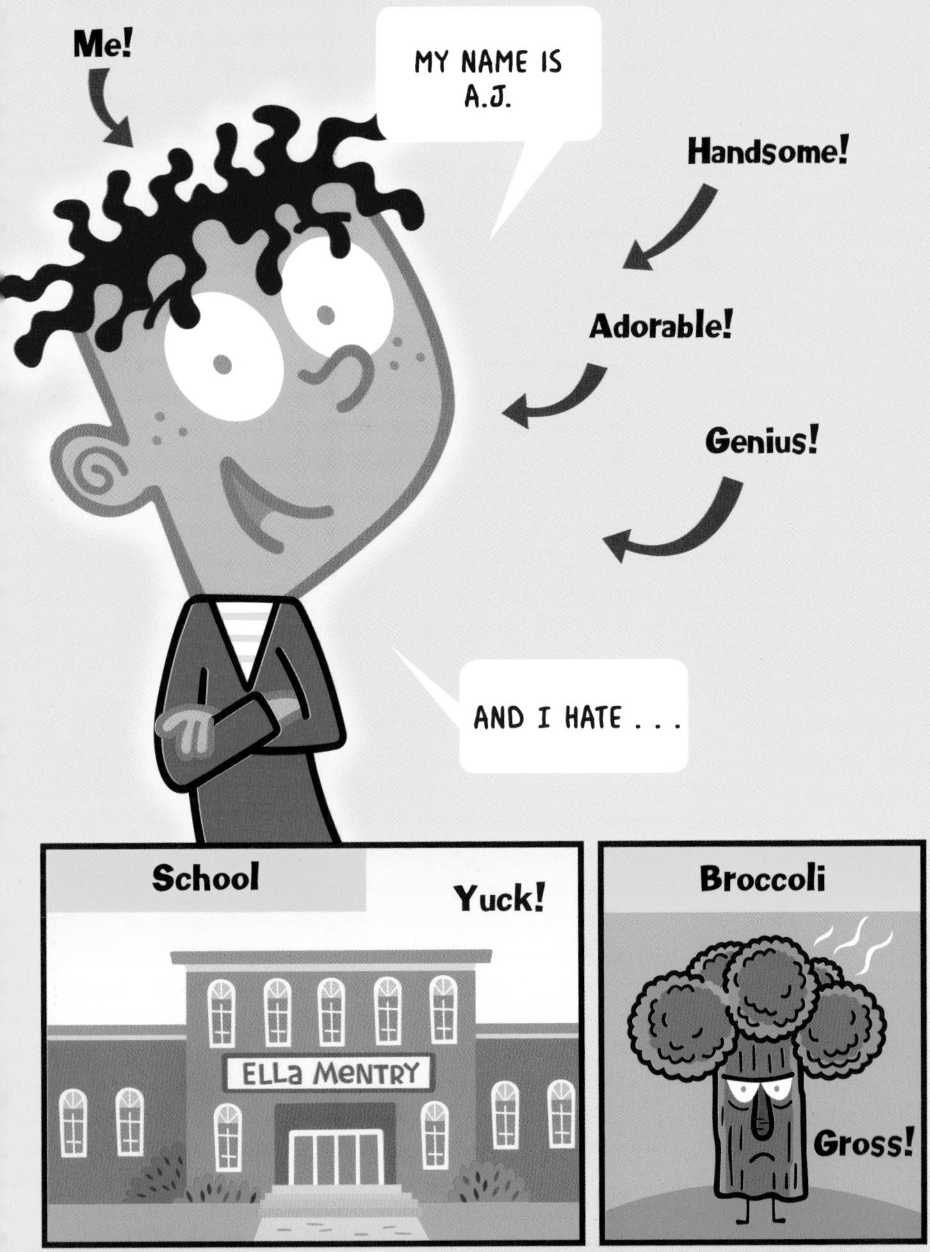
Me!
MY NAME IS A.J.
Handsome!
Adorable!
Genius!
AND I HATE . . .
School
Yuck!
ELLa MENTRY
Broccoli
Gross!

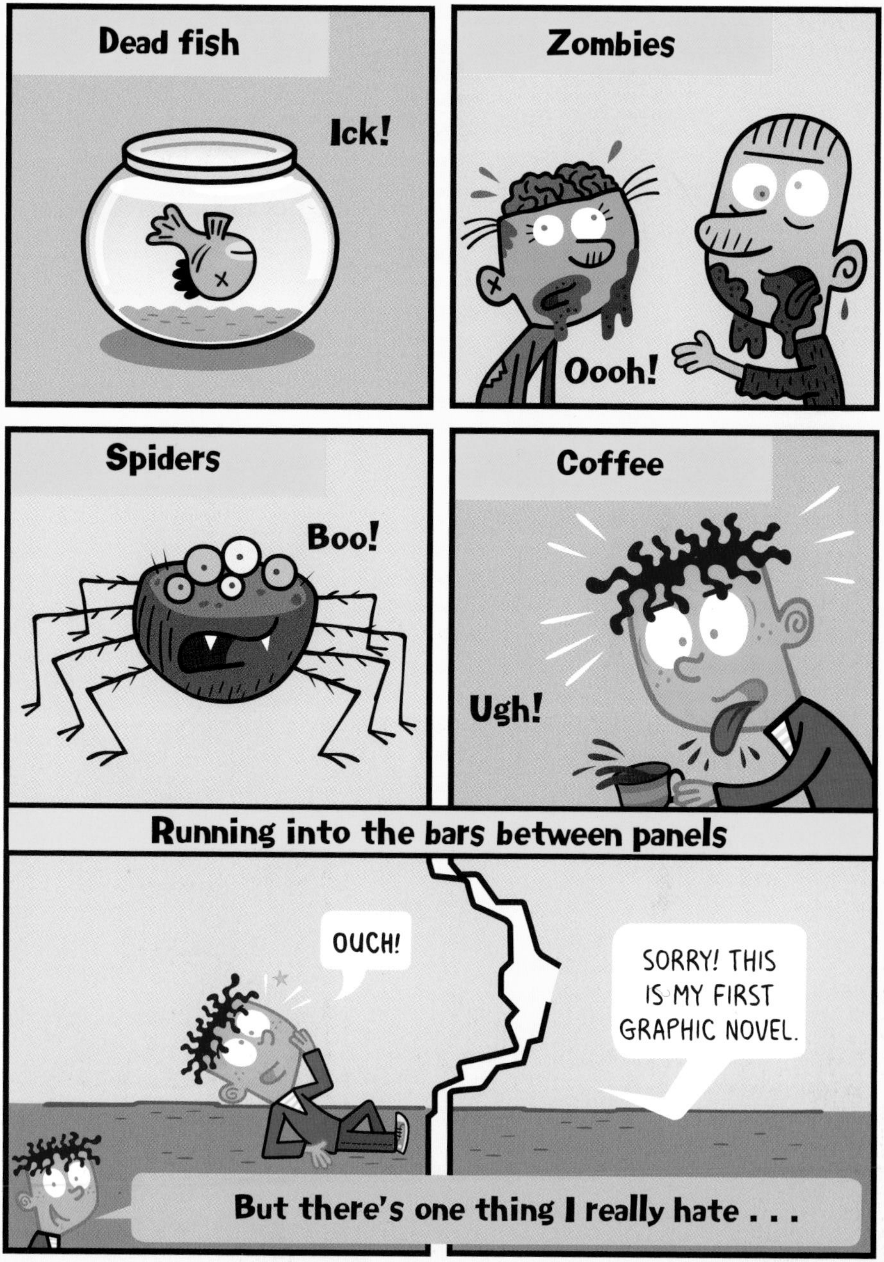
Dead fish
Ick!
Zombies
Oooh!
Spiders
Boo!
Coffee
Ugh!
Running into the bars between panels
OUCH!
SORRY! THIS IS MY FIRST GRAPHIC NOVEL.
But there's one thing I really hate . . .

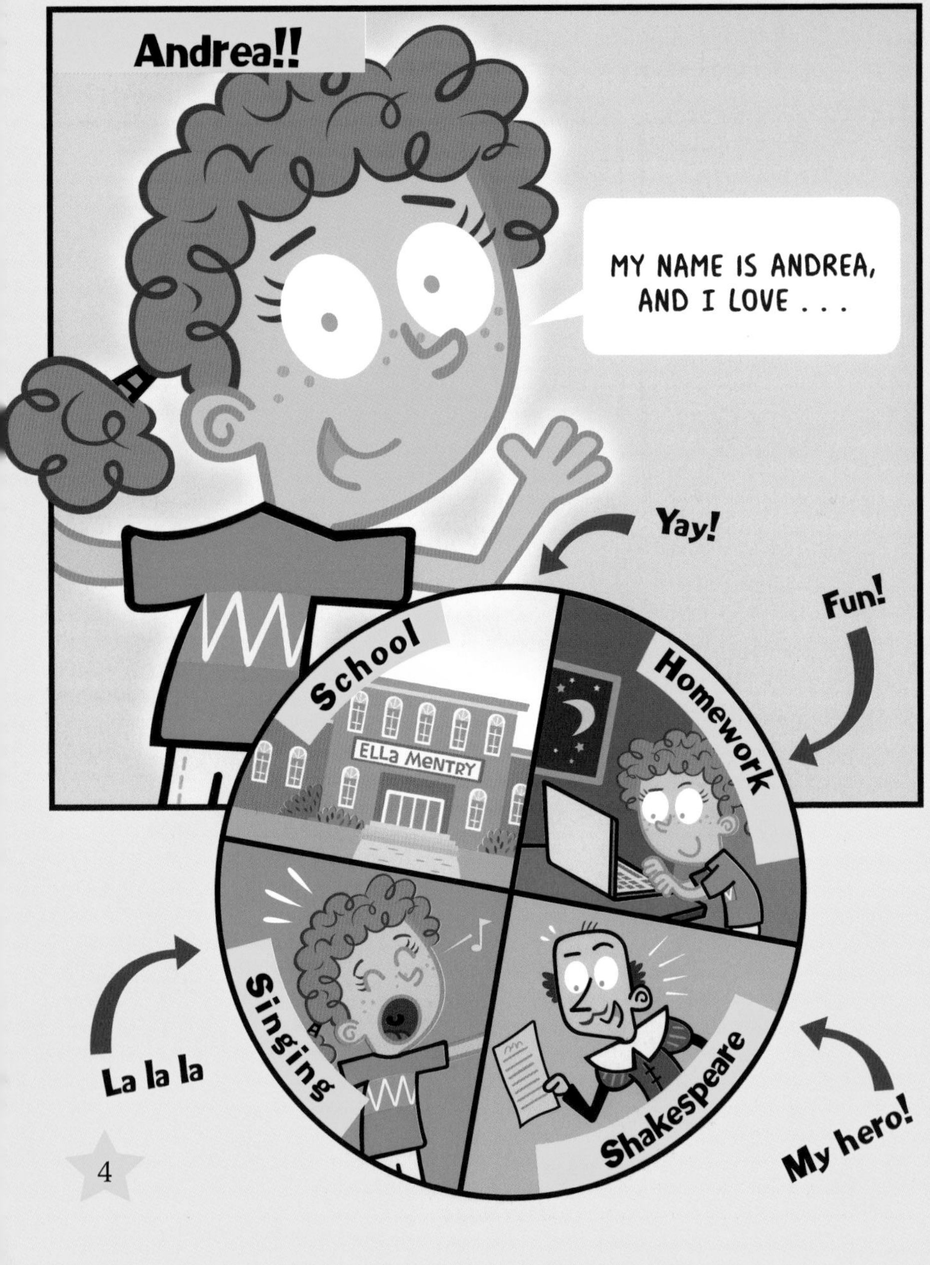
Andrea!!
MY NAME IS ANDREA, AND I LOVE . . .
Yay!
School
ELLa MENTRY
Fun!
Homework
La la la
Singing
My hero!
Shakespeare

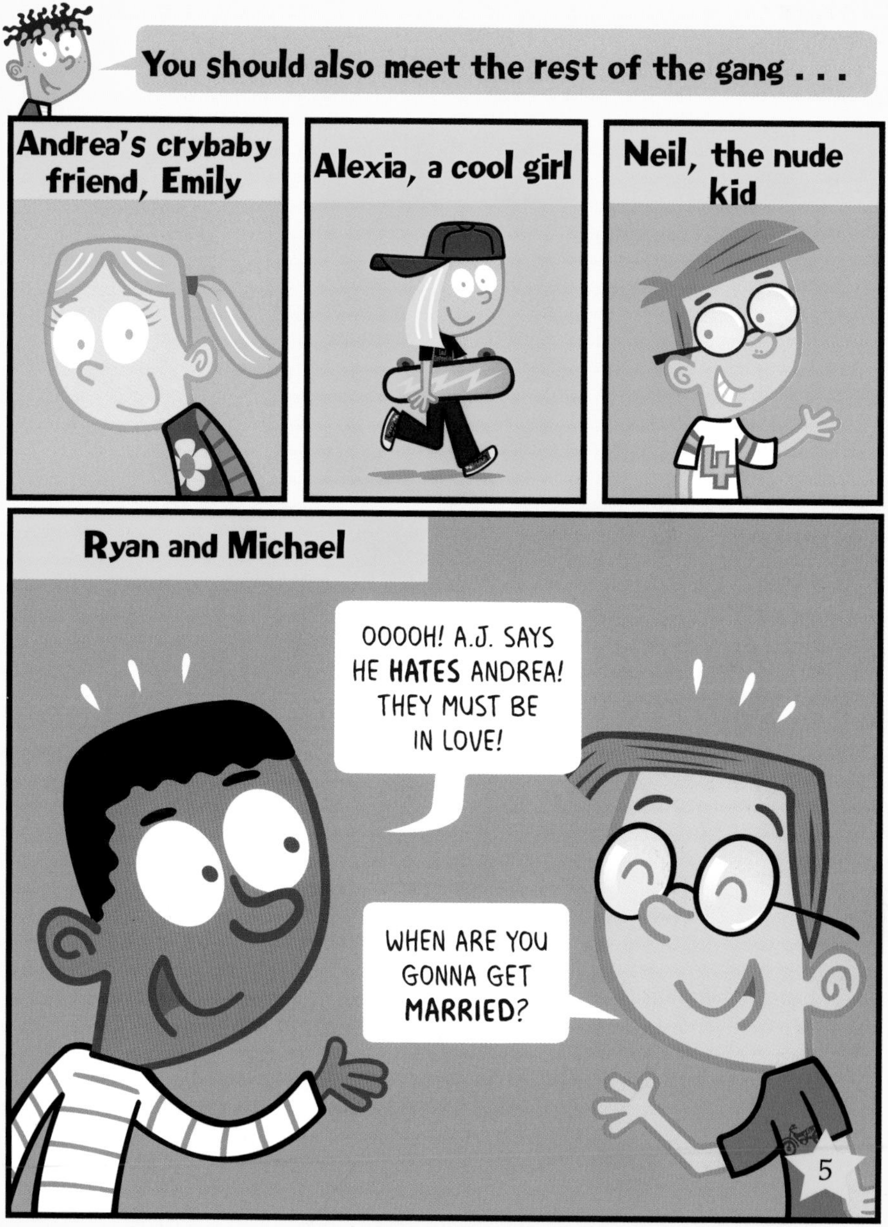
You should also meet the rest of the gang . . .
Andrea's crybaby friend, Emily
Alexia, a cool girl
Neil, the nude kid
Ryan and Michael
OOOOH! A.J. SAYS HE **HATES** ANDREA! THEY MUST BE IN LOVE!
WHEN ARE YOU GONNA GET **MARRIED**?

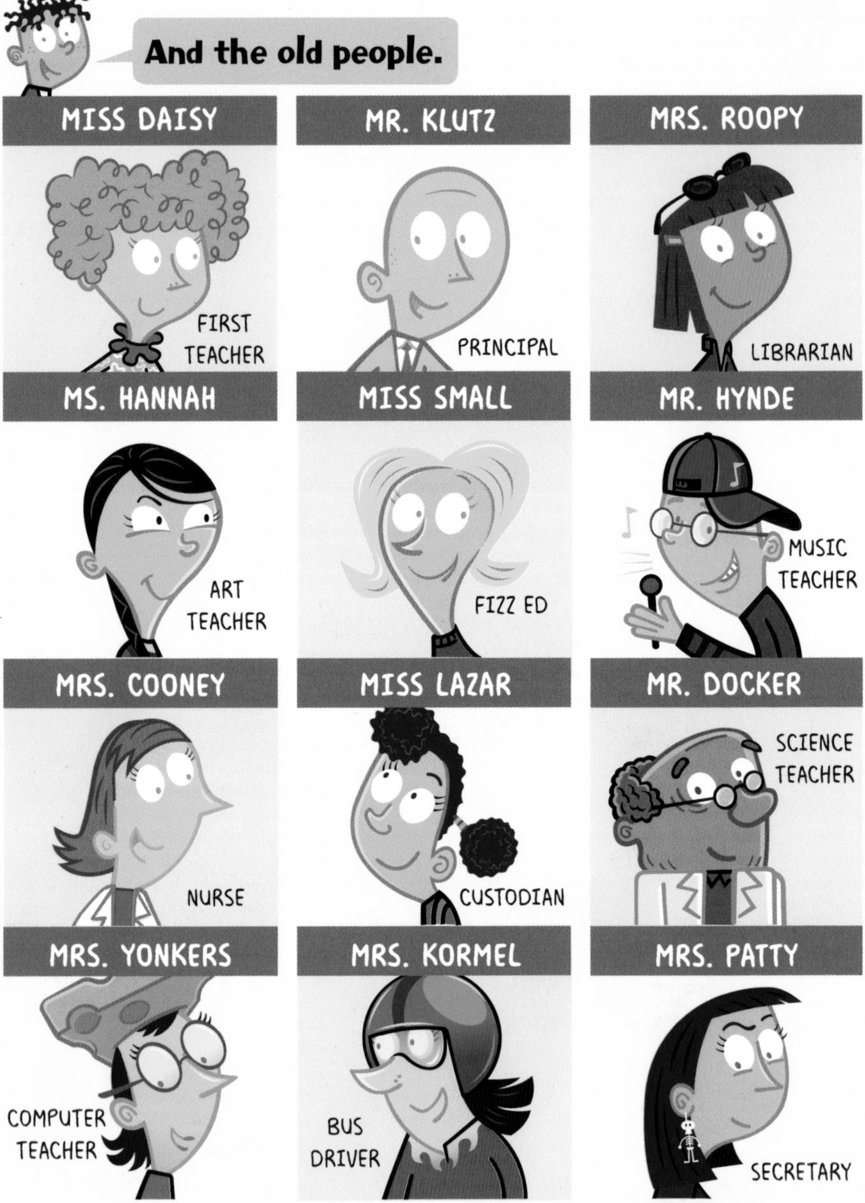
And the old people.
MISS DAISY
FIRST TEACHER
MR. KLUTZ
PRINCIPAL
MRS. ROOPY
LIBRARIAN
MS. HANNAH
ART TEACHER
MISS SMALL
FIZZ ED
MR. HYNDE
MUSIC TEACHER
MRS. COONEY
NURSE
MISS LAZAR
CUSTODIAN
MR. DOCKER
SCIENCE TEACHER
MRS. YONKERS
COMPUTER TEACHER
MRS. KORMEL
BUS DRIVER
MRS. PATTY
SECRETARY

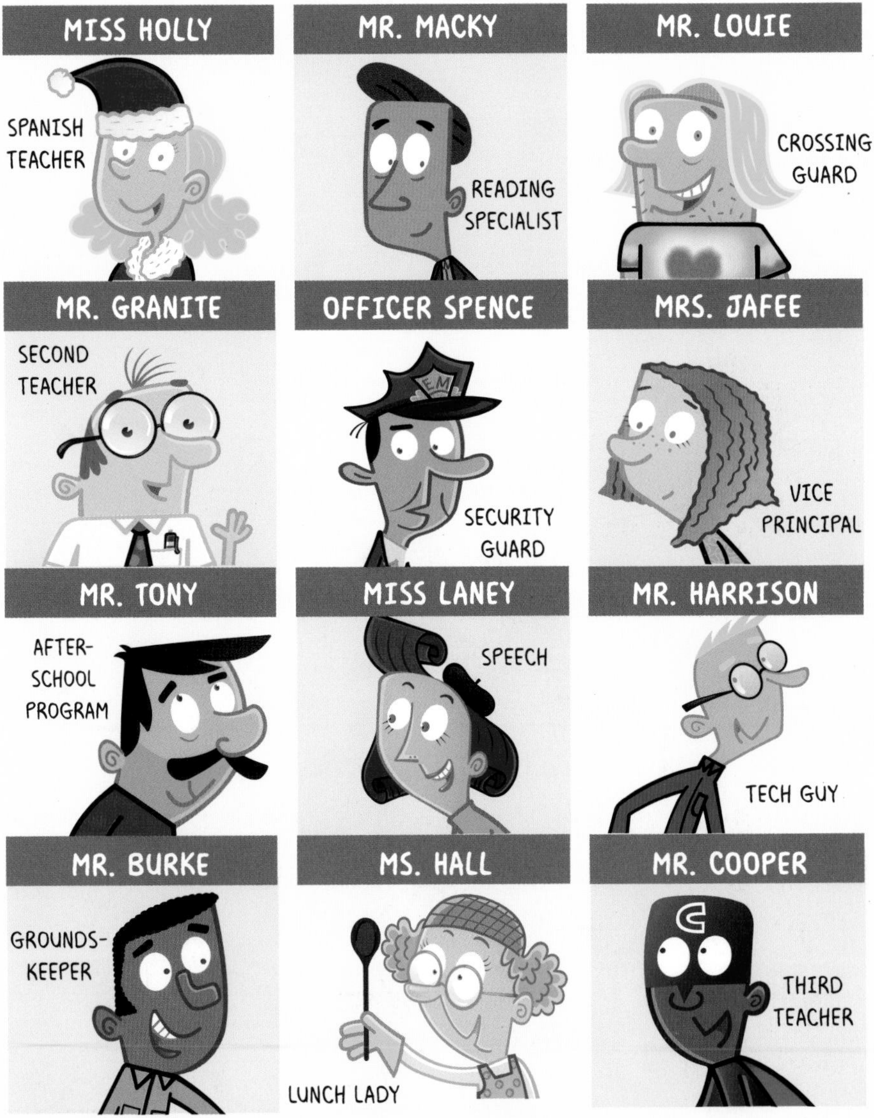
MISS HOLLY
SPANISH TEACHER
MR. MACKY
READING SPECIALIST
MR. LOUIE
CROSSING GUARD
MR. GRANITE
SECOND TEACHER
OFFICER SPENCE
E.M.
SECURITY GUARD
MRS. JAFEE
VICE PRINCIPAL
MR. TONY
AFTER-SCHOOL PROGRAM
MISS LANEY
SPEECH
MR. HARRISON
TECH GUY
MR. BURKE
GROUNDS-KEEPER
MS. HALL
LUNCH LADY
MR. COOPER
THIRD TEACHER

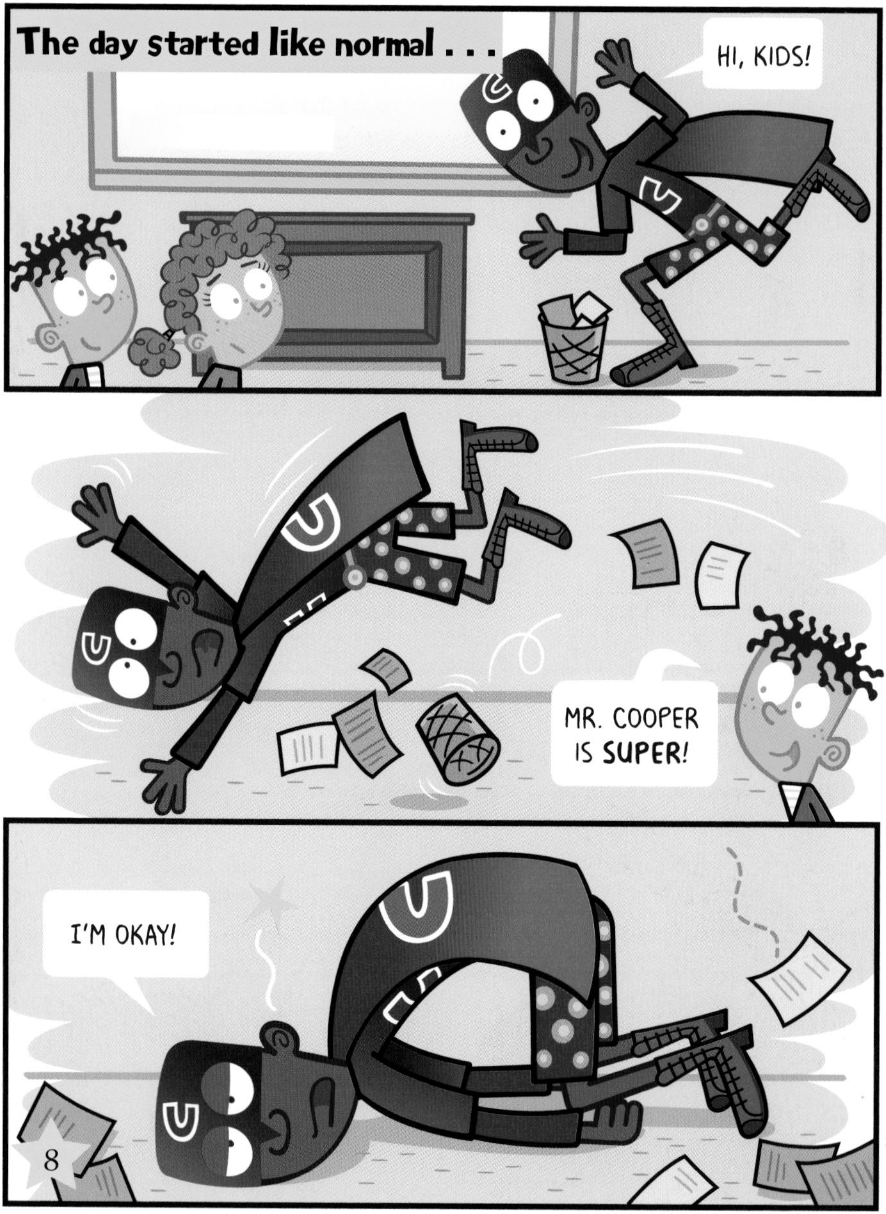
The day started like normal . . .
HI, KIDS!
MR. COOPER IS SUPER!
I'M OKAY!

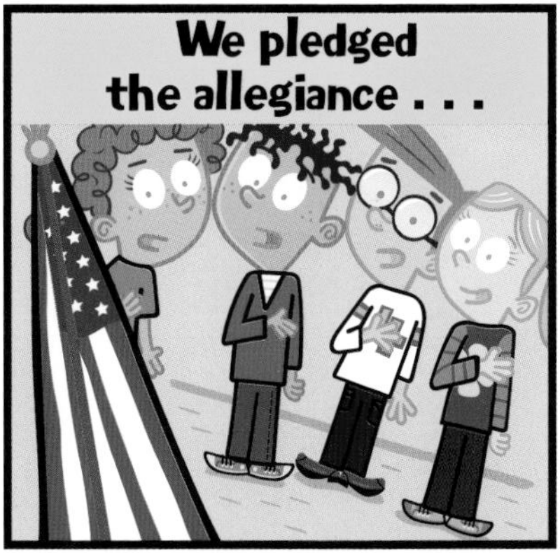
We pledged the allegiance . . .

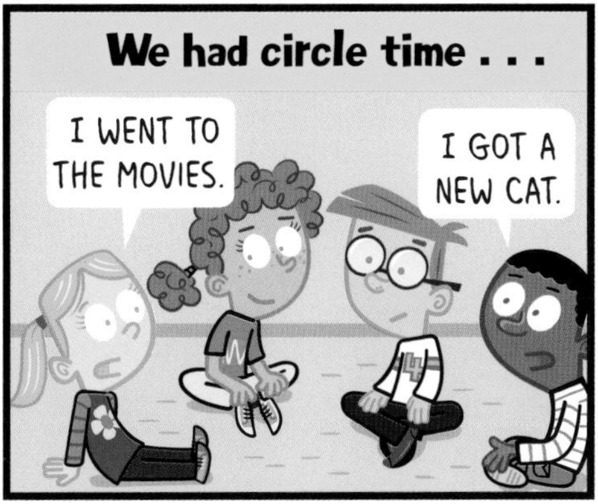
We had circle time . . .
I WENT TO THE MOVIES.
I GOT A NEW CAT.

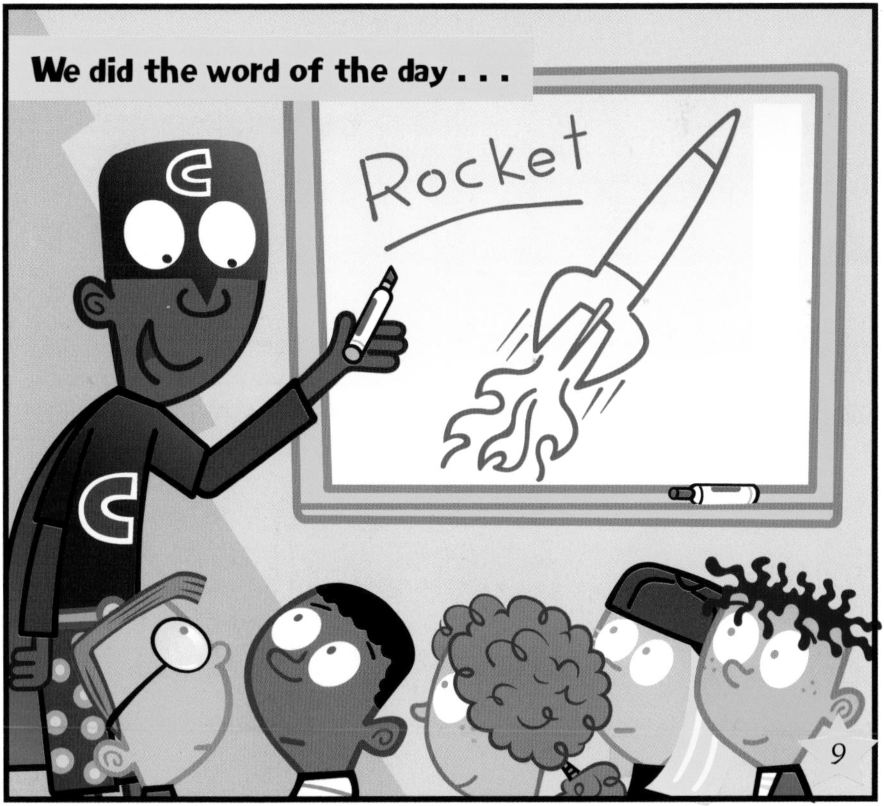
We did the word of the day . . .
Rocket

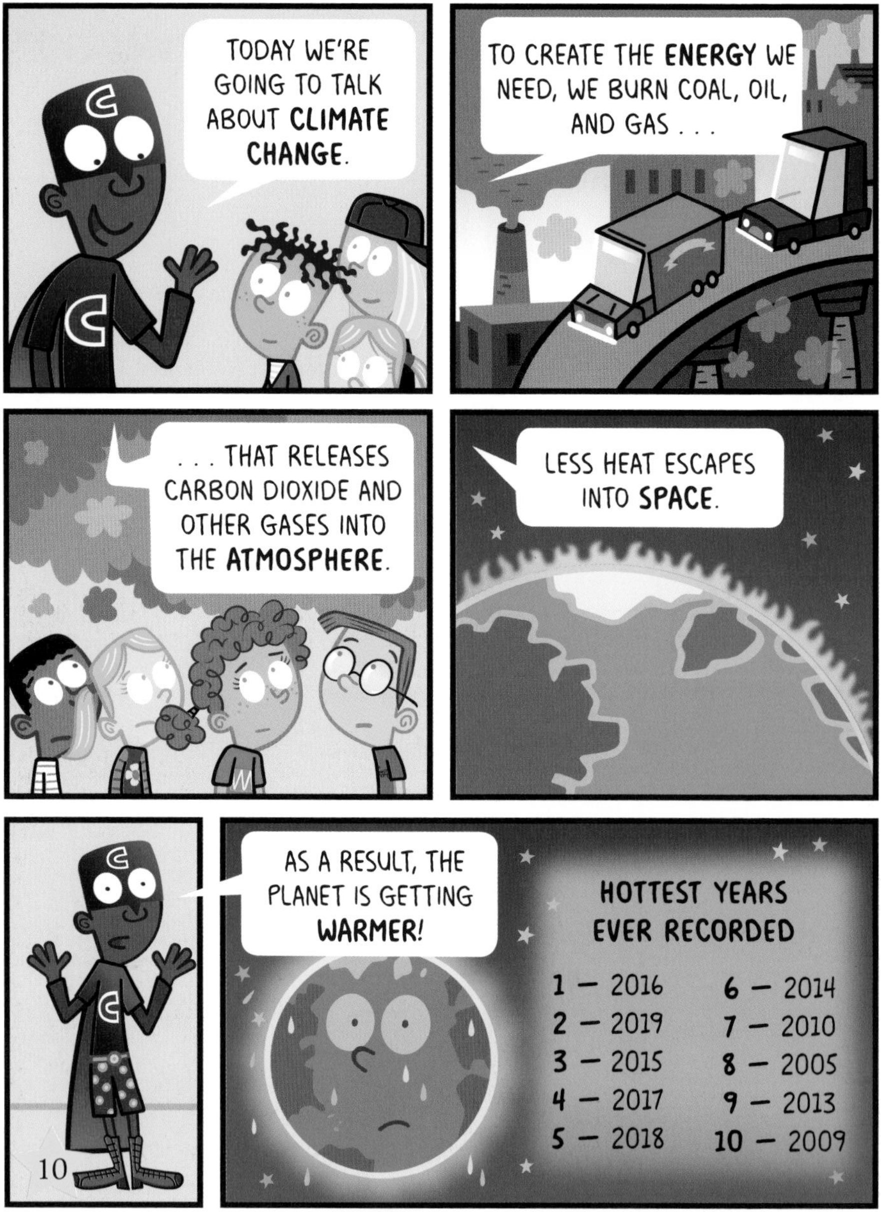
TODAY WE'RE GOING TO TALK ABOUT **CLIMATE CHANGE**.
TO CREATE THE **ENERGY** WE NEED, WE BURN COAL, OIL, AND GAS . . .
. . . THAT RELEASES CARBON DIOXIDE AND OTHER GASES INTO THE **ATMOSPHERE**.
LESS HEAT ESCAPES INTO **SPACE**.
AS A RESULT, THE PLANET IS GETTING **WARMER!**
HOTTEST YEARS EVER RECORDED
1 — 2016
2 — 2019
3 — 2015
4 — 2017
5 — 2018
6 — 2014
7 — 2010
8 — 2005
9 — 2013
10 — 2009

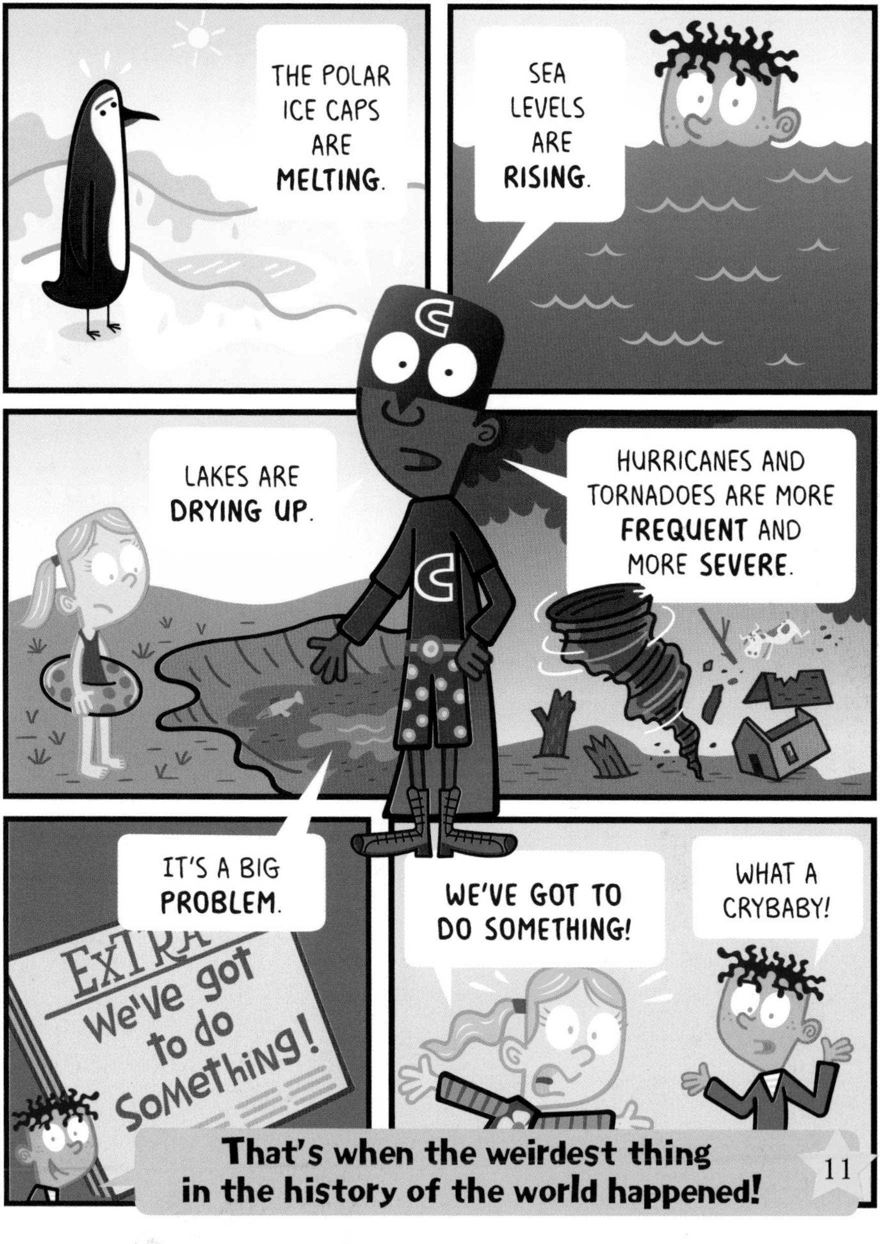
THE POLAR ICE CAPS ARE MELTING.
SEA LEVELS ARE RISING.
LAKES ARE DRYING UP.
HURRICANES AND TORNADOES ARE MORE FREQUENT AND MORE SEVERE.
IT'S A BIG PROBLEM.
EXTRA
We've got to do Something!
WE'VE GOT TO DO SOMETHING!
WHAT A CRYBABY!
That's when the weirdest thing in the history of the world happened!

READER SURVEY

THIS IS OUR FIRST MY WEIRD SCHOOL GRAPHIC NOVEL. PLEASE TAKE THIS
SHORT SURVEY TO HELP US KNOW WHAT YOU LIKE OR DON'T LIKE . . .

WHAT DO YOU THINK OF THE BOOK SO FAR?
- I LIKE IT
- I DON'T LIKE IT
- NONE OF YOUR BEESWAX
- I LIKE HOT DOGS
- WHAT DO HOT DOGS HAVE TO DO WITH ANYTHING?

DID THIS BOOK MAKE YOU . . .
- LAUGH
- CRY
- WANT TO READ ANOTHER MY WEIRD SCHOOL BOOK
- VOMIT

IF YOU WERE STRANDED ON A DESERT ISLAND AND THIS BOOK WAS WATERPROOF, WOULD YOU USE IT TO BUILD A LIFE RAFT?

WOULD YOU RECOMMEND THIS BOOK TO A DOG?
- YES
- NO
- YES AND NO
- IT DEPENDS ON THE DOG

HOW ABOUT TO A HAMSTER?

WHERE DID YOU GET THIS BOOK?
- AT A BOOKSTORE
- AT A LIBRARY
- ONLINE
- FROM A FRIEND
- FROM A GUY ON THE CORNER WEARING A TRENCH COAT

DID YOU TAKE A SHOWER OR BATH THIS WEEK? IF SO, PLEASE GIVE IT BACK.

WHAT DO YOU CALL A GUY HANGING ON A WALL?
- BOB
- WALLY
- ART
- DUMBHEAD

WHY DO BAGPIPERS WALK WHILE THEY PLAY?
- TO GET TO THE OTHER SIDE
- THEY'RE TRYING TO FIND A BATHROOM
- SO PEOPLE DON'T THROW ROTTEN FRUIT AT THEM
- THEY'RE TRYING TO GET AWAY FROM THE MUSIC

WHEN YOU FINISH READING THIS BOOK, YOU WILL . . .
- READ IT AGAIN
- DONATE IT TO A LIBRARY
- LEND IT TO A FRIEND
- USE IT TO GET YOUR CAMPFIRE STARTED
- EAT IT

13

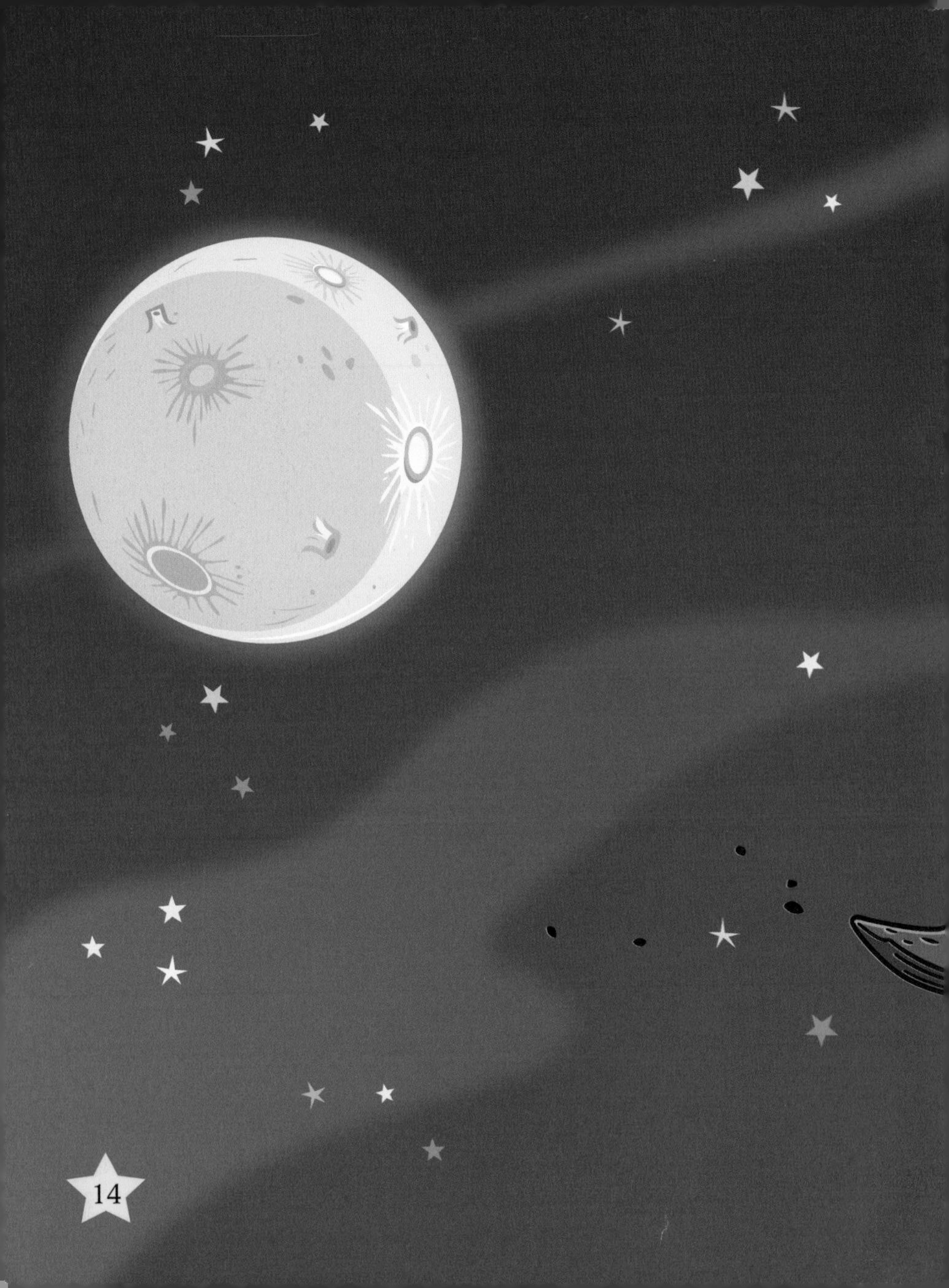

CHAPTER 2
After the Beginning

I HOPE I GET AN A!

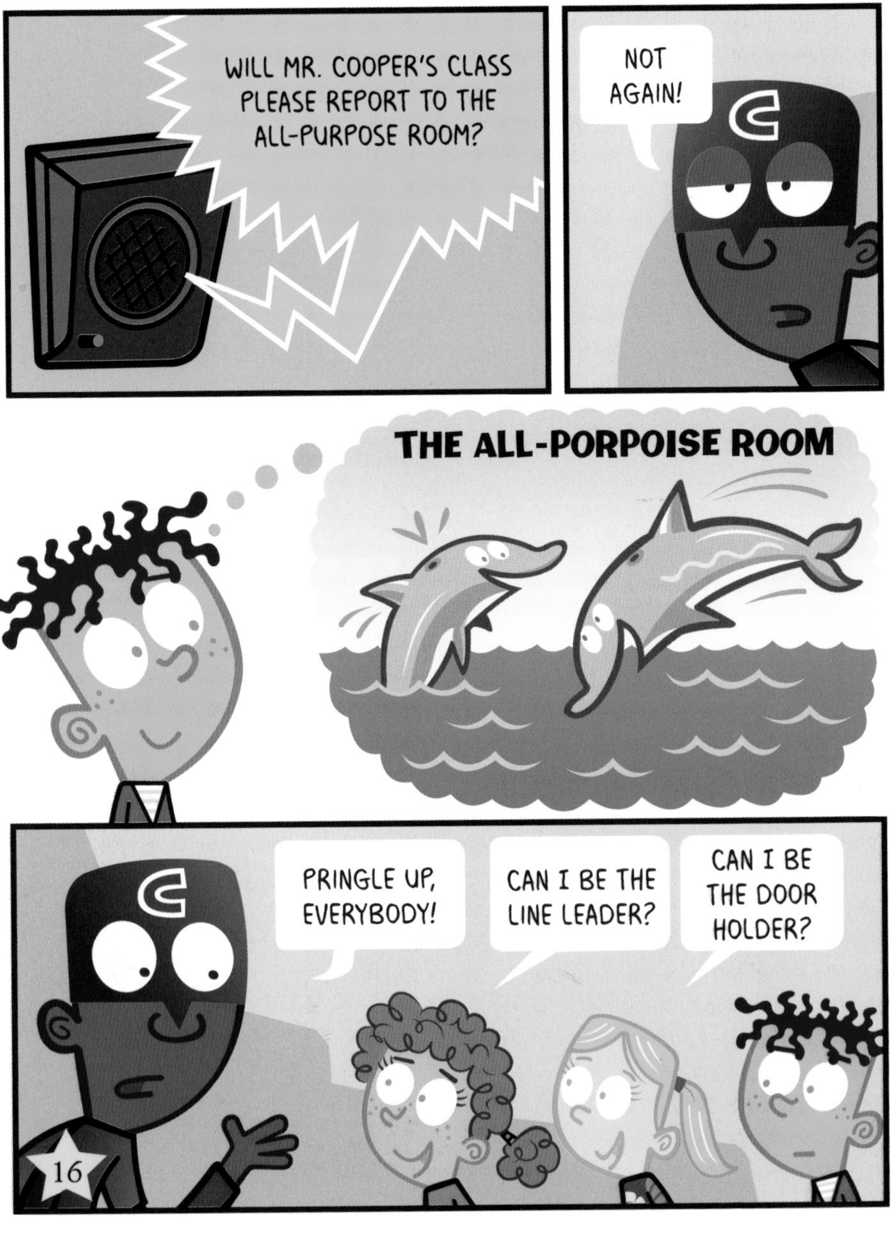
WILL MR. COOPER'S CLASS PLEASE REPORT TO THE ALL-PURPOSE ROOM?
NOT AGAIN!
THE ALL-PORPOISE ROOM
PRINGLE UP, EVERYBODY!
CAN I BE THE LINE LEADER?
CAN I BE THE DOOR HOLDER?

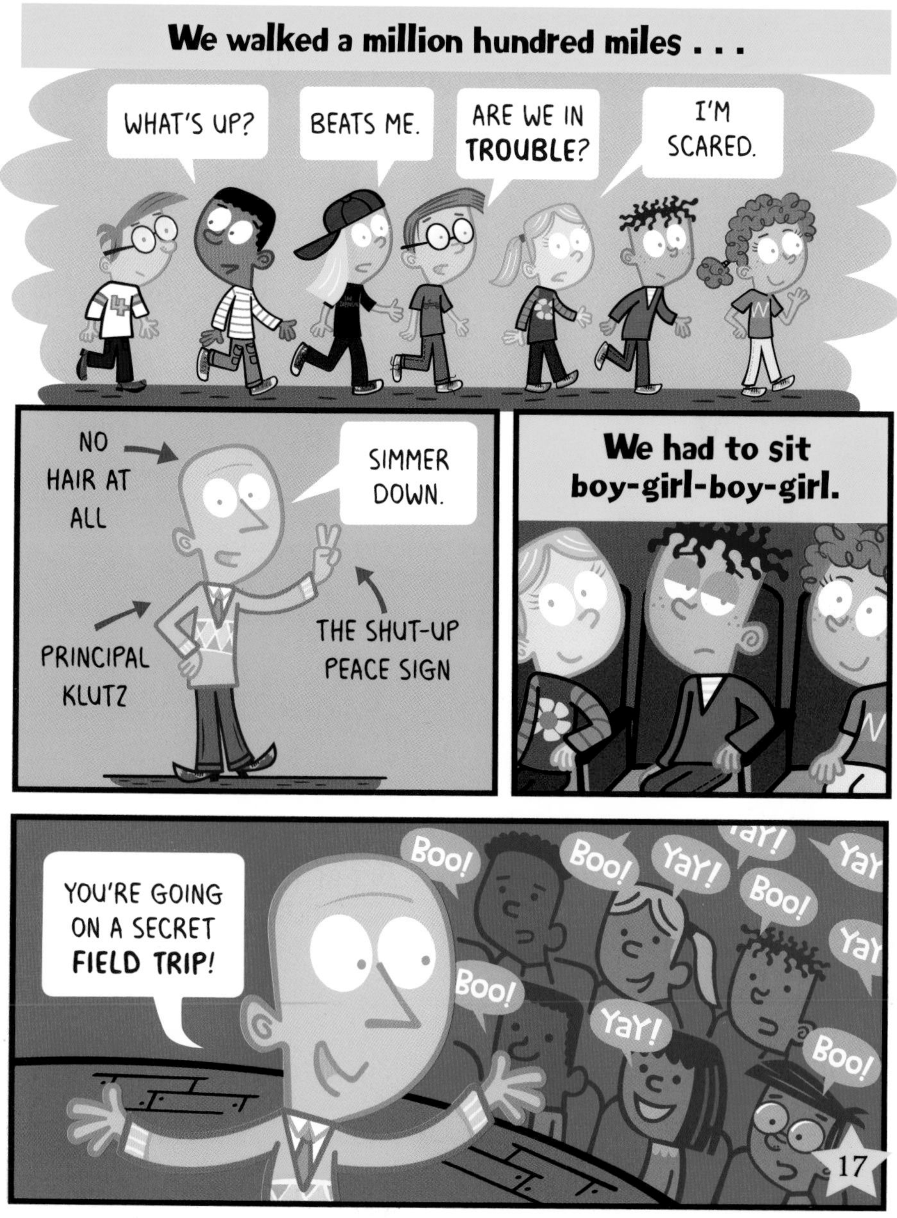
We walked a million hundred miles . . .
WHAT'S UP?
BEATS ME.
ARE WE IN TROUBLE?
I'M SCARED.
NO HAIR AT ALL
SIMMER DOWN.
PRINCIPAL KLUTZ
THE SHUT-UP PEACE SIGN
We had to sit boy-girl-boy-girl.
YOU'RE GOING ON A SECRET FIELD TRIP!
Boo!
Boo!
YaY!
Boo!
Boo!
YaY!
Boo!

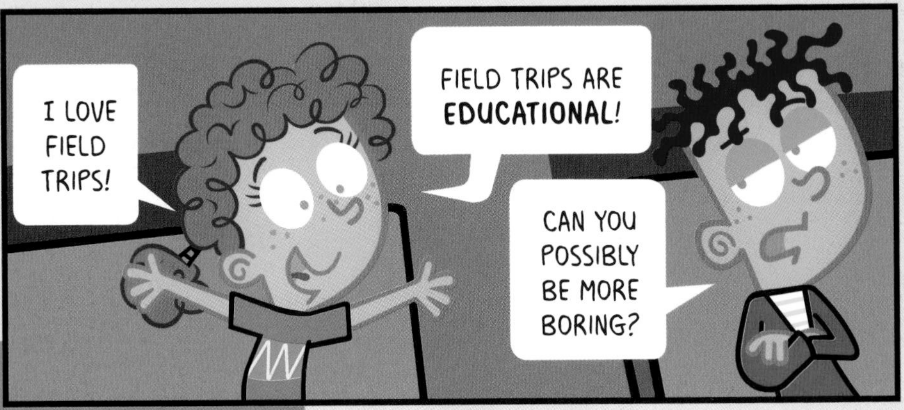
I LOVE FIELD TRIPS!
FIELD TRIPS ARE EDUCATIONAL!
CAN YOU POSSIBLY BE MORE BORING?

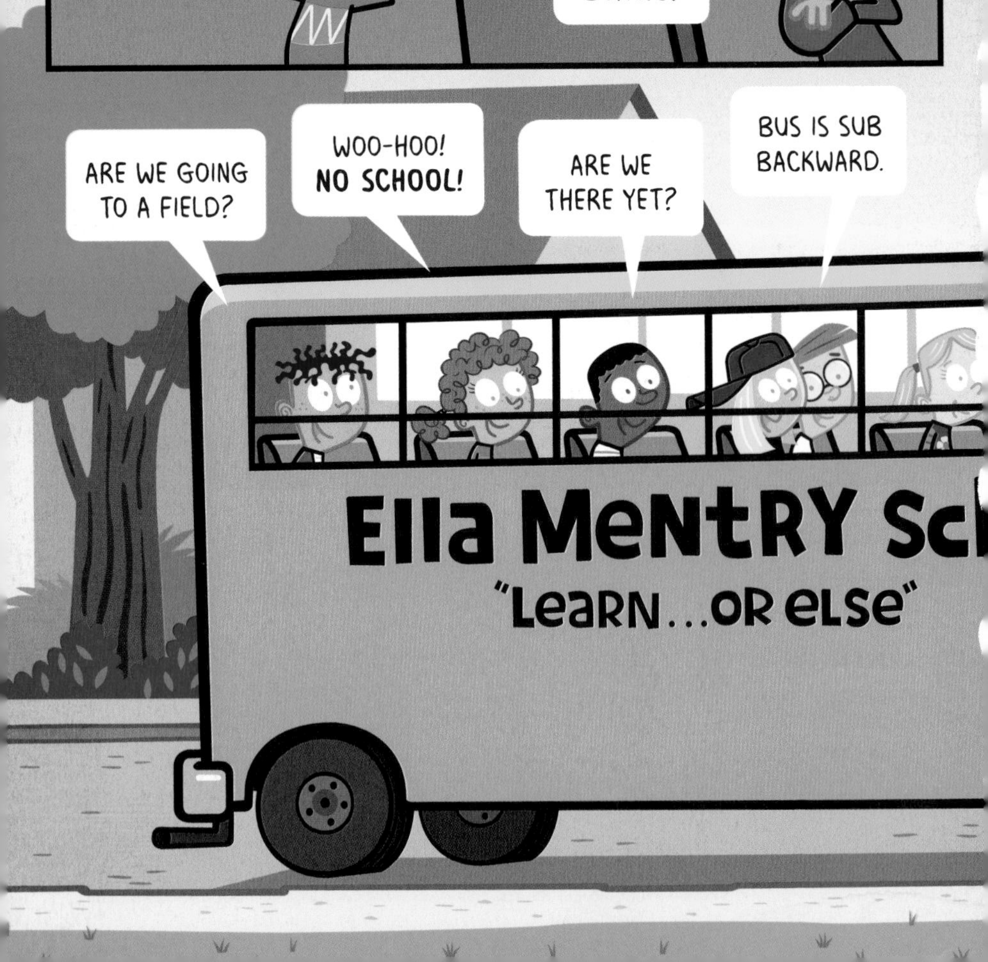
ARE WE GOING TO A FIELD?
WOO-HOO! NO SCHOOL!
ARE WE THERE YET?
BUS IS SUB BACKWARD.
"LEARN...OR ELSE"

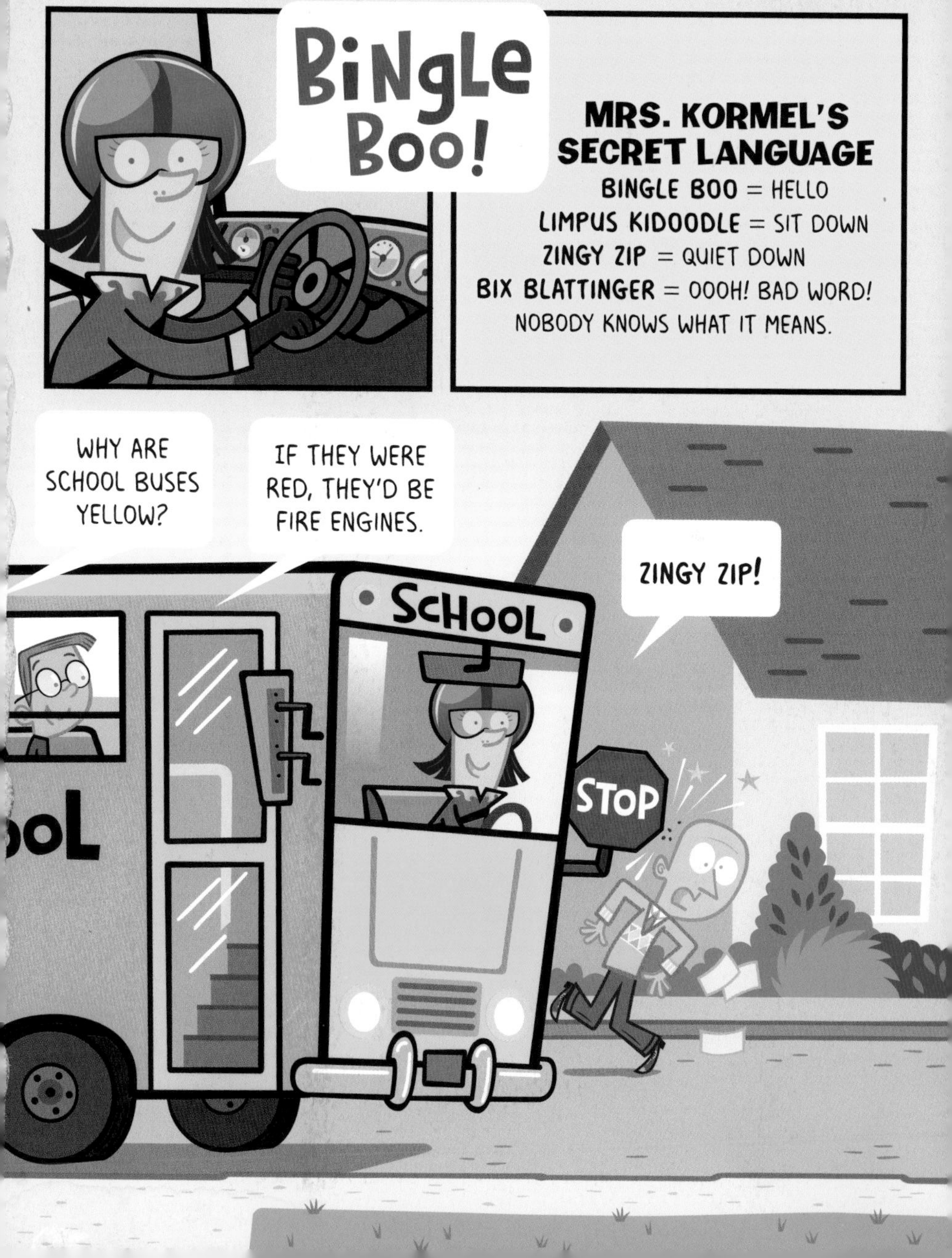
Bingle Boo!
MRS. KORMEL'S SECRET LANGUAGE
BINGLE BOO = HELLO
LIMPUS KIDOODLE = SIT DOWN
ZINGY ZIP = QUIET DOWN
BIX BLATTINGER = OOOH! BAD WORD! NOBODY KNOWS WHAT IT MEANS.
WHY ARE SCHOOL BUSES YELLOW?
IF THEY WERE RED, THEY'D BE FIRE ENGINES.
ZINGY ZIP!
SCHOOL
STOP

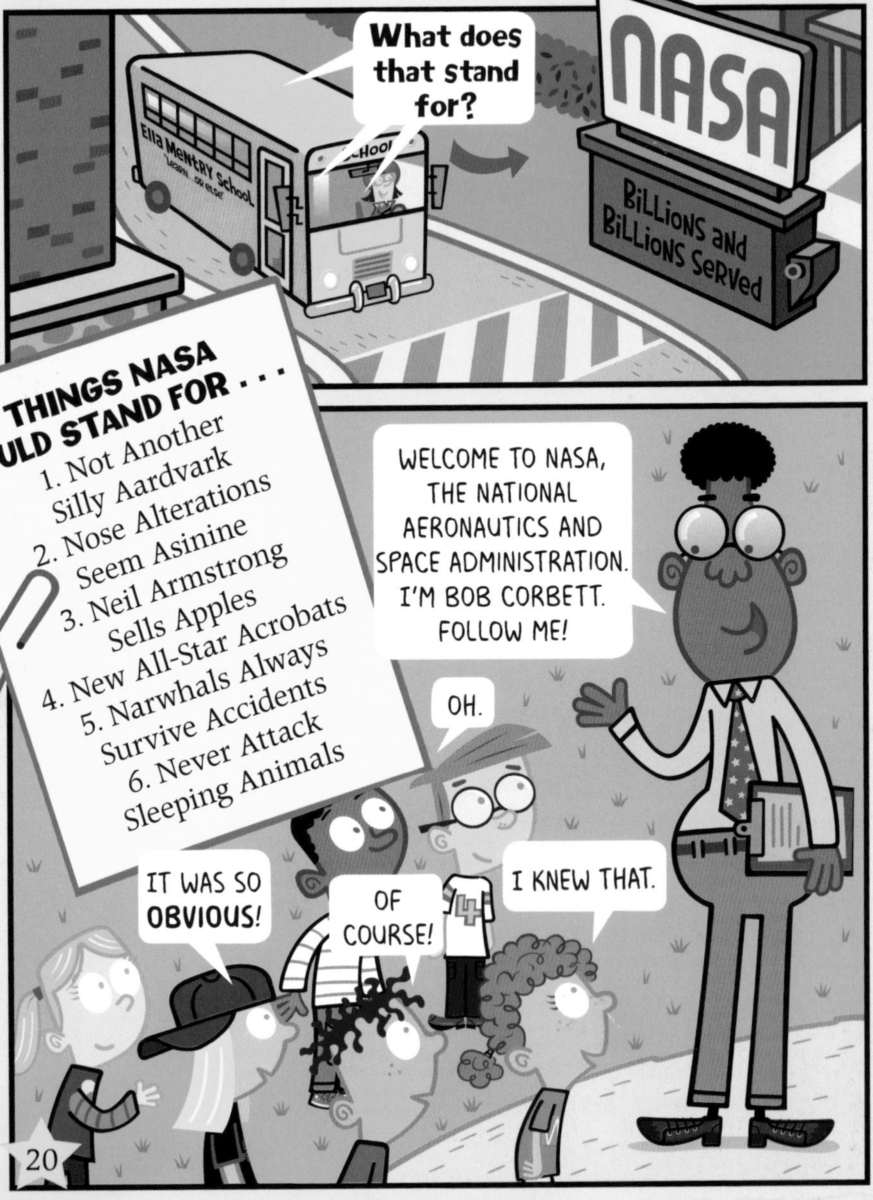

Ella Mentry School
"Learn... or else"
School
What does that stand for?
NASA
Billions and Billions Served
THINGS NASA COULD STAND FOR . . .
1. Not Another Silly Aardvark
2. Nose Alterations Seem Asinine
3. Neil Armstrong Sells Apples
4. New All-Star Acrobats
5. Narwhals Always Survive Accidents
6. Never Attack Sleeping Animals
WELCOME TO NASA, THE NATIONAL AERONAUTICS AND SPACE ADMINISTRATION. I'M BOB CORBETT. FOLLOW ME!
OH.
IT WAS SO OBVIOUS!
OF COURSE!
I KNEW THAT.

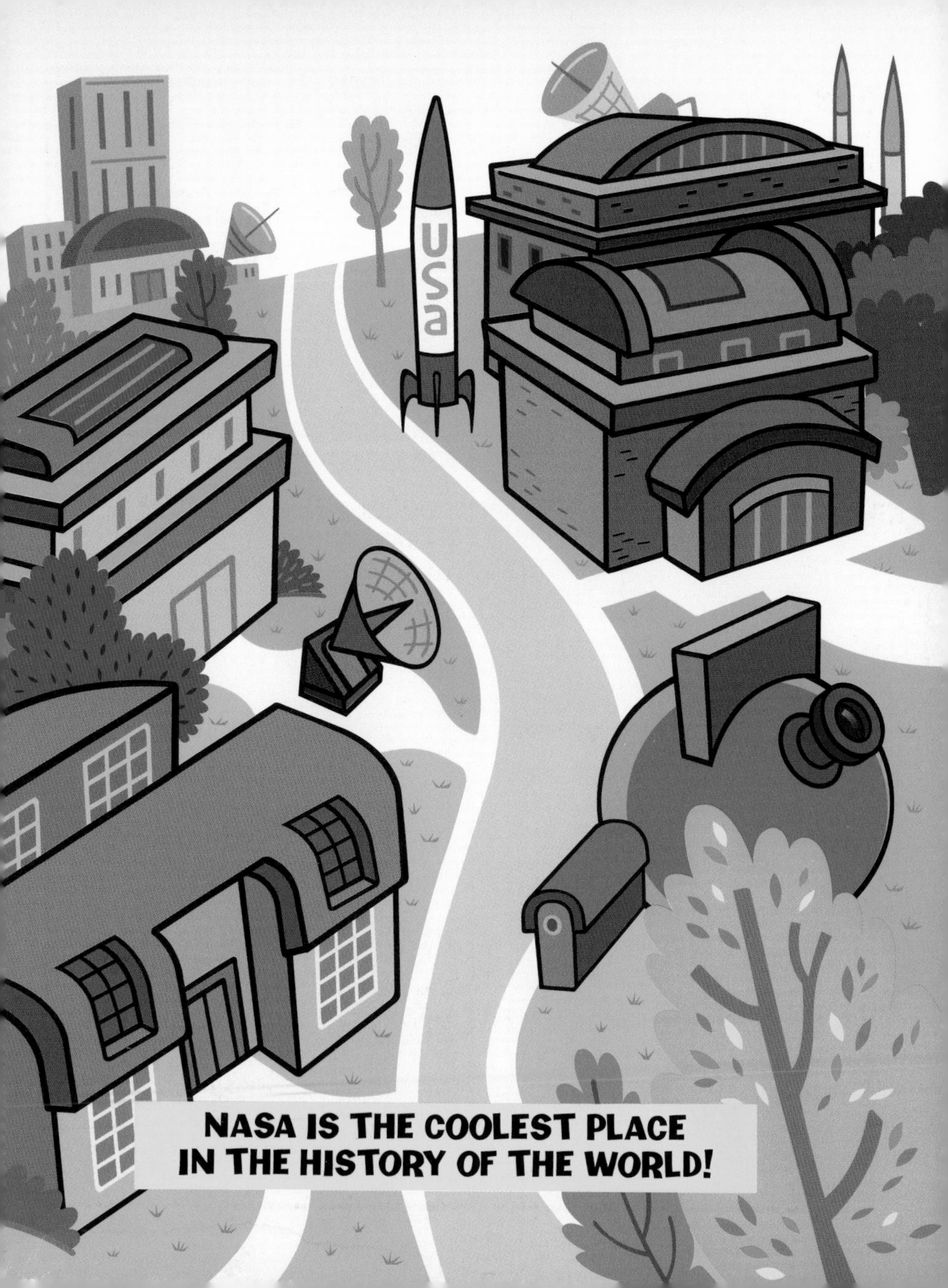
USA
NASA IS THE COOLEST PLACE
IN THE HISTORY OF THE WORLD!

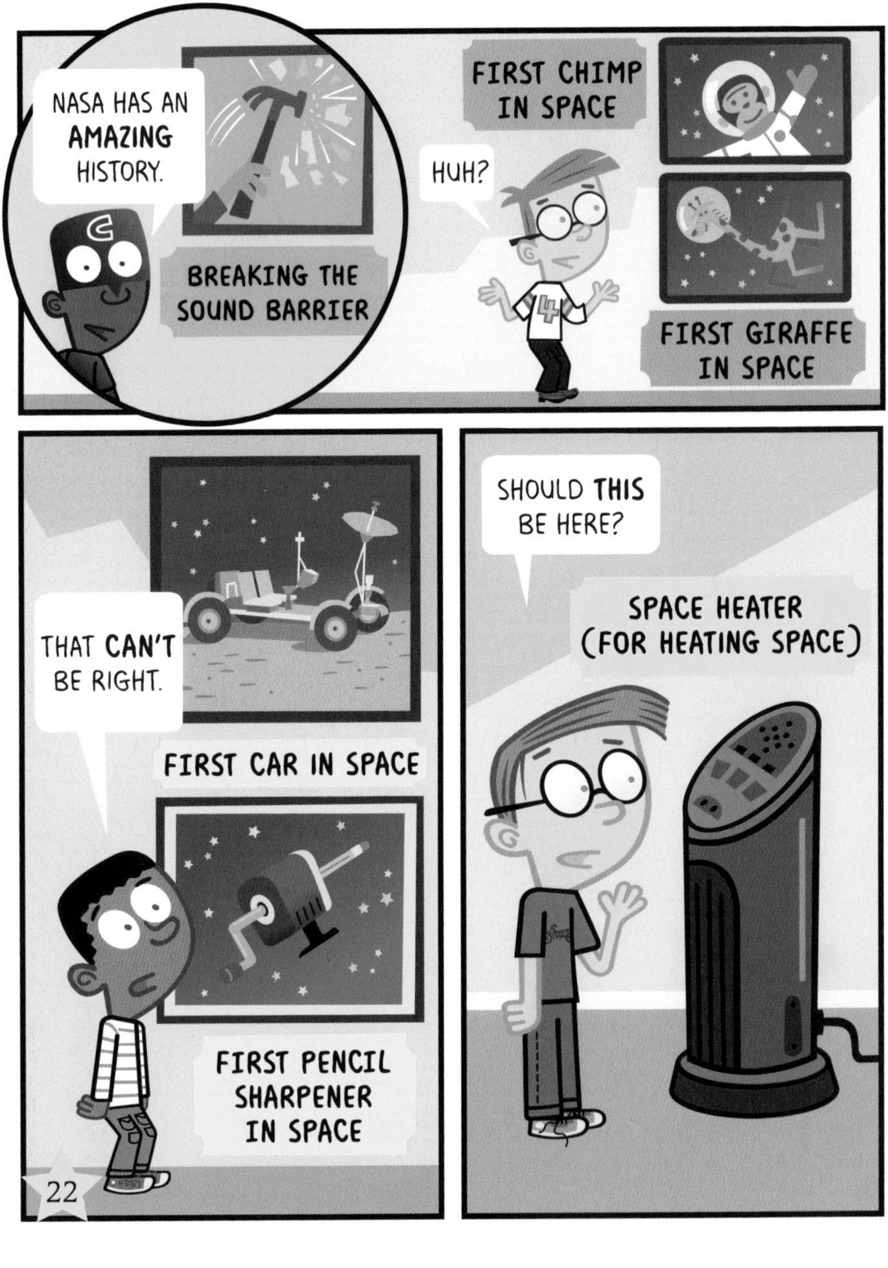
NASA HAS AN AMAZING HISTORY.
BREAKING THE SOUND BARRIER
FIRST CHIMP IN SPACE
HUH?
FIRST GIRAFFE IN SPACE
THAT CAN'T BE RIGHT.
FIRST CAR IN SPACE
FIRST PENCIL SHARPENER IN SPACE
SHOULD THIS BE HERE?
SPACE HEATER (FOR HEATING SPACE)

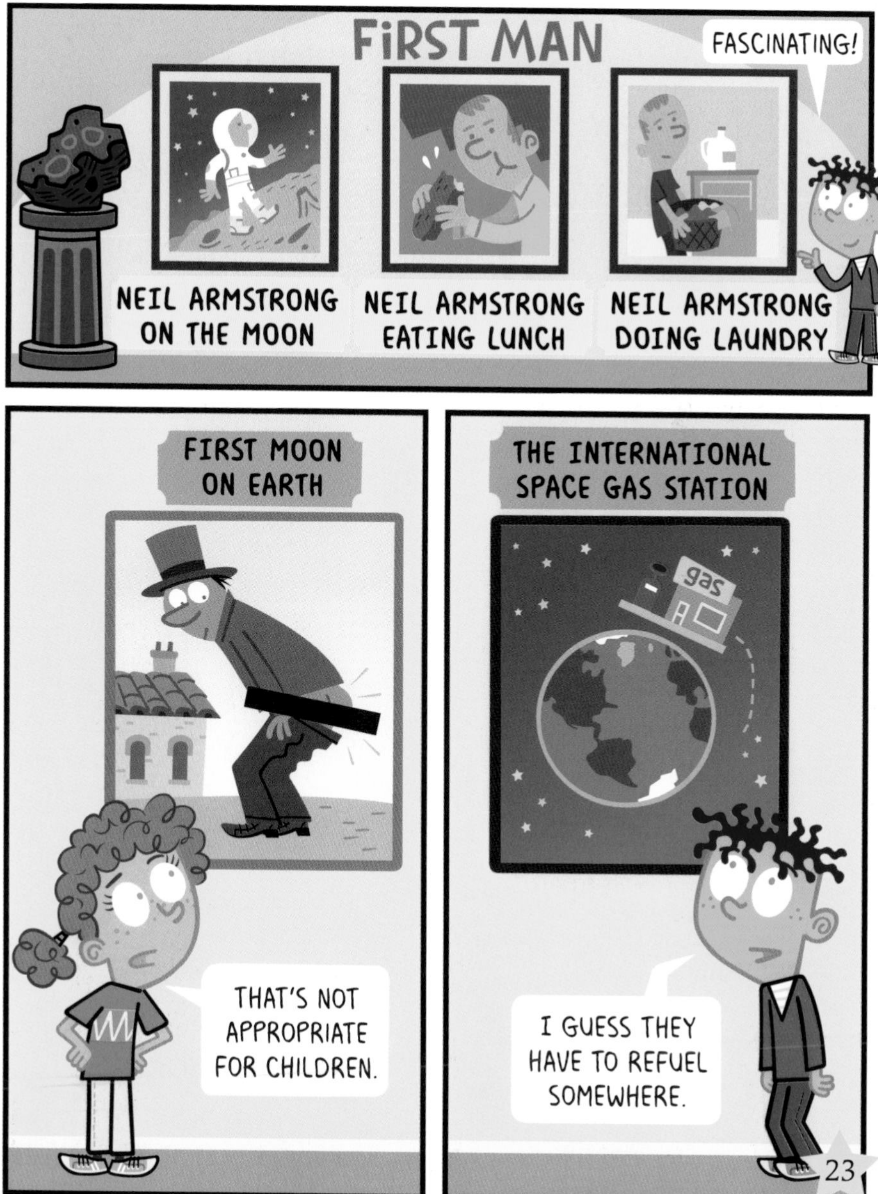
FIRST MAN
NEIL ARMSTRONG ON THE MOON
NEIL ARMSTRONG EATING LUNCH
NEIL ARMSTRONG DOING LAUNDRY
FASCINATING!
FIRST MOON ON EARTH
THAT'S NOT APPROPRIATE FOR CHILDREN.
THE INTERNATIONAL SPACE GAS STATION
gas
I GUESS THEY HAVE TO REFUEL SOMEWHERE.

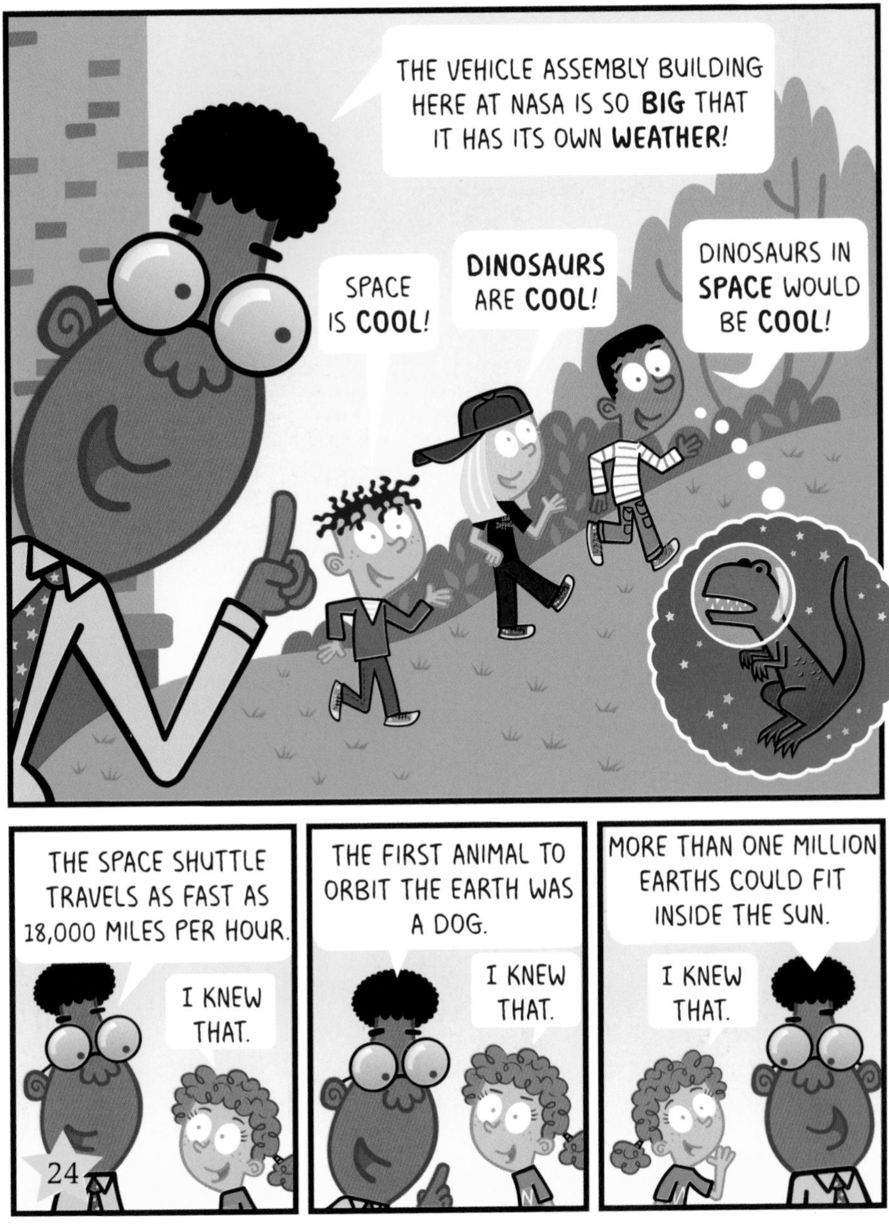
THE VEHICLE ASSEMBLY BUILDING HERE AT NASA IS SO BIG THAT IT HAS ITS OWN WEATHER!
SPACE IS COOL!
DINOSAURS ARE COOL!
DINOSAURS IN SPACE WOULD BE COOL!
THE SPACE SHUTTLE TRAVELS AS FAST AS 18,000 MILES PER HOUR.
I KNEW THAT.
THE FIRST ANIMAL TO ORBIT THE EARTH WAS A DOG.
I KNEW THAT.
MORE THAN ONE MILLION EARTHS COULD FIT INSIDE THE SUN.
I KNEW THAT.

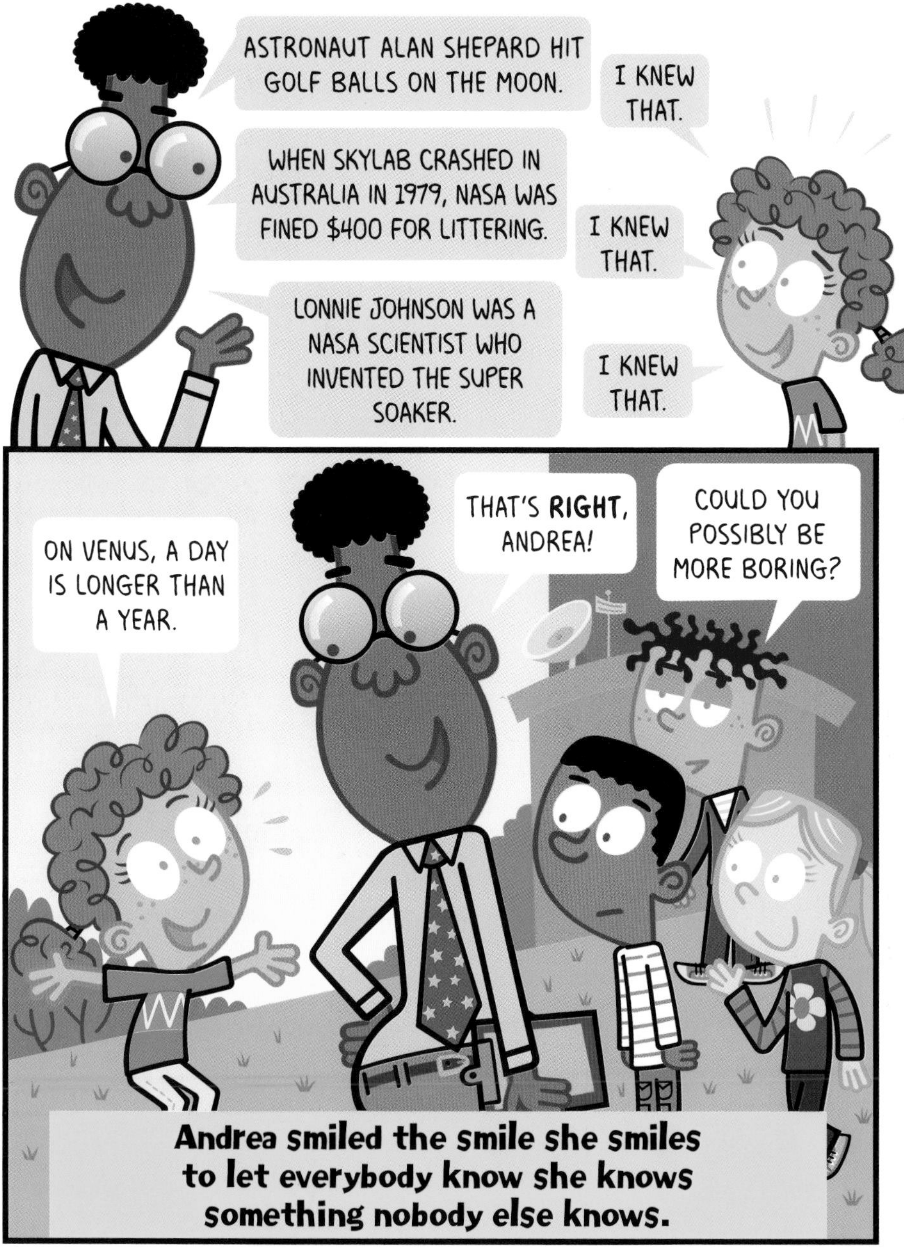
ASTRONAUT ALAN SHEPARD HIT GOLF BALLS ON THE MOON.
I KNEW THAT.
WHEN SKYLAB CRASHED IN AUSTRALIA IN 1979, NASA WAS FINED $400 FOR LITTERING.
I KNEW THAT.
LONNIE JOHNSON WAS A NASA SCIENTIST WHO INVENTED THE SUPER SOAKER.
I KNEW THAT.
ON VENUS, A DAY IS LONGER THAN A YEAR.
THAT'S **RIGHT**, ANDREA!
COULD YOU POSSIBLY BE MORE BORING?
Andrea smiled the smile she smiles to let everybody know she knows something nobody else knows.

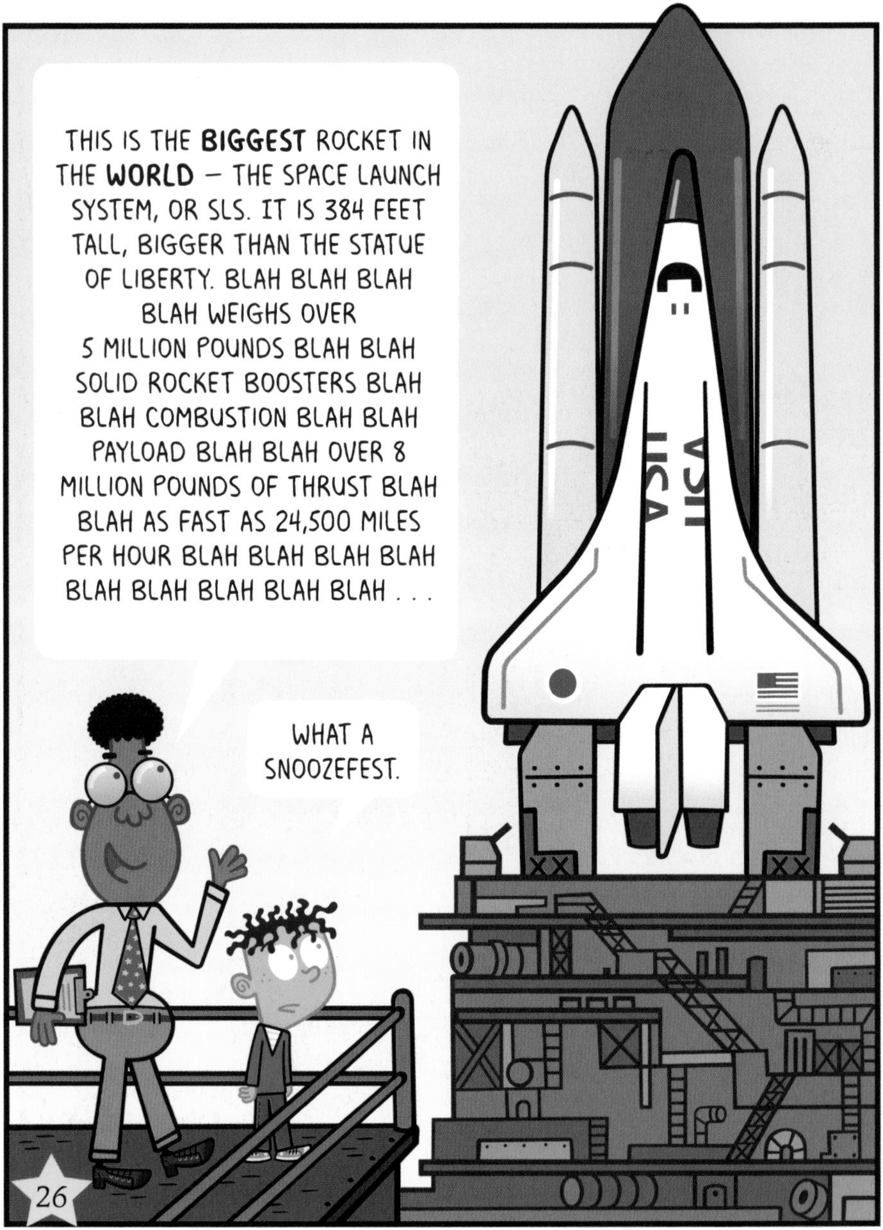
THIS IS THE BIGGEST ROCKET IN THE WORLD — THE SPACE LAUNCH SYSTEM, OR SLS. IT IS 384 FEET TALL, BIGGER THAN THE STATUE OF LIBERTY. BLAH BLAH BLAH BLAH WEIGHS OVER 5 MILLION POUNDS BLAH BLAH SOLID ROCKET BOOSTERS BLAH BLAH COMBUSTION BLAH BLAH PAYLOAD BLAH BLAH OVER 8 MILLION POUNDS OF THRUST BLAH BLAH AS FAST AS 24,500 MILES PER HOUR BLAH BLAH BLAH BLAH BLAH BLAH BLAH BLAH BLAH . . .
WHAT A SNOOZEFEST.
USA
USA

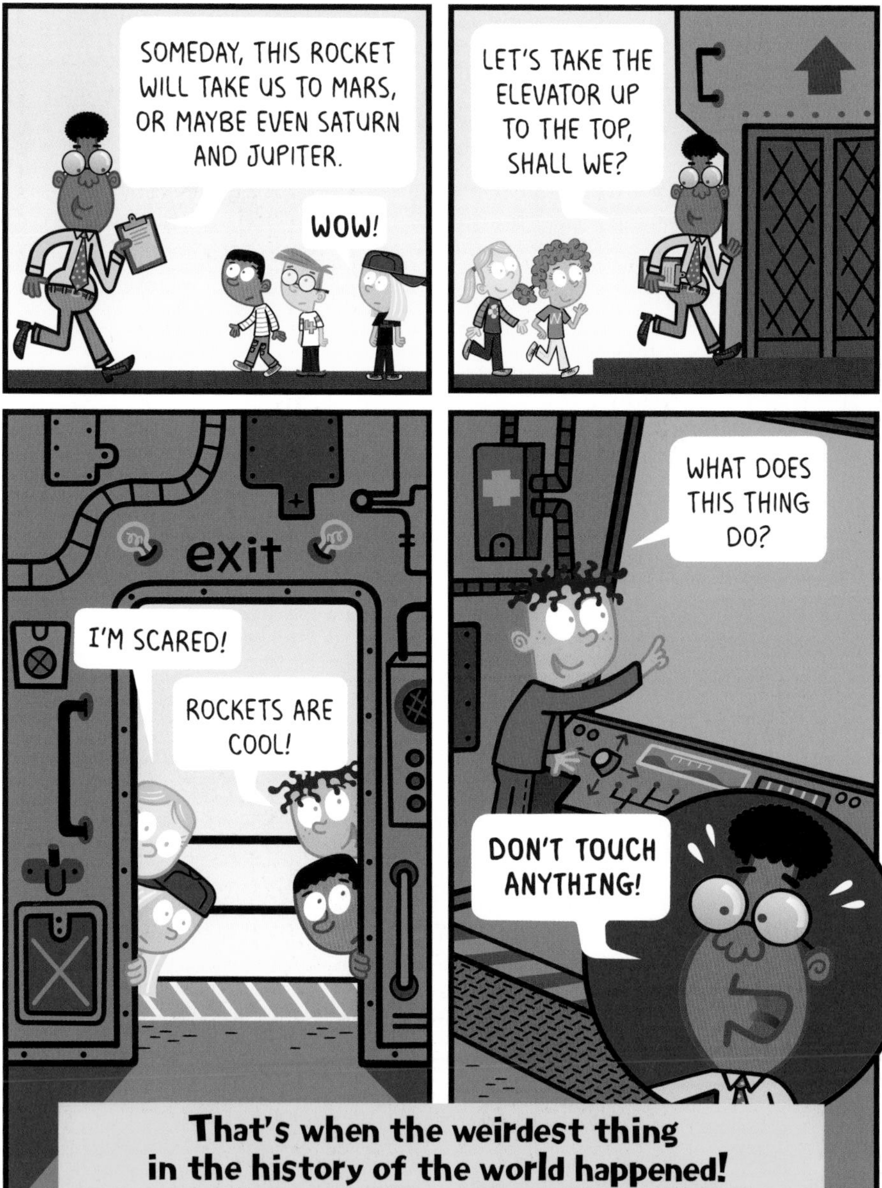
SOMEDAY, THIS ROCKET WILL TAKE US TO MARS, OR MAYBE EVEN SATURN AND JUPITER.
WOW!
LET'S TAKE THE ELEVATOR UP TO THE TOP, SHALL WE?
exit
I'M SCARED!
ROCKETS ARE COOL!
WHAT DOES THIS THING DO?
DON'T TOUCH ANYTHING!
That's when the weirdest thing in the history of the world happened!

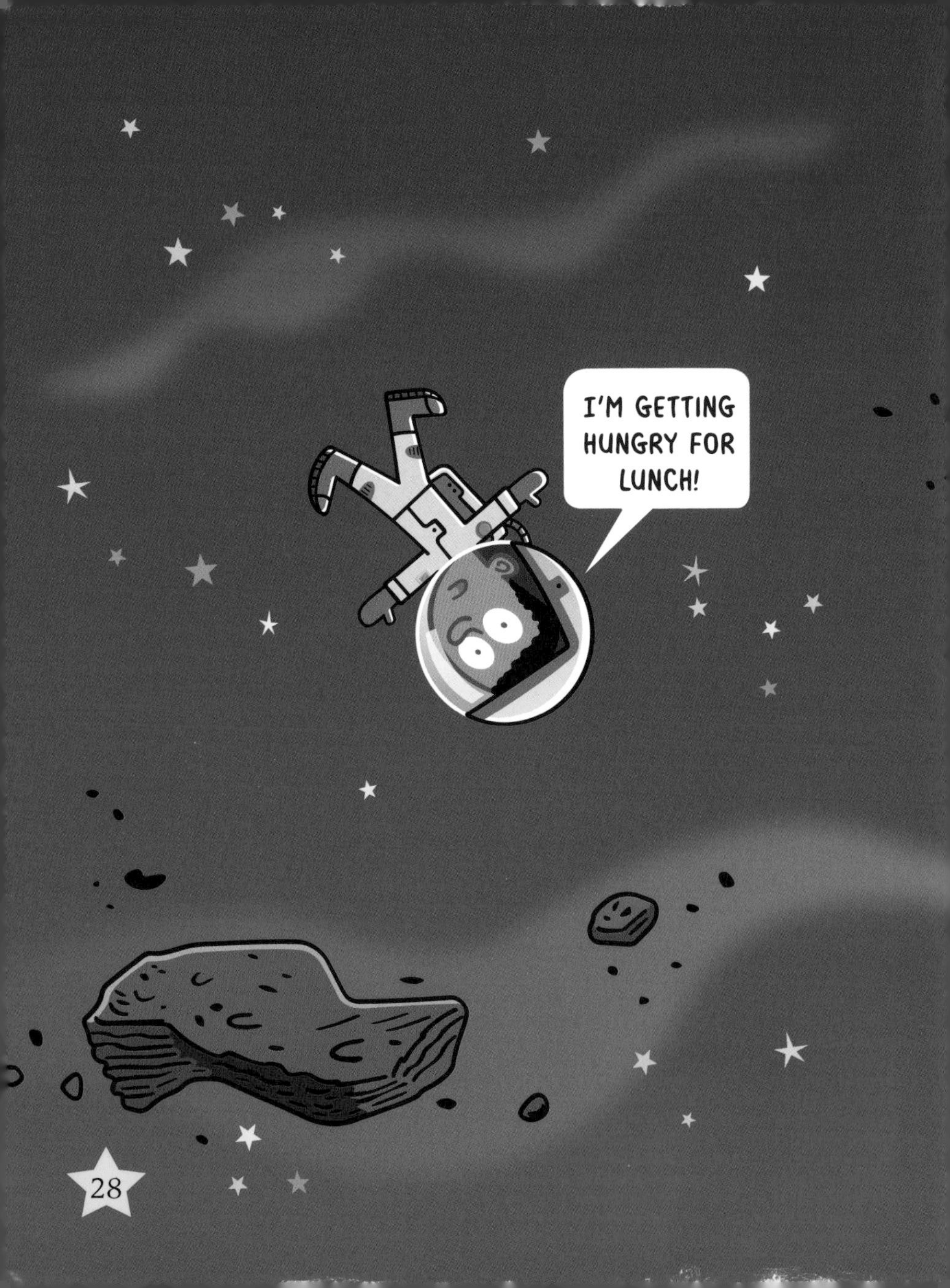
I'M GETTING HUNGRY FOR LUNCH!

CHAPTER 3

Almost the Middle

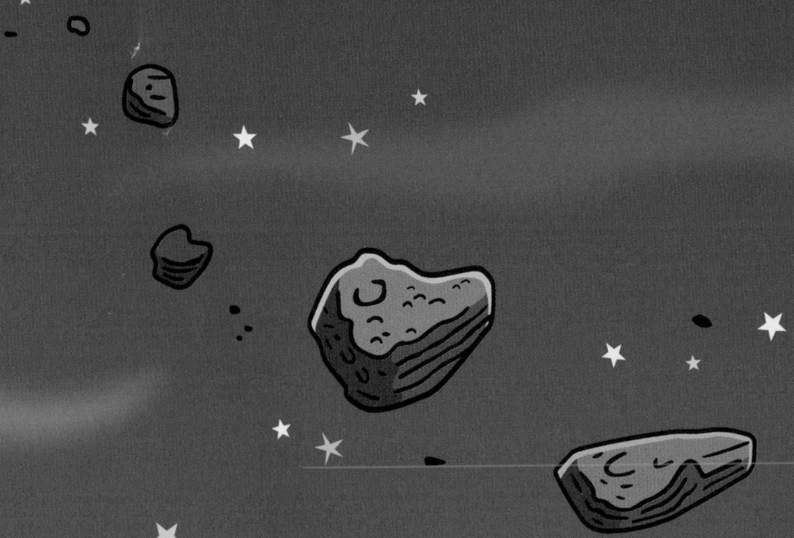

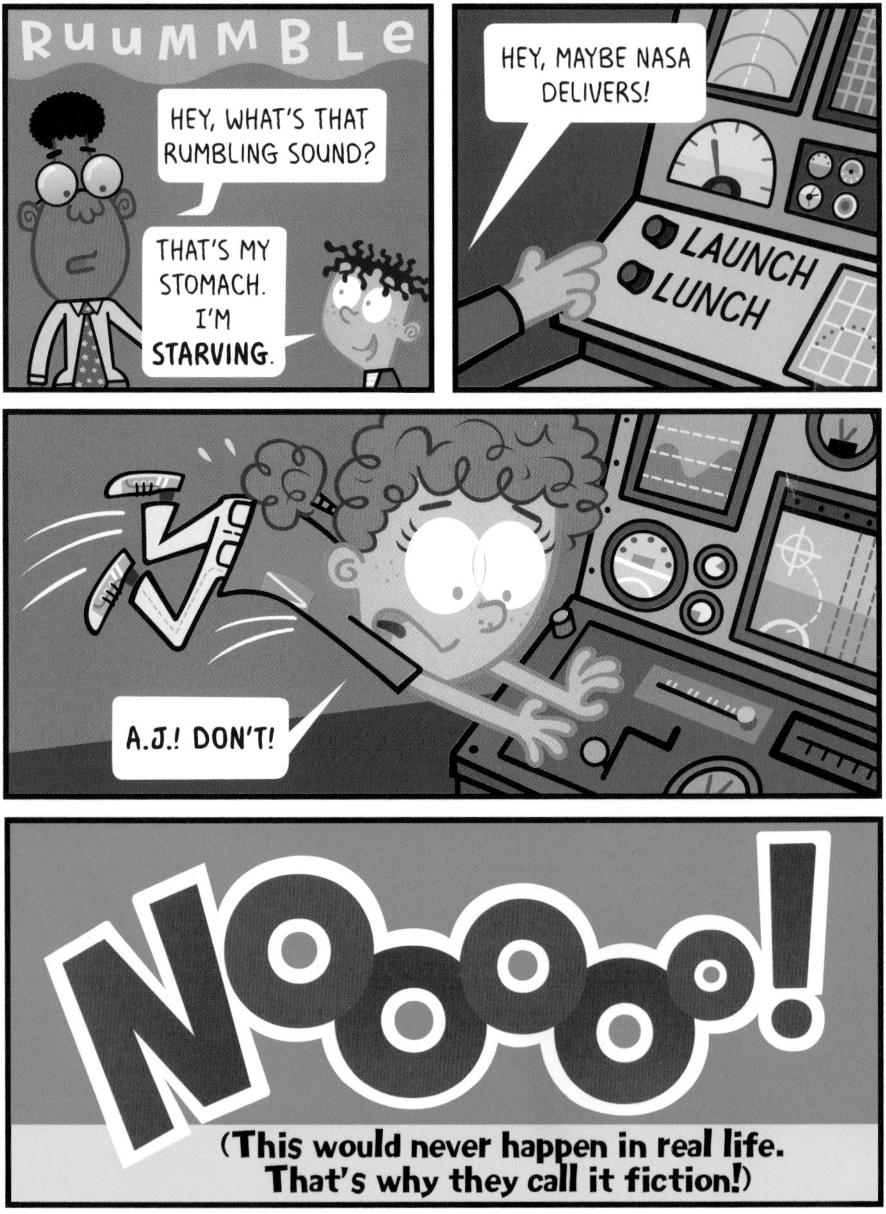
RUUMMBLE
HEY, WHAT'S THAT RUMBLING SOUND?
THAT'S MY STOMACH. I'M STARVING.
HEY, MAYBE NASA DELIVERS!
LAUNCH
LUNCH
A.J.! DON'T!
NOOOOO!
(This would never happen in real life. That's why they call it fiction!)

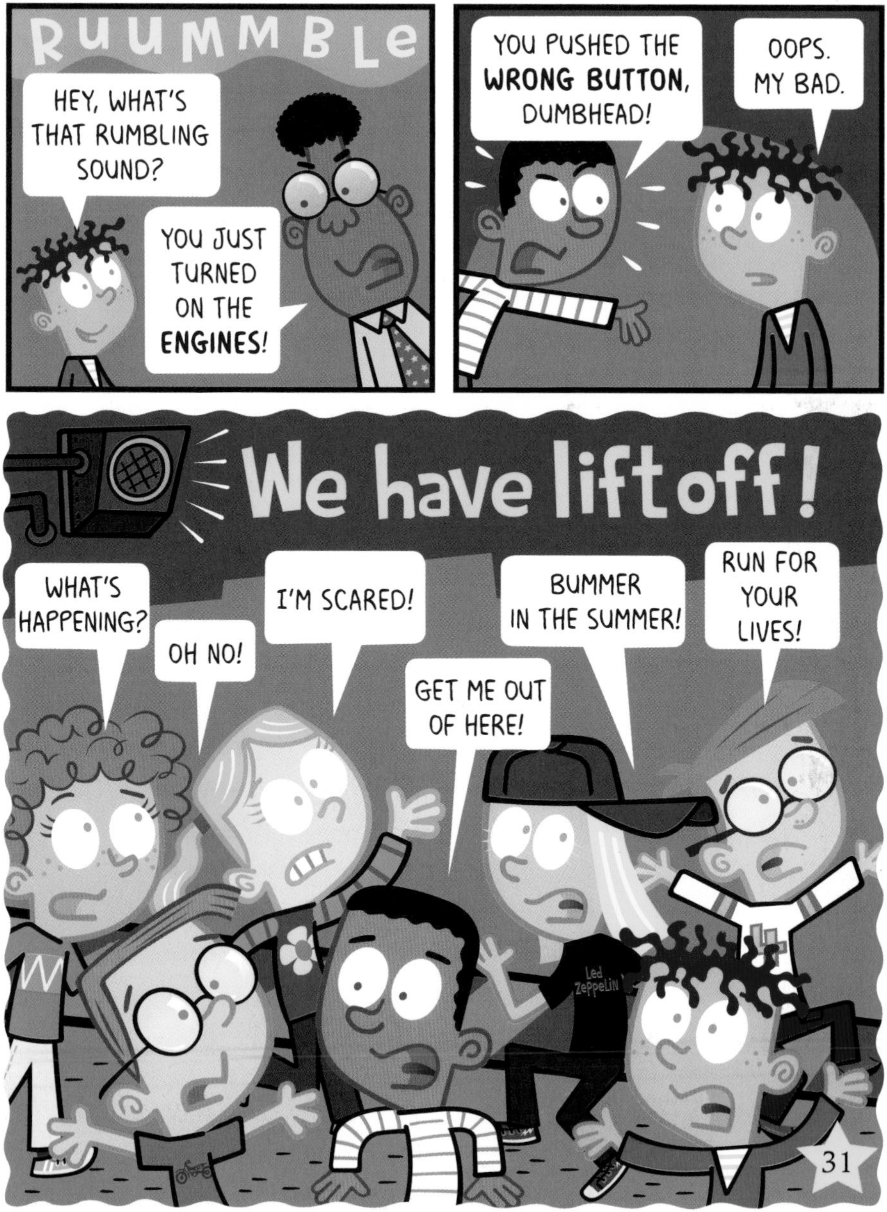
RUUMMBLE
HEY, WHAT'S THAT RUMBLING SOUND?
YOU JUST TURNED ON THE **ENGINES**!
YOU PUSHED THE **WRONG BUTTON**, DUMBHEAD!
OOPS. MY BAD.
We have lift off!
WHAT'S HAPPENING?
OH NO!
I'M SCARED!
GET ME OUT OF HERE!
BUMMER IN THE SUMMER!
RUN FOR YOUR LIVES!
Led ZePPeLIN

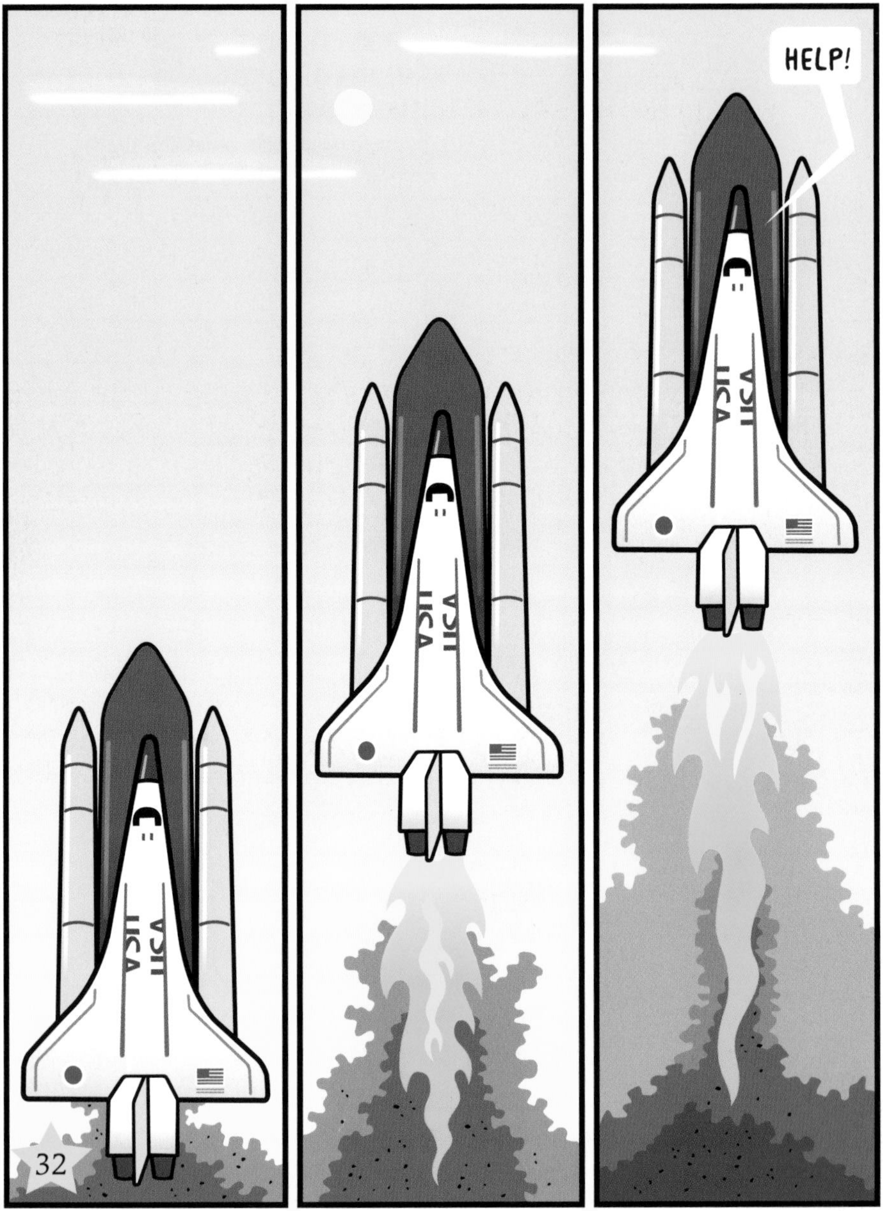
HELP!

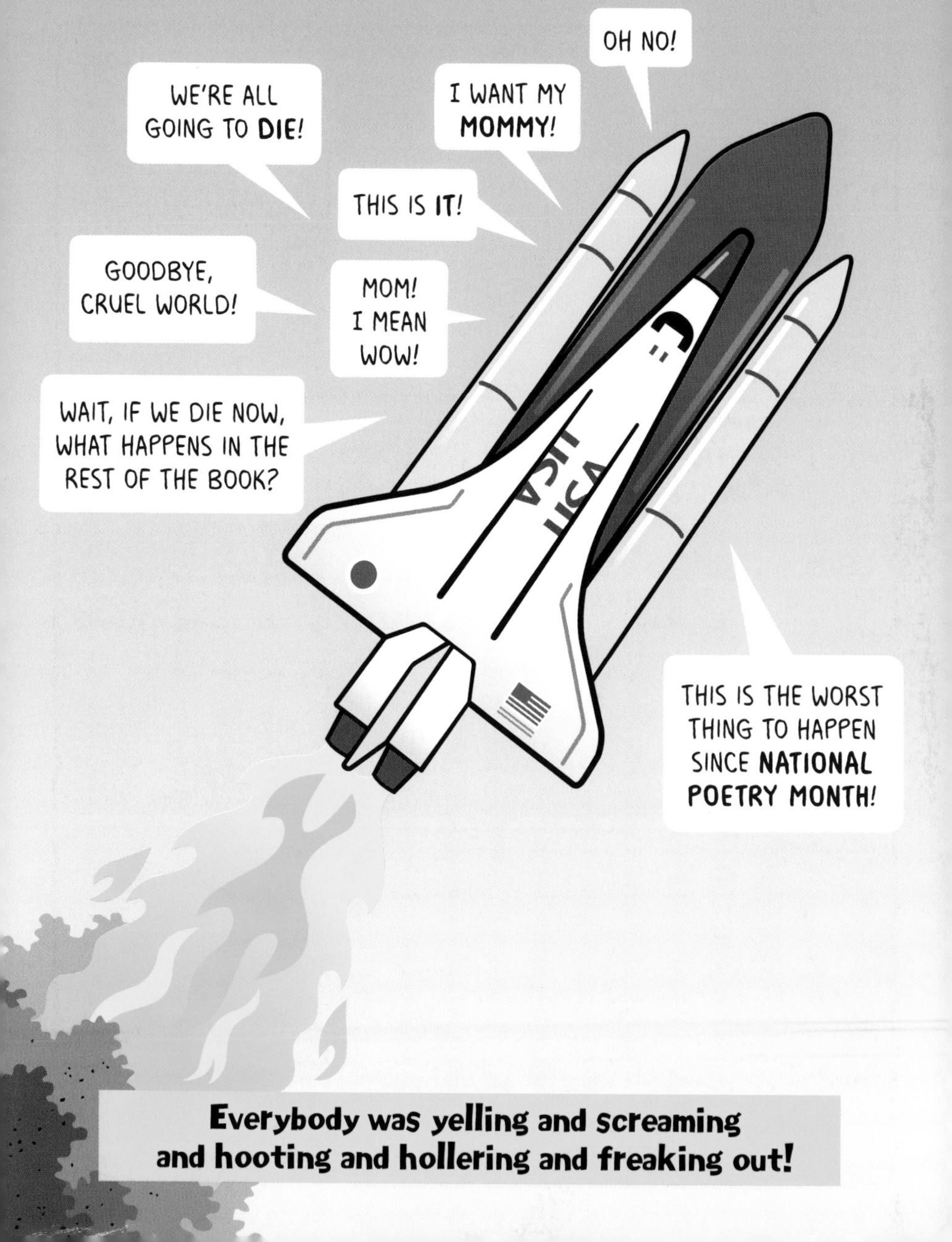

OH NO!
WE'RE ALL GOING TO DIE!
I WANT MY MOMMY!
THIS IS IT!
GOODBYE, CRUEL WORLD!
MOM! I MEAN WOW!
WAIT, IF WE DIE NOW, WHAT HAPPENS IN THE REST OF THE BOOK?
THIS IS THE WORST THING TO HAPPEN SINCE NATIONAL POETRY MONTH!

Everybody was yelling and screaming and hooting and hollering and freaking out!

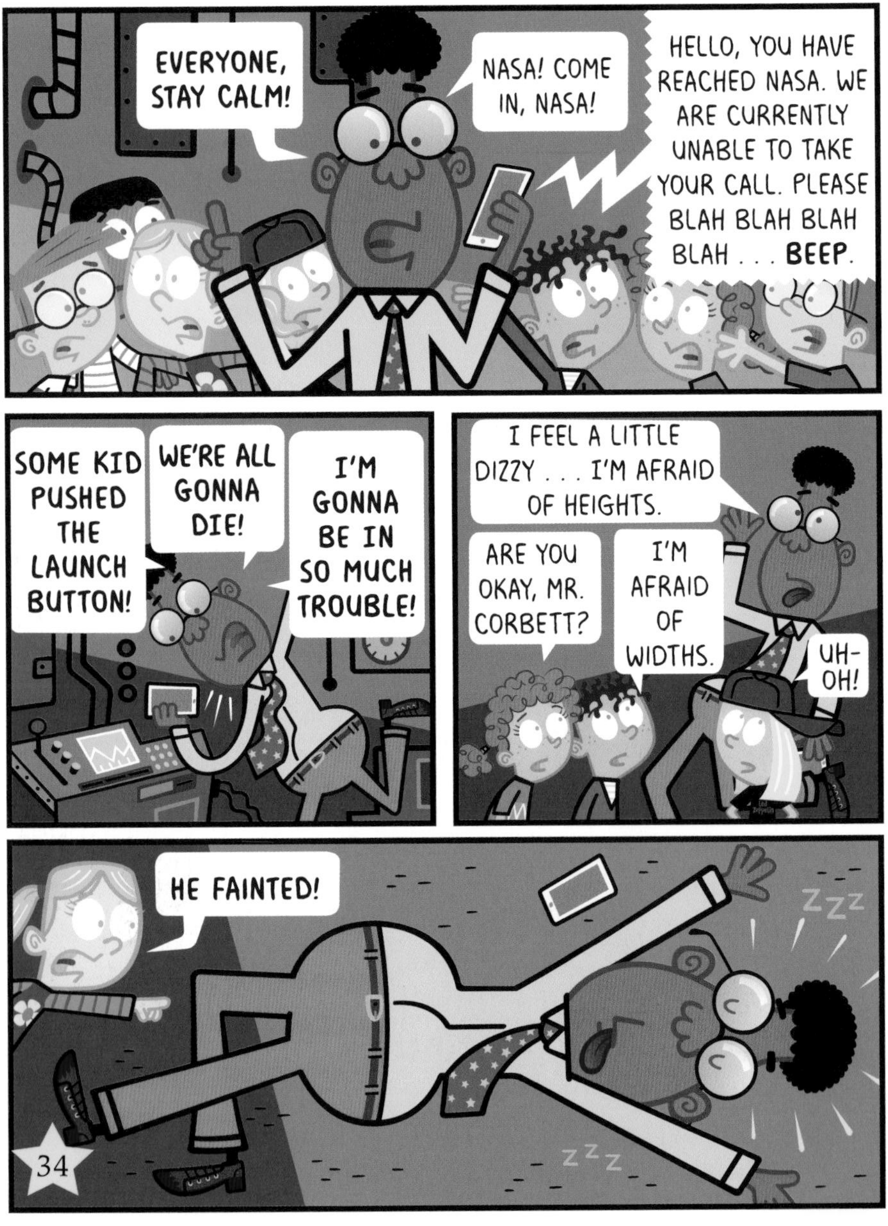
EVERYONE, STAY CALM!
NASA! COME IN, NASA!
HELLO, YOU HAVE REACHED NASA. WE ARE CURRENTLY UNABLE TO TAKE YOUR CALL. PLEASE BLAH BLAH BLAH BLAH . . . **BEEP**.
SOME KID PUSHED THE LAUNCH BUTTON!
WE'RE ALL GONNA DIE!
I'M GONNA BE IN SO MUCH TROUBLE!
I FEEL A LITTLE DIZZY . . . I'M AFRAID OF HEIGHTS.
ARE YOU OKAY, MR. CORBETT?
I'M AFRAID OF WIDTHS.
UH-OH!
HE FAINTED!
ZZZ
ZZZ

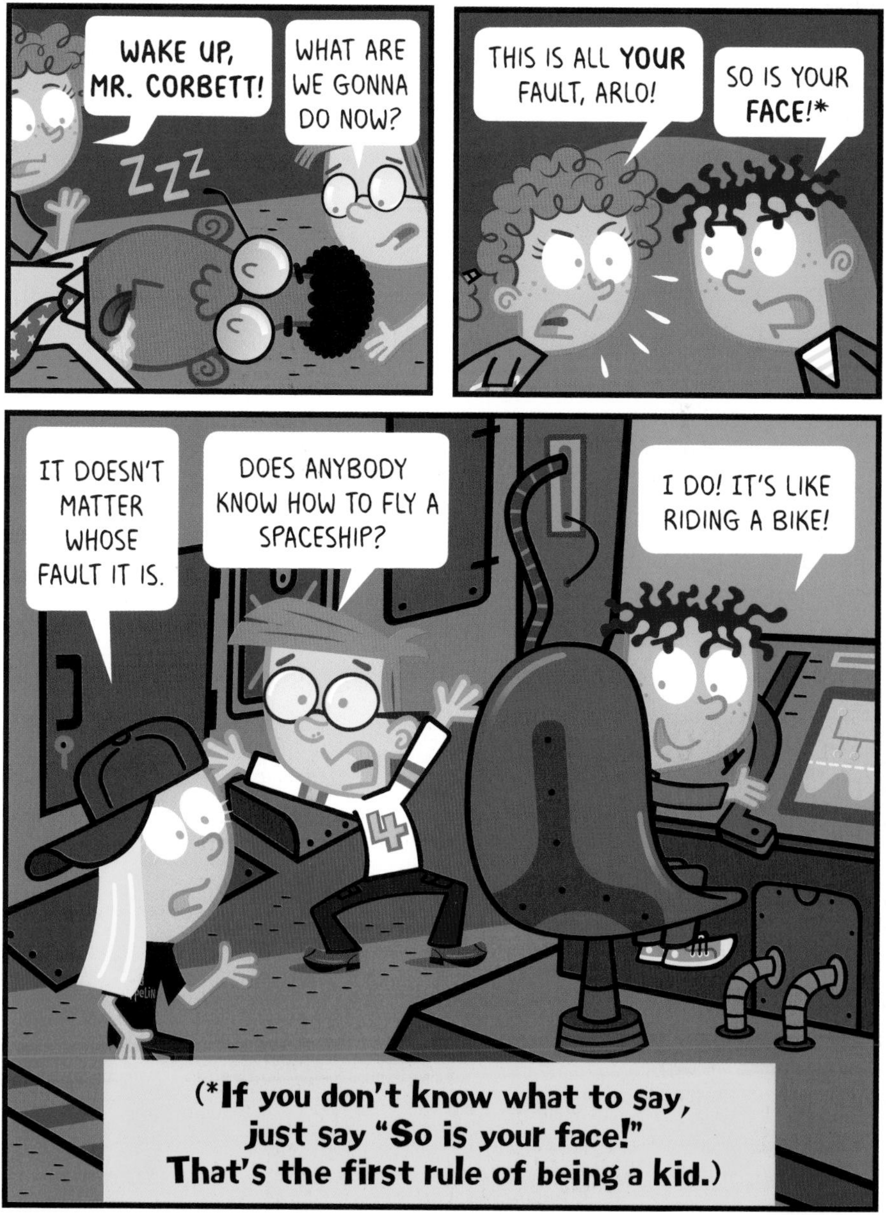
WAKE UP, MR. CORBETT!
ZZZ
WHAT ARE WE GONNA DO NOW?
THIS IS ALL YOUR FAULT, ARLO!
SO IS YOUR FACE!*
IT DOESN'T MATTER WHOSE FAULT IT IS.
DOES ANYBODY KNOW HOW TO FLY A SPACESHIP?
I DO! IT'S LIKE RIDING A BIKE!
(*If you don't know what to say, just say "So is your face!" That's the first rule of being a kid.)

THE FIRST RULE OF BEING A KID

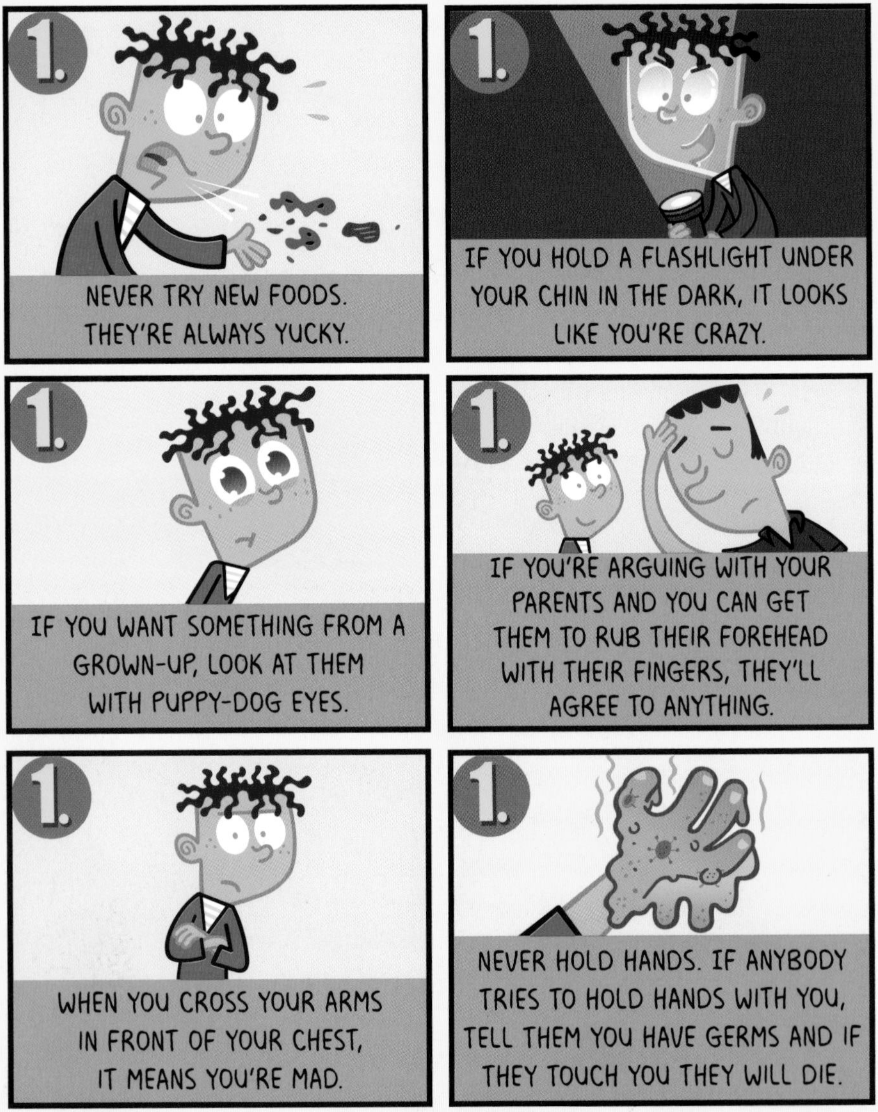
1.
NEVER TRY NEW FOODS. THEY'RE ALWAYS YUCKY.
1.
IF YOU HOLD A FLASHLIGHT UNDER YOUR CHIN IN THE DARK, IT LOOKS LIKE YOU'RE CRAZY.
1.
IF YOU WANT SOMETHING FROM A GROWN-UP, LOOK AT THEM WITH PUPPY-DOG EYES.
1.
IF YOU'RE ARGUING WITH YOUR PARENTS AND YOU CAN GET THEM TO RUB THEIR FOREHEAD WITH THEIR FINGERS, THEY'LL AGREE TO ANYTHING.
1.
WHEN YOU CROSS YOUR ARMS IN FRONT OF YOUR CHEST, IT MEANS YOU'RE MAD.
1.
NEVER HOLD HANDS. IF ANYBODY TRIES TO HOLD HANDS WITH YOU, TELL THEM YOU HAVE GERMS AND IF THEY TOUCH YOU THEY WILL DIE.

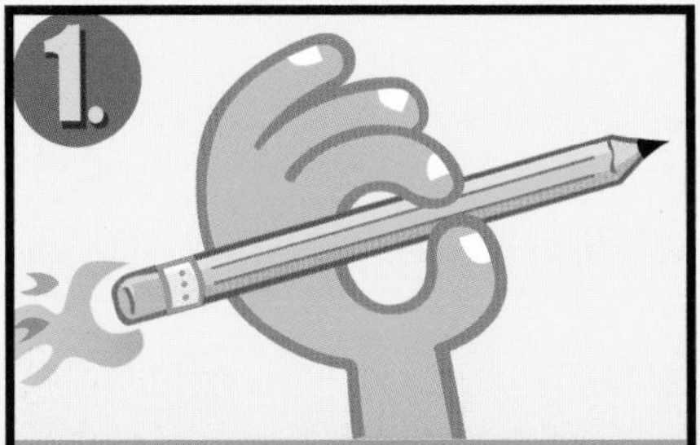
1.

IF YOU'RE BORED AT SCHOOL, PRETEND YOUR PENCIL IS A ROCKET SHIP.

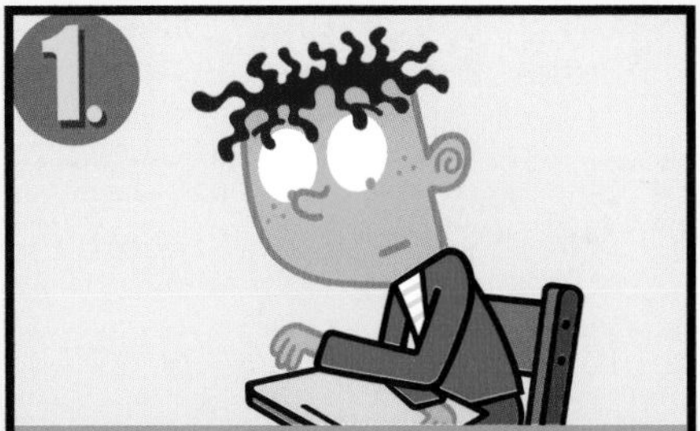
1.

IF YOU DON'T WANT THE TEACHER TO CALL ON YOU, ALWAYS LOOK AT THE FLOOR.

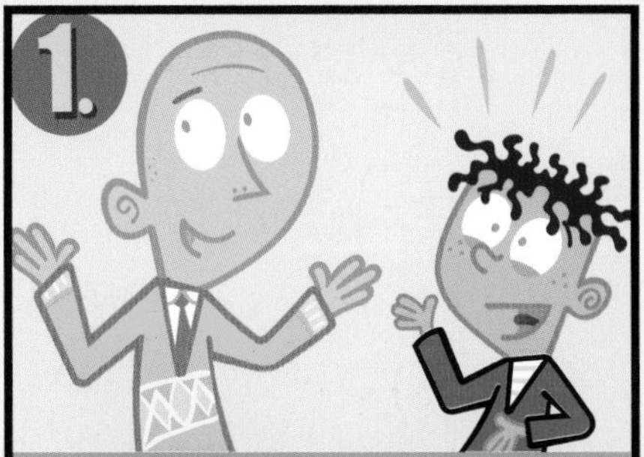
1.

WHEN GROWN-UPS TELL JOKES, ALWAYS PRETEND TO LAUGH.

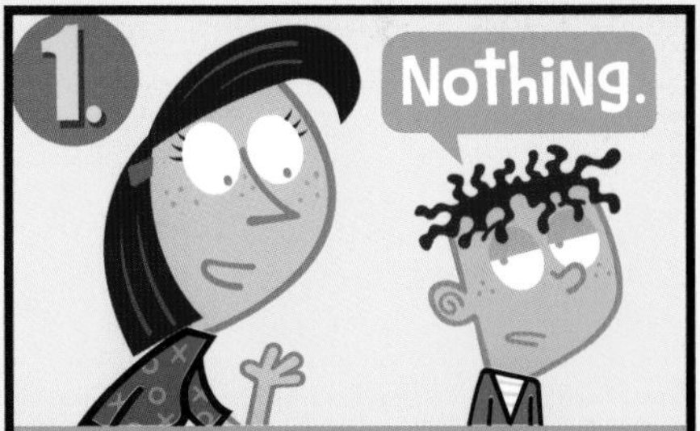
1.
Nothing.

WHEN YOUR PARENTS ASK WHAT YOU LEARNED AT SCHOOL TODAY, ALWAYS REPLY "NOTHING."

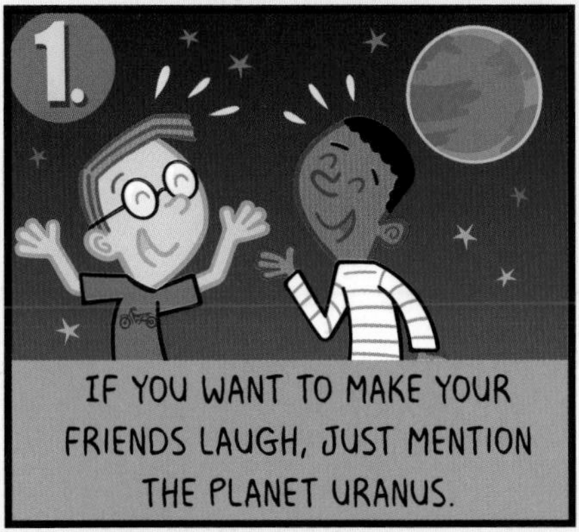
1.

IF YOU WANT TO MAKE YOUR FRIENDS LAUGH, JUST MENTION THE PLANET URANUS.

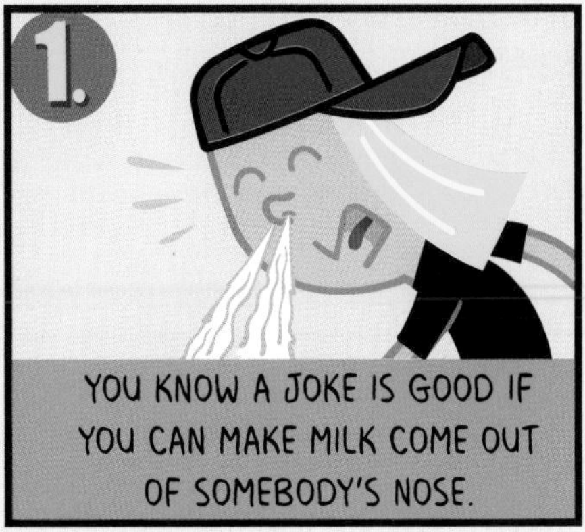
1.

YOU KNOW A JOKE IS GOOD IF YOU CAN MAKE MILK COME OUT OF SOMEBODY'S NOSE.

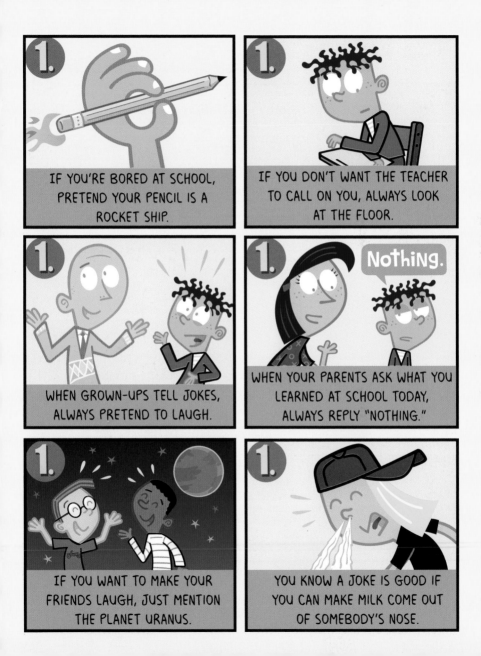

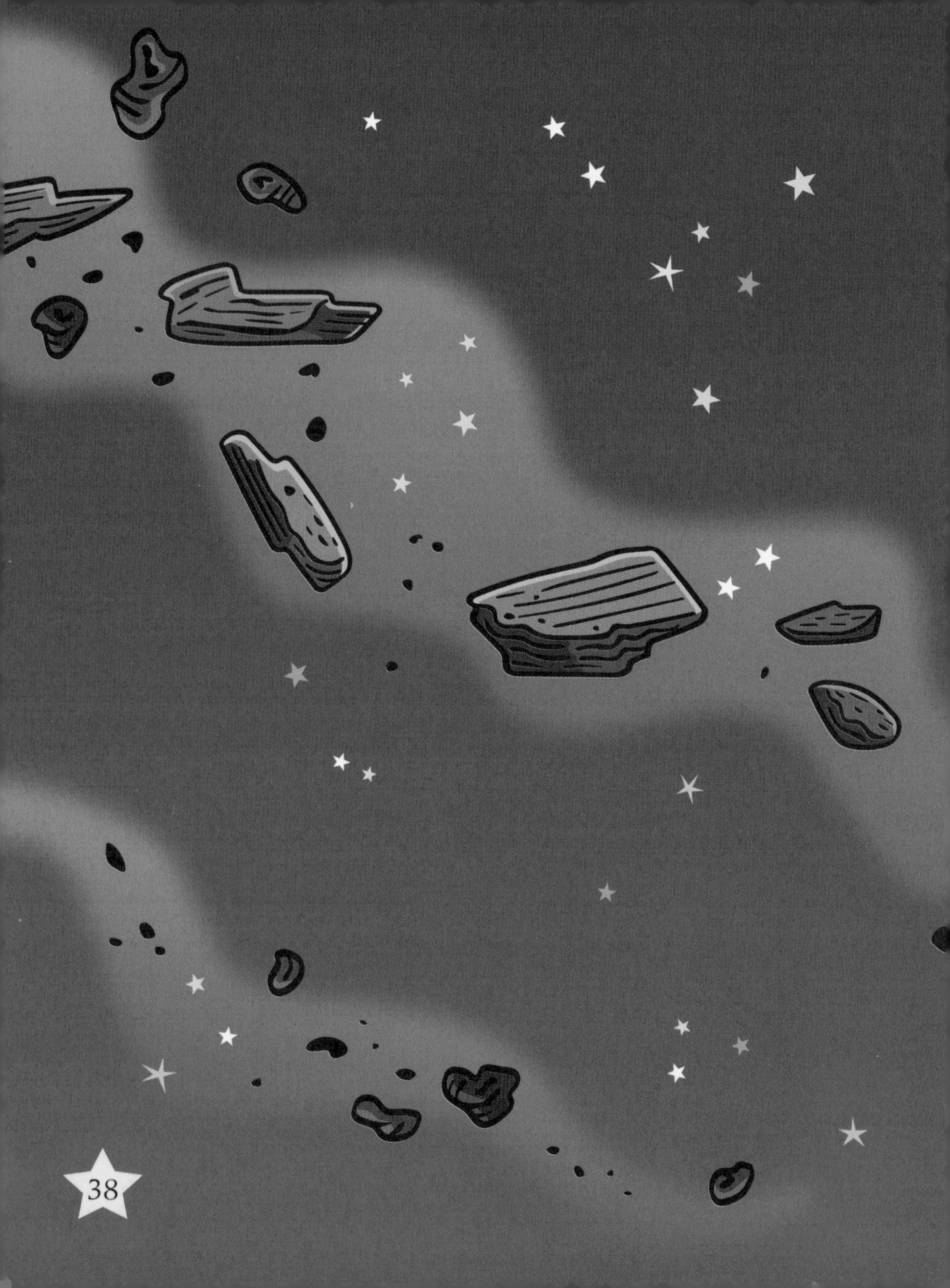

CHAPTER 4

The Middle

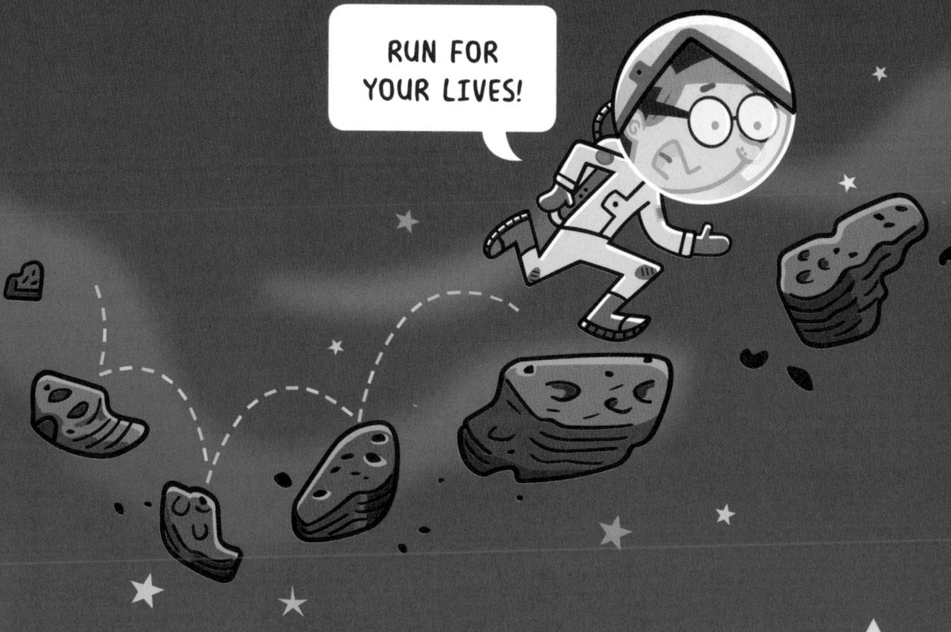
RUN FOR YOUR LIVES!

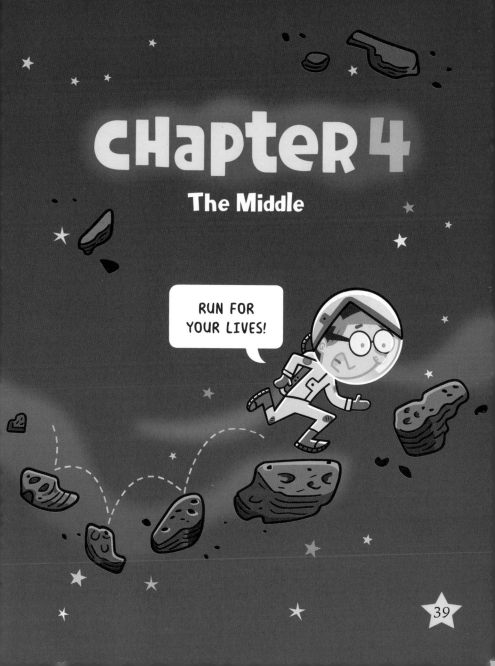

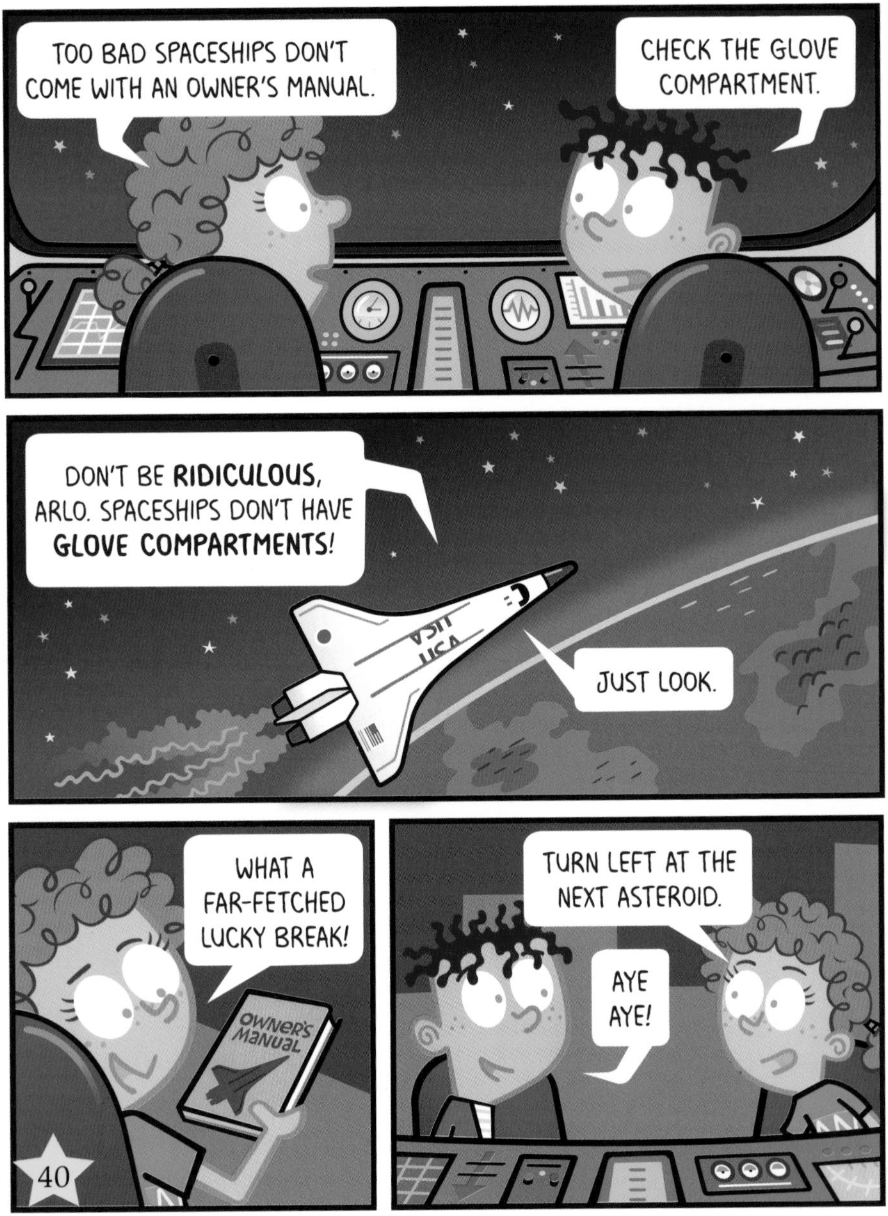
TOO BAD SPACESHIPS DON'T COME WITH AN OWNER'S MANUAL.
CHECK THE GLOVE COMPARTMENT.
DON'T BE RIDICULOUS, ARLO. SPACESHIPS DON'T HAVE GLOVE COMPARTMENTS!
JUST LOOK.
WHAT A FAR-FETCHED LUCKY BREAK!
OWNER'S MANUAL
TURN LEFT AT THE NEXT ASTEROID.
AYE AYE!

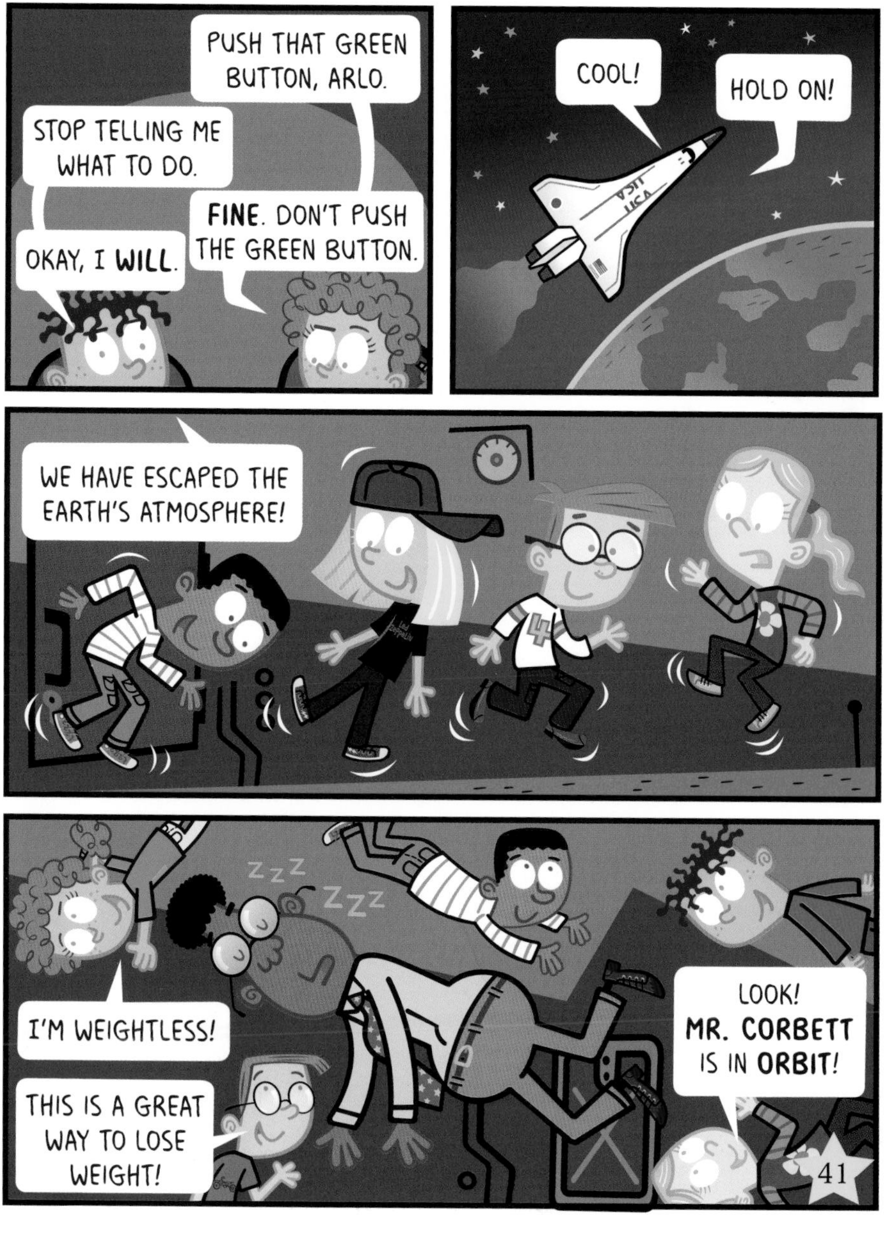
PUSH THAT GREEN BUTTON, ARLO.
STOP TELLING ME WHAT TO DO.
FINE. DON'T PUSH THE GREEN BUTTON.
OKAY, I WILL.
COOL!
HOLD ON!
WE HAVE ESCAPED THE EARTH'S ATMOSPHERE!
I'M WEIGHTLESS!
THIS IS A GREAT WAY TO LOSE WEIGHT!
LOOK! MR. CORBETT IS IN ORBIT!

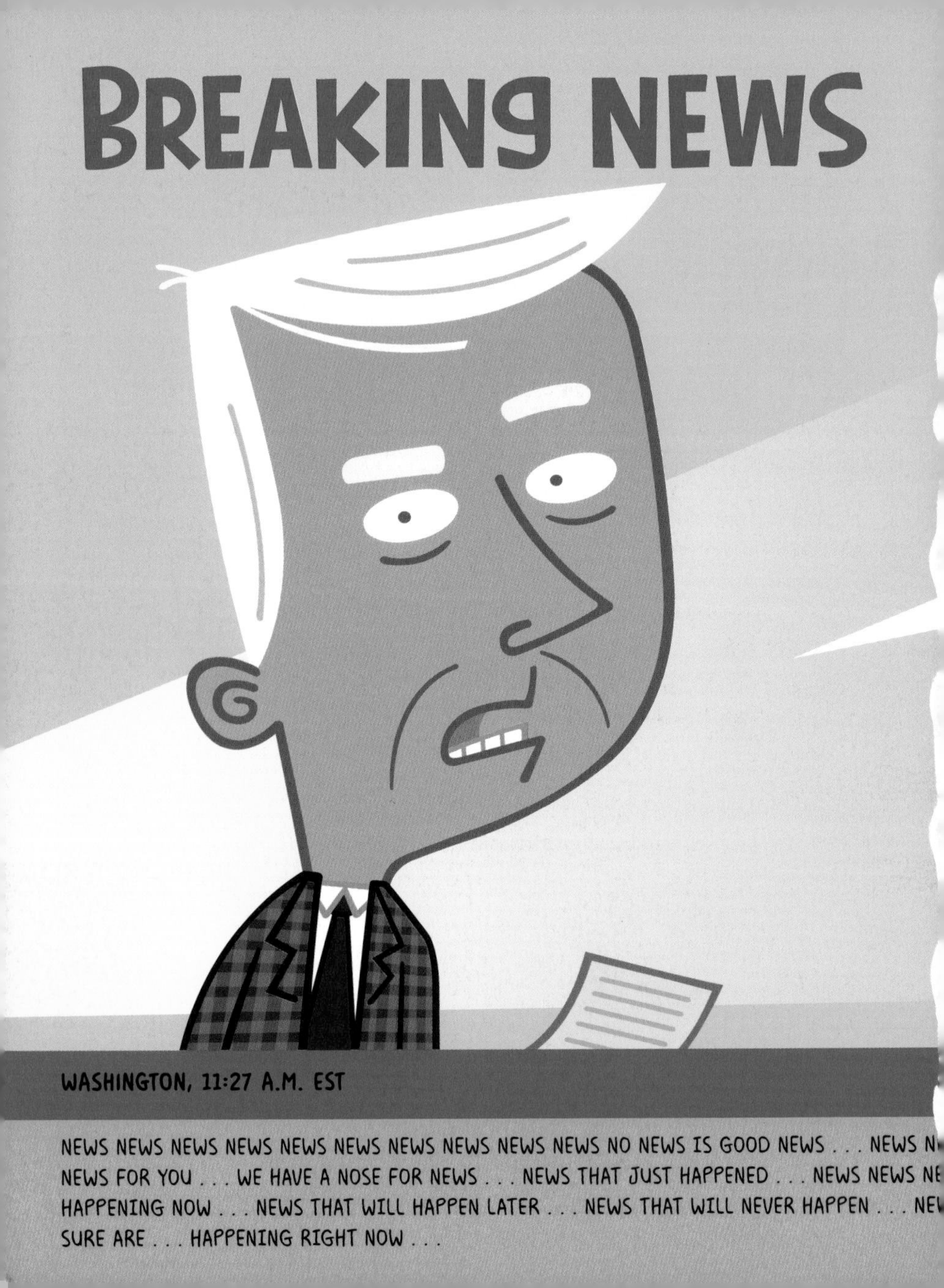
BREAKING NEWS
WASHINGTON, 11:27 A.M. EST
NEWS NEWS NEWS NEWS NEWS NEWS NEWS NEWS NEWS NEWS NO NEWS IS GOOD NEWS . . . NEWS
NEWS FOR YOU . . . WE HAVE A NOSE FOR NEWS . . . NEWS THAT JUST HAPPENED . . . NEWS NEWS
HAPPENING NOW . . . NEWS THAT WILL HAPPEN LATER . . . NEWS THAT WILL NEVER HAPPEN . . .
SURE ARE . . . HAPPENING RIGHT NOW . . .

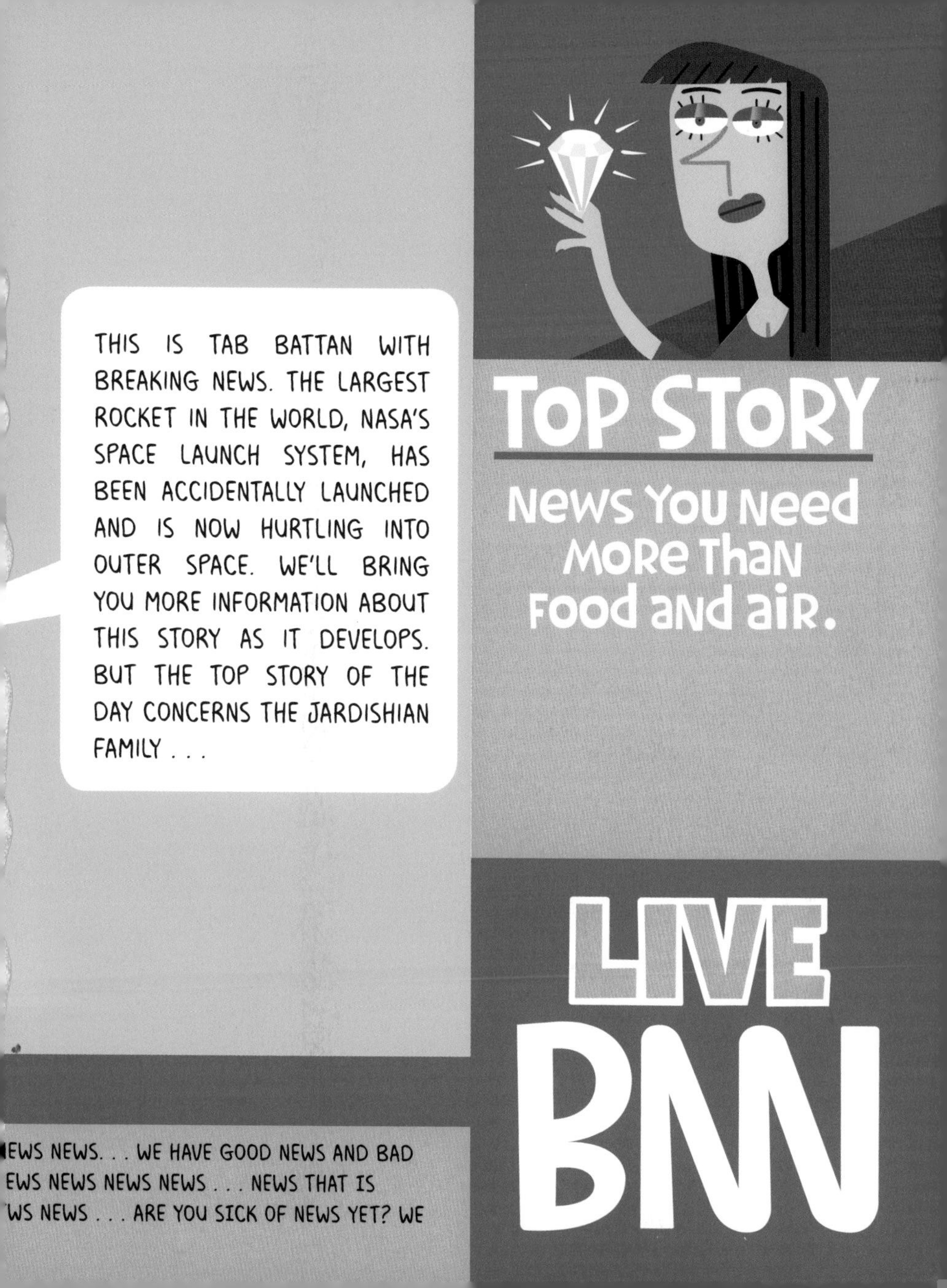
THIS IS TAB BATTAN WITH BREAKING NEWS. THE LARGEST ROCKET IN THE WORLD, NASA'S SPACE LAUNCH SYSTEM, HAS BEEN ACCIDENTALLY LAUNCHED AND IS NOW HURTLING INTO OUTER SPACE. WE'LL BRING YOU MORE INFORMATION ABOUT THIS STORY AS IT DEVELOPS. BUT THE TOP STORY OF THE DAY CONCERNS THE JARDISHIAN FAMILY . . .
TOP STORY
News You Need More Than Food and air.
LIVE
BNN
EWS NEWS. . . WE HAVE GOOD NEWS AND BAD
EWS NEWS NEWS NEWS . . . NEWS THAT IS
WS NEWS . . . ARE YOU SICK OF NEWS YET? WE

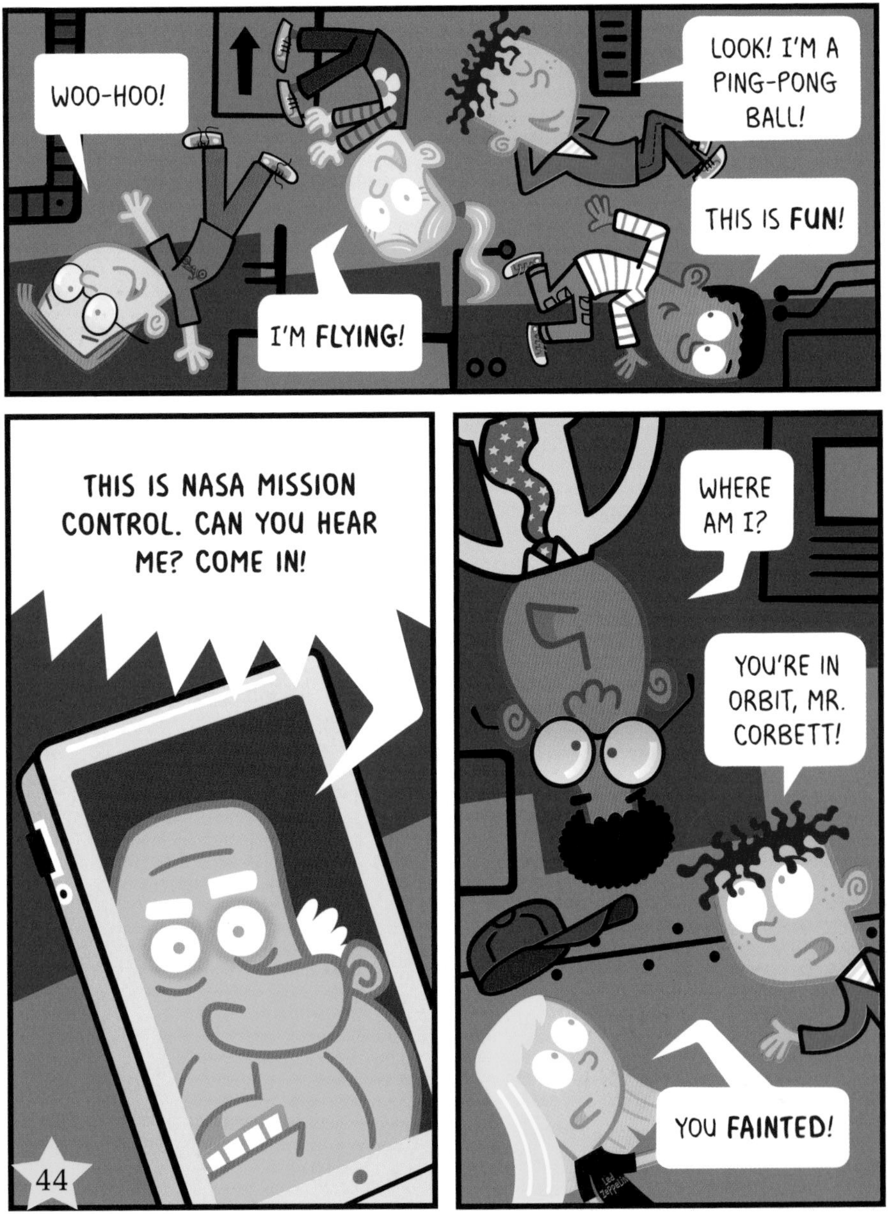
WOO-HOO!
I'M **FLYING**!
LOOK! I'M A PING-PONG BALL!
THIS IS **FUN**!
THIS IS NASA MISSION CONTROL. CAN YOU HEAR ME? COME IN!
WHERE AM I?
YOU'RE IN ORBIT, MR. CORBETT!
YOU **FAINTED**!

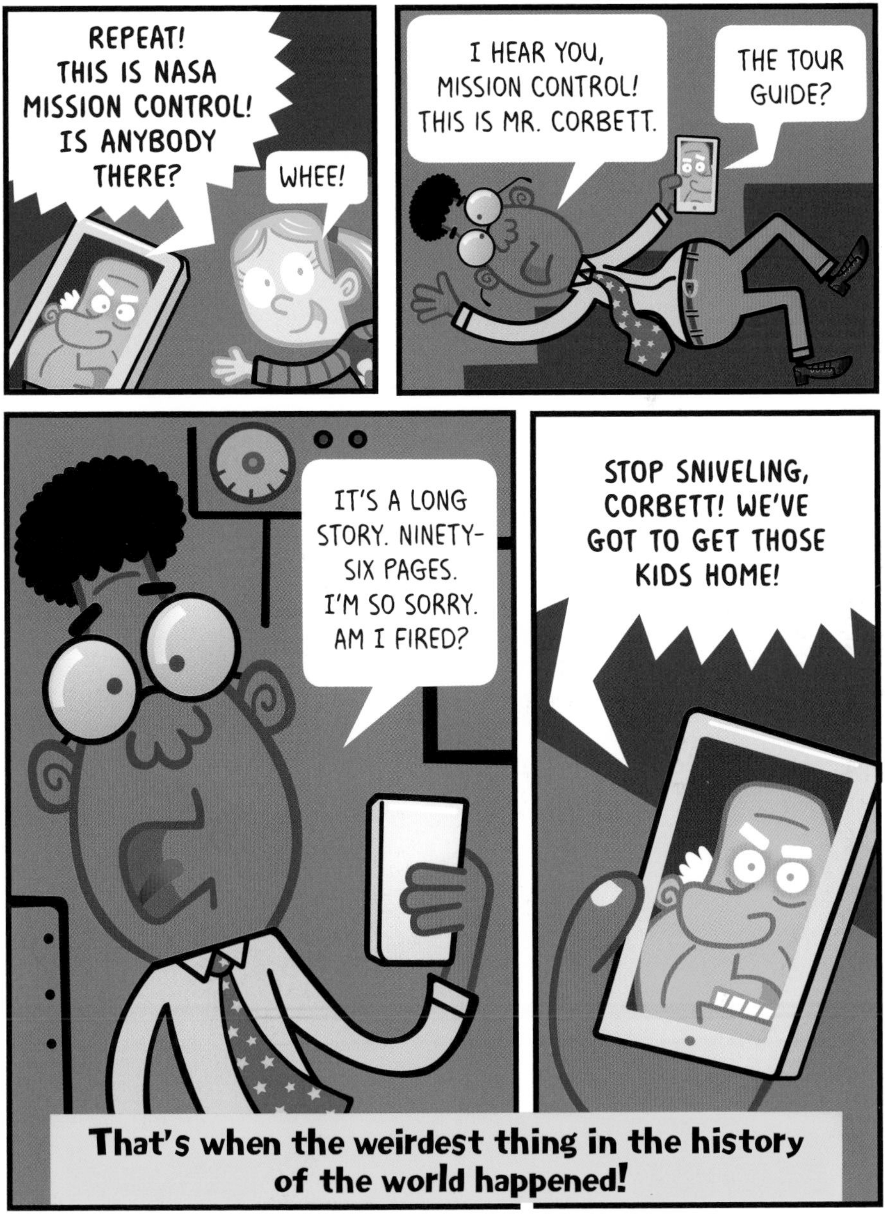
REPEAT! THIS IS NASA MISSION CONTROL! IS ANYBODY THERE?
WHEE!
I HEAR YOU, MISSION CONTROL! THIS IS MR. CORBETT.
THE TOUR GUIDE?
IT'S A LONG STORY. NINETY-SIX PAGES. I'M SO SORRY. AM I FIRED?
STOP SNIVELING, CORBETT! WE'VE GOT TO GET THOSE KIDS HOME!
That's when the weirdest thing in the history of the world happened!

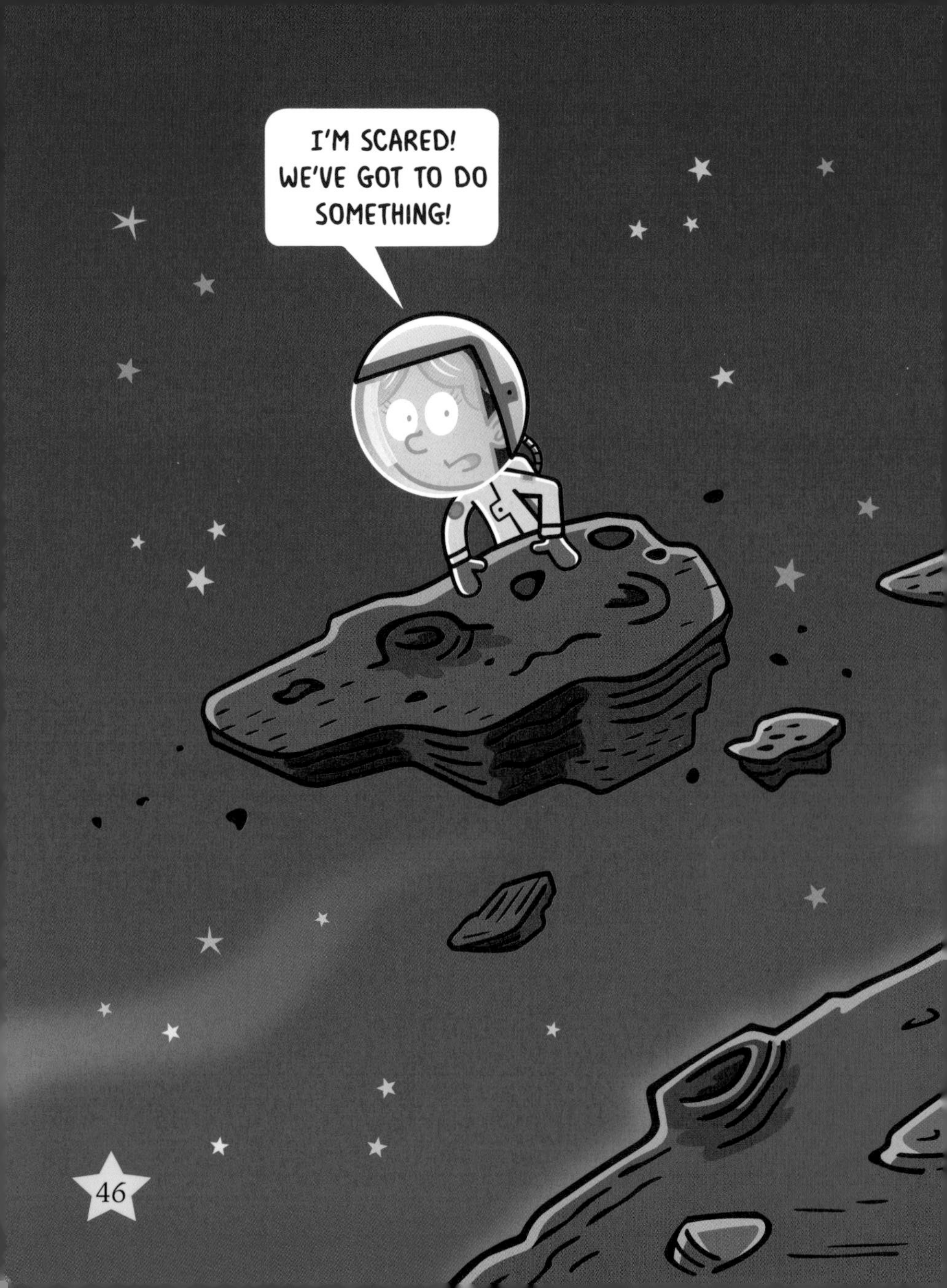
I'M SCARED! WE'VE GOT TO DO SOMETHING!

CHAPTER 5

After the Middle

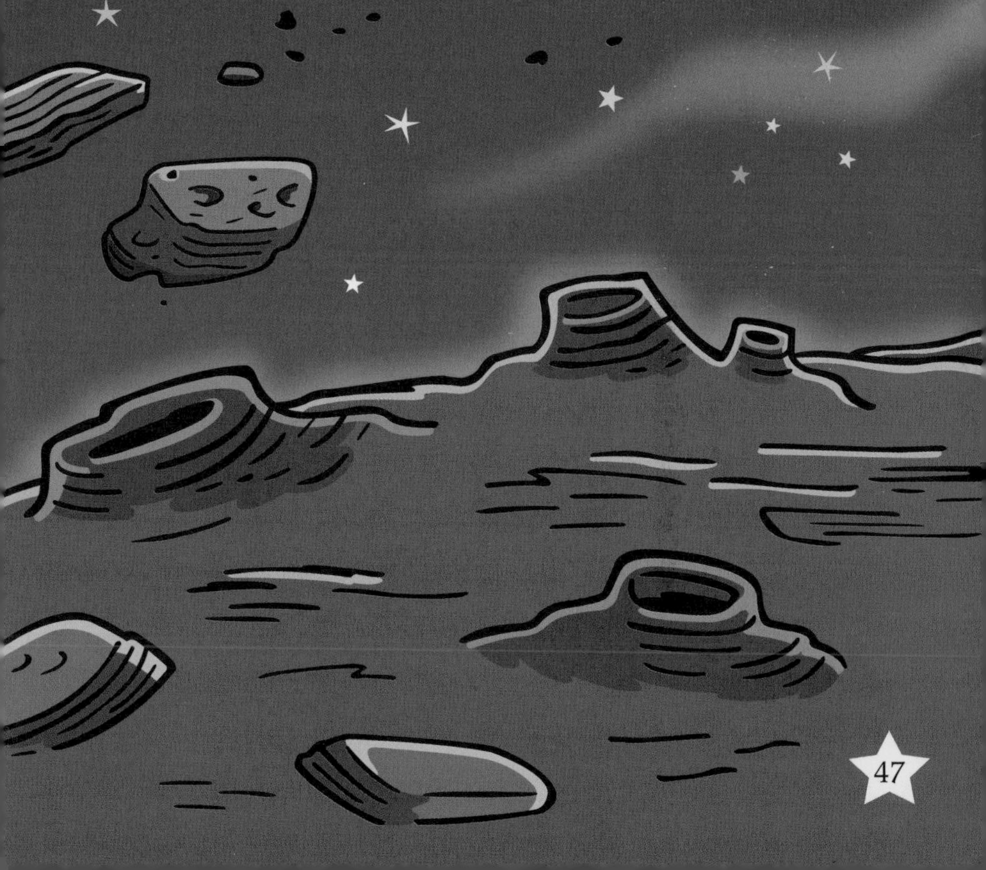

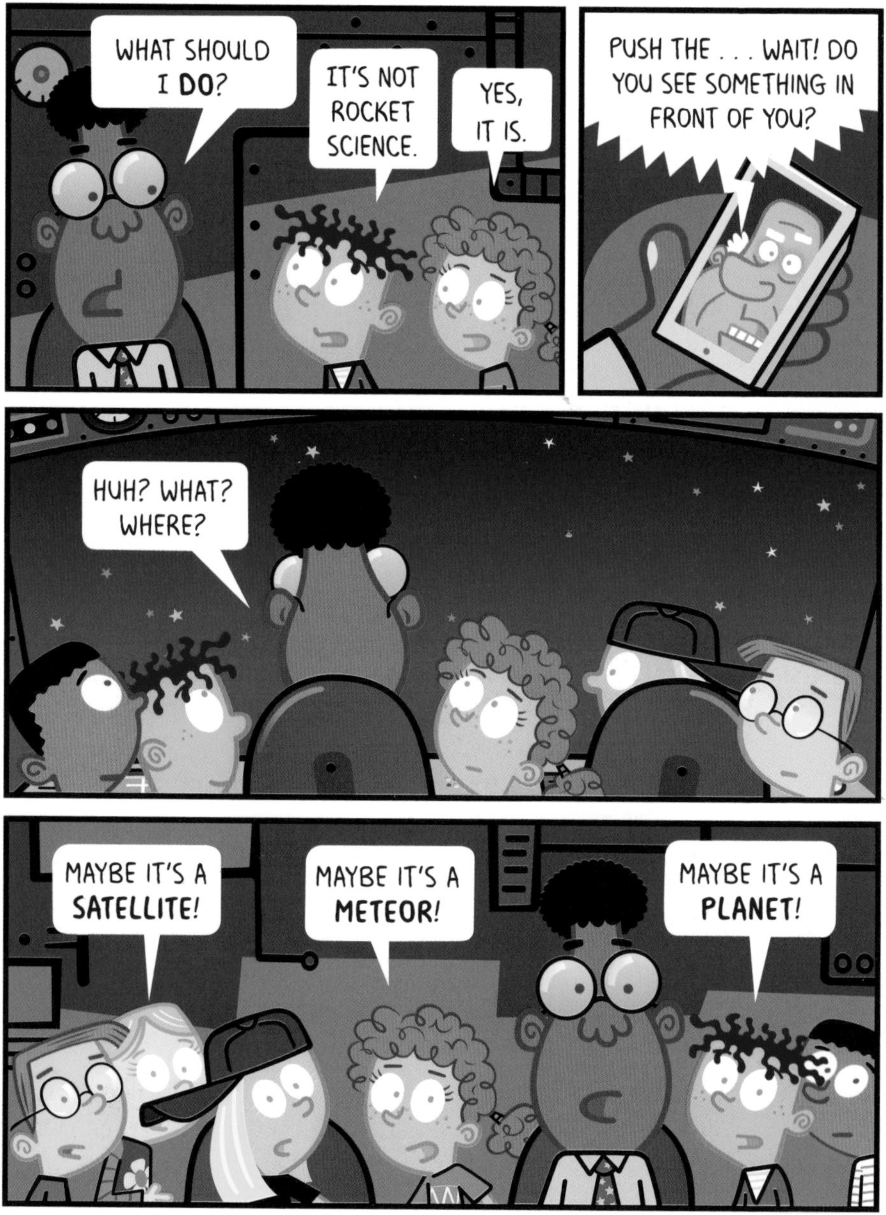
WHAT SHOULD I **DO**?
IT'S NOT ROCKET SCIENCE.
YES, IT IS.
PUSH THE . . . WAIT! DO YOU SEE SOMETHING IN FRONT OF YOU?
HUH? WHAT? WHERE?
MAYBE IT'S A **SATELLITE**!
MAYBE IT'S A **METEOR**!
MAYBE IT'S A **PLANET**!

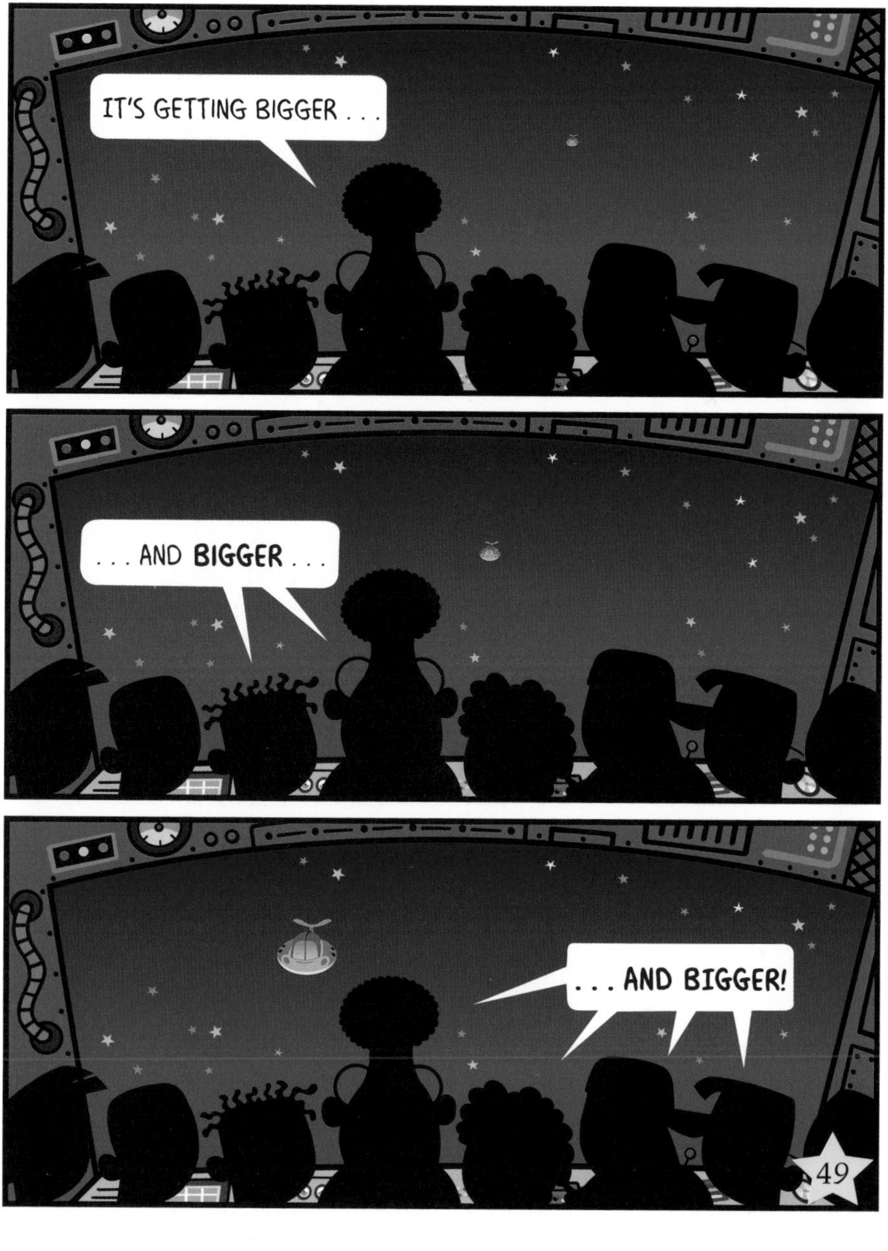
IT'S GETTING BIGGER . . .
. . . AND **BIGGER** . . .
. . . AND BIGGER!

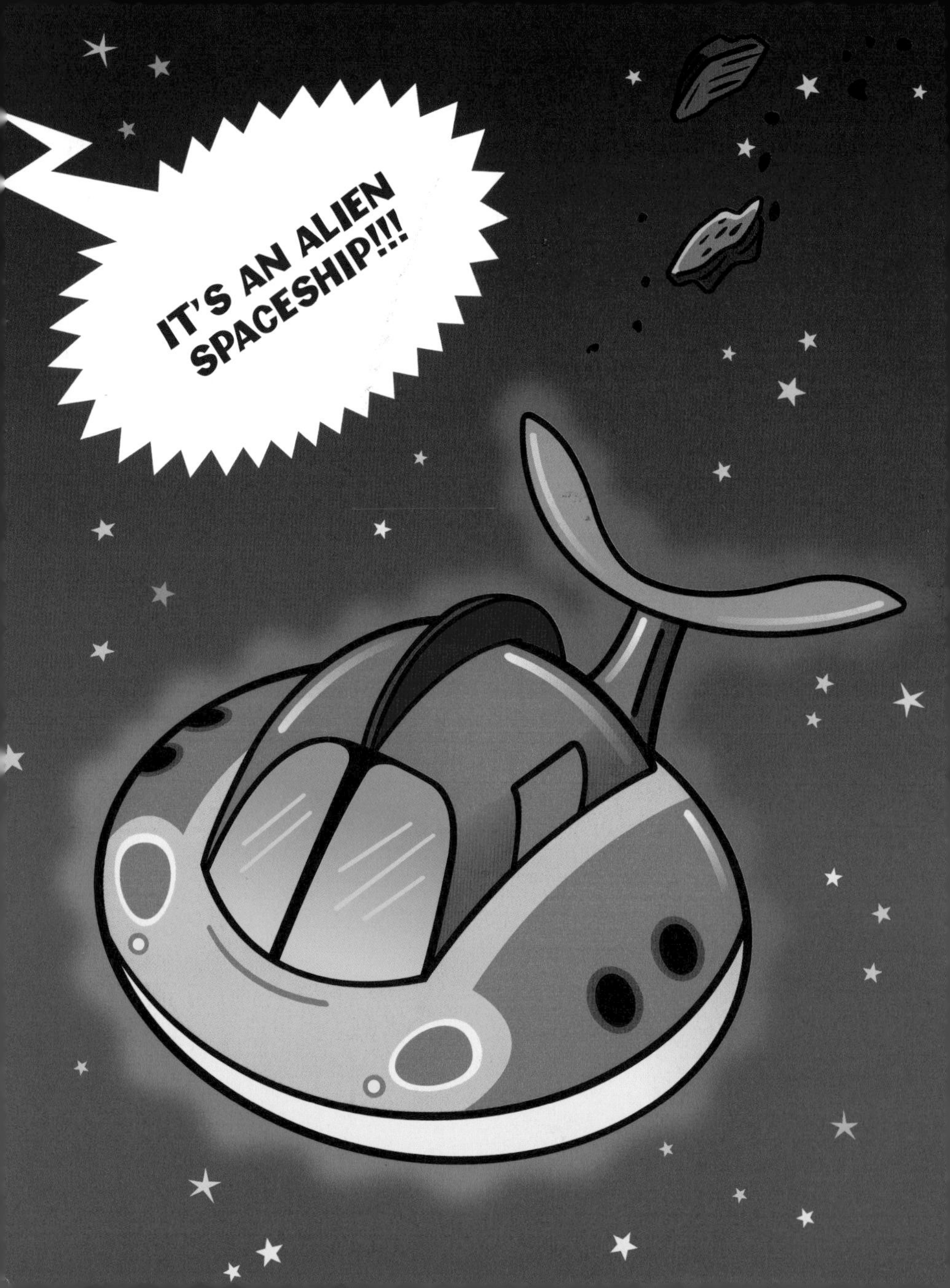
IT'S AN ALIEN SPACESHIP!!!

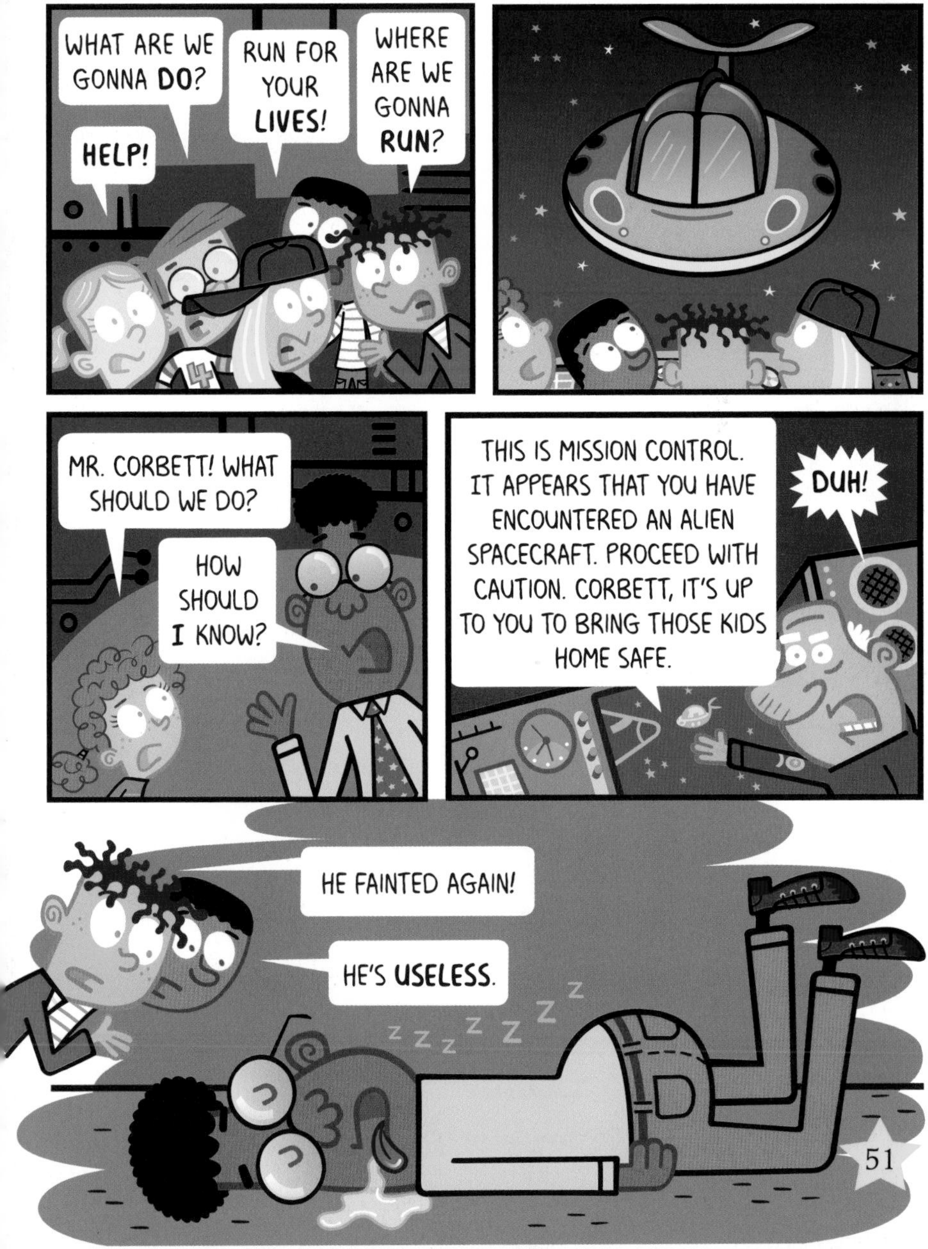

WHAT ARE WE GONNA **DO**?
HELP!
RUN FOR YOUR **LIVES**!
WHERE ARE WE GONNA **RUN**?
MR. CORBETT! WHAT SHOULD WE DO?
HOW SHOULD **I** KNOW?
THIS IS MISSION CONTROL. IT APPEARS THAT YOU HAVE ENCOUNTERED AN ALIEN SPACECRAFT. PROCEED WITH CAUTION. CORBETT, IT'S UP TO YOU TO BRING THOSE KIDS HOME SAFE.
DUH!
HE FAINTED AGAIN!
HE'S **USELESS**.
Z Z Z Z Z Z Z

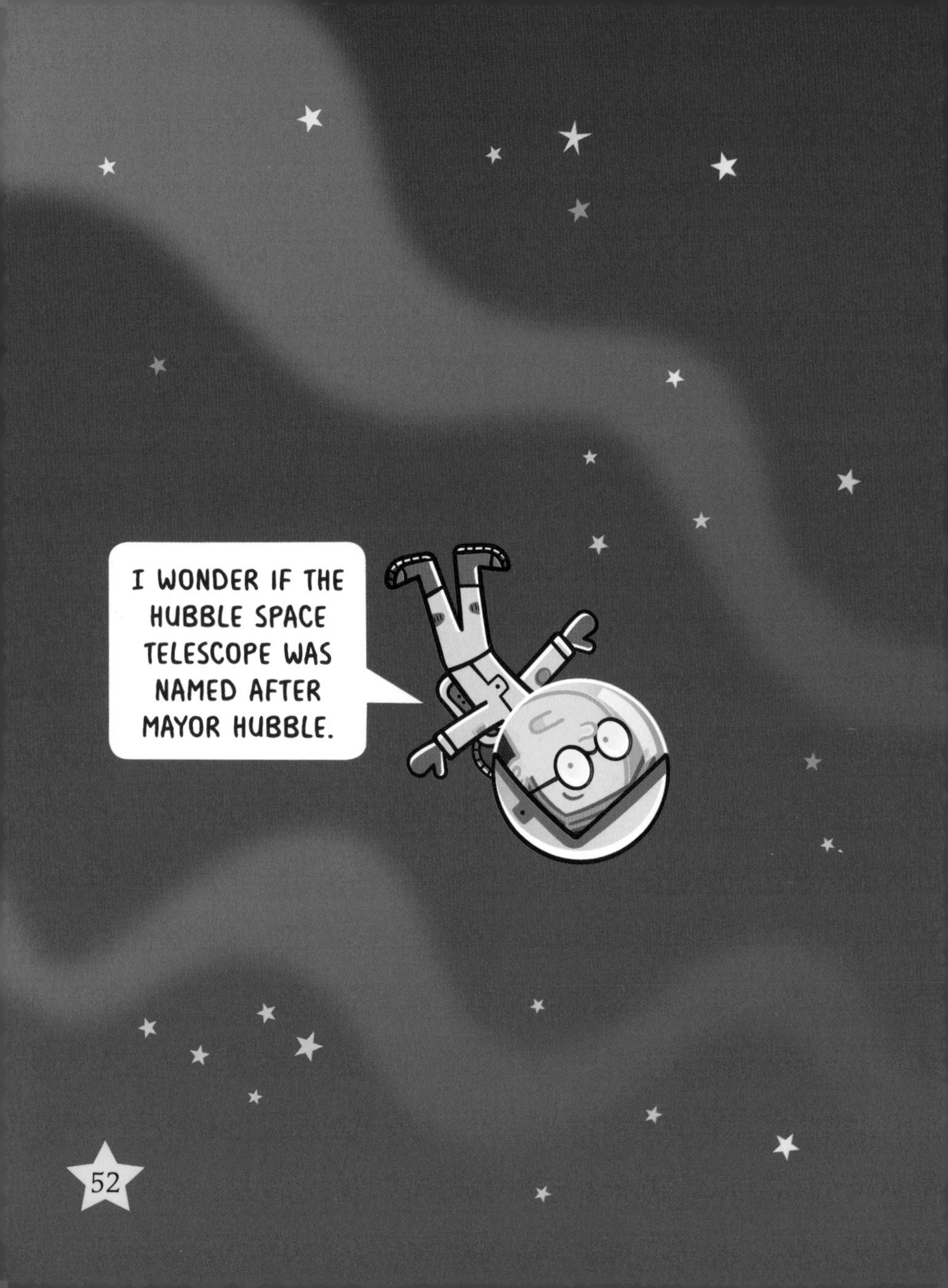
I WONDER IF THE HUBBLE SPACE TELESCOPE WAS NAMED AFTER MAYOR HUBBLE.

CHAPTER 6

More Stuff Happens Here

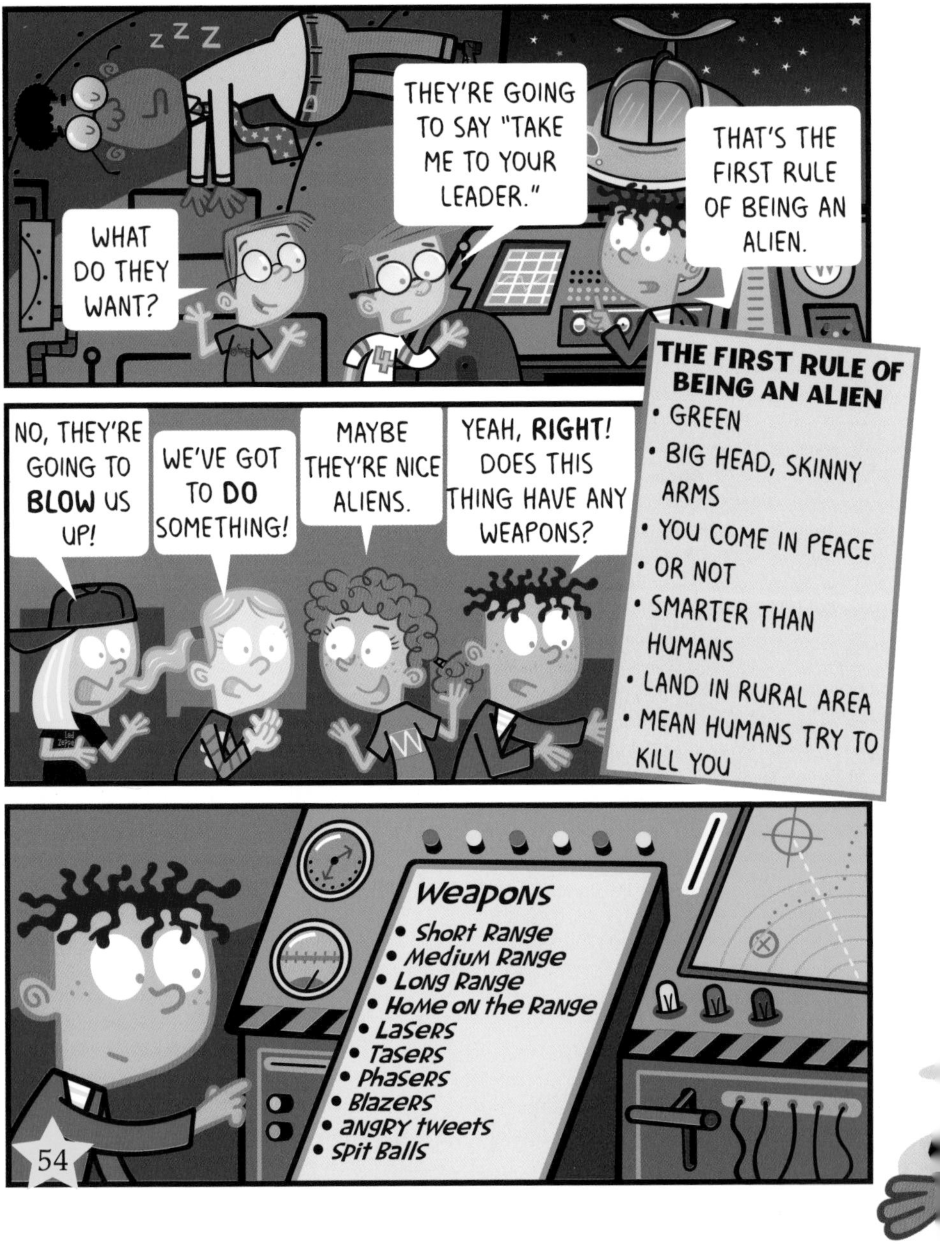
Z Z Z
WHAT DO THEY WANT?
THEY'RE GOING TO SAY "TAKE ME TO YOUR LEADER."
THAT'S THE FIRST RULE OF BEING AN ALIEN.
NO, THEY'RE GOING TO **BLOW** US UP!
WE'VE GOT TO **DO** SOMETHING!
MAYBE THEY'RE NICE ALIENS.
YEAH, **RIGHT**! DOES THIS THING HAVE ANY WEAPONS?
THE FIRST RULE OF BEING AN ALIEN
• GREEN
• BIG HEAD, SKINNY ARMS
• YOU COME IN PEACE
• OR NOT
• SMARTER THAN HUMANS
• LAND IN RURAL AREA
• MEAN HUMANS TRY TO KILL YOU
Weapons
• Short Range
• Medium Range
• Long Range
• Home on the Range
• Lasers
• Tasers
• Phasers
• Blazers
• angry tweets
• Spit Balls

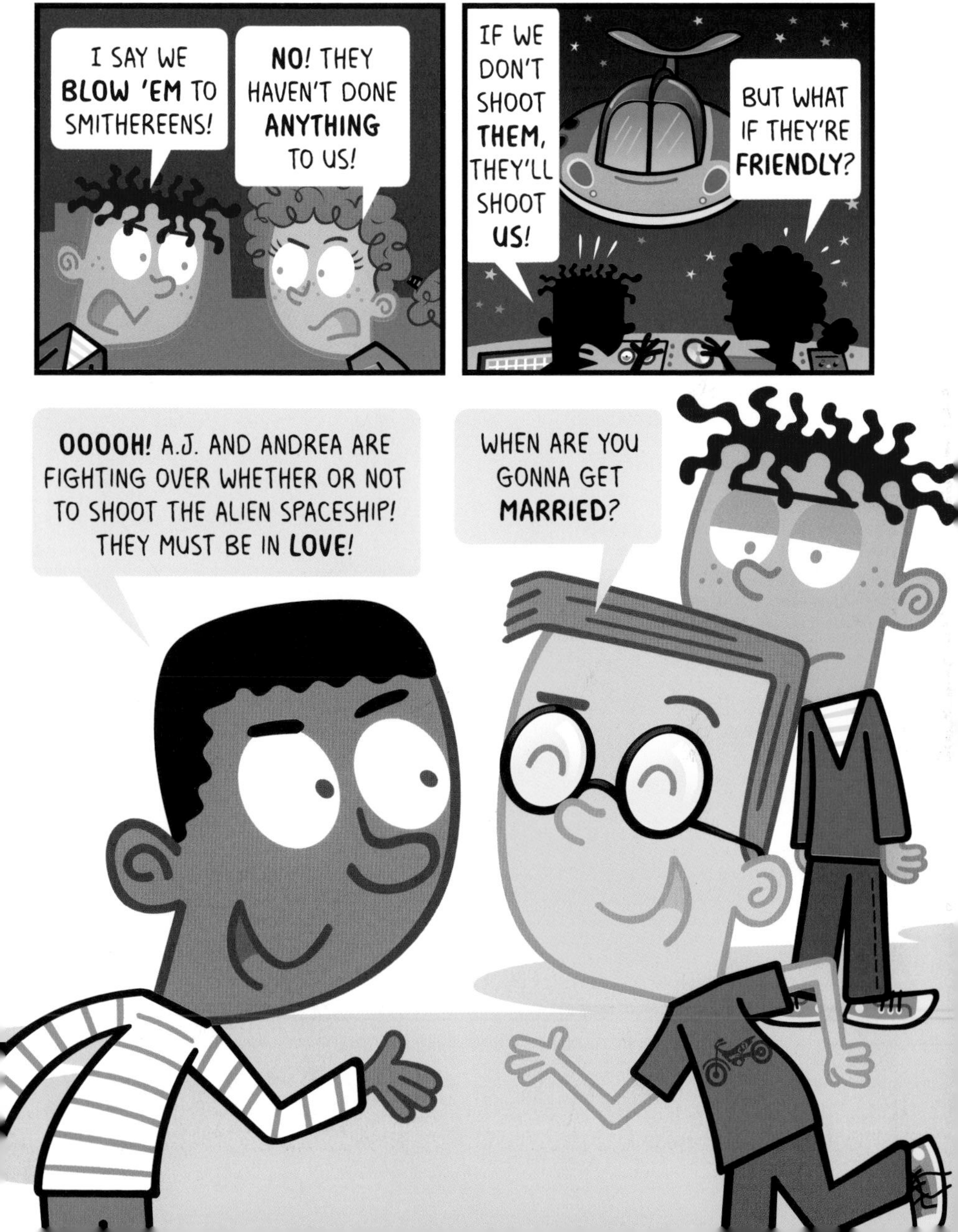
I SAY WE BLOW 'EM TO SMITHEREENS!
NO! THEY HAVEN'T DONE ANYTHING TO US!
IF WE DON'T SHOOT THEM, THEY'LL SHOOT US!
BUT WHAT IF THEY'RE FRIENDLY?
OOOOH! A.J. AND ANDREA ARE FIGHTING OVER WHETHER OR NOT TO SHOOT THE ALIEN SPACESHIP! THEY MUST BE IN LOVE!
WHEN ARE YOU GONNA GET MARRIED?

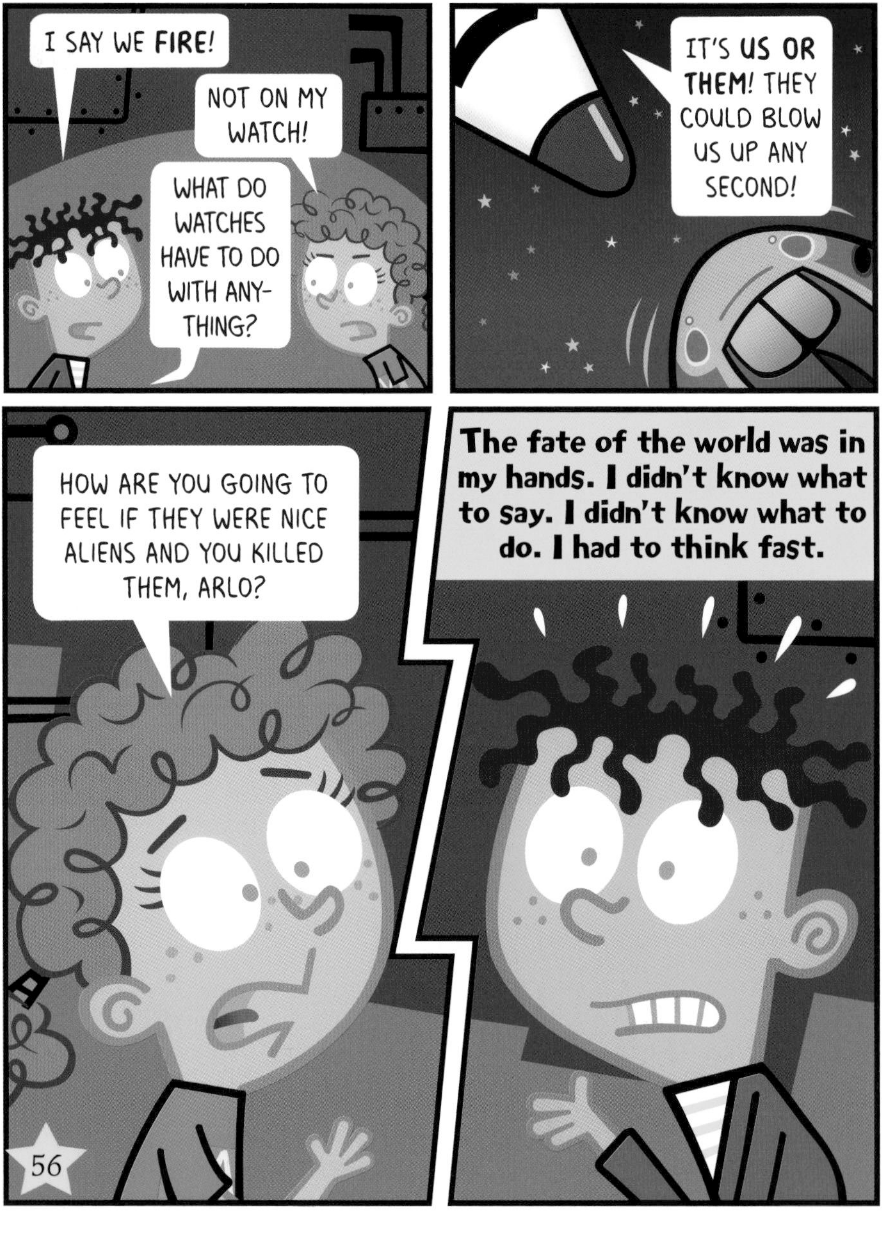
I SAY WE **FIRE**!
NOT ON MY WATCH!
WHAT DO WATCHES HAVE TO DO WITH ANY-THING?
IT'S **US OR THEM**! THEY COULD BLOW US UP ANY SECOND!
HOW ARE YOU GOING TO FEEL IF THEY WERE NICE ALIENS AND YOU KILLED THEM, ARLO?
The fate of the world was in my hands. I didn't know what to say. I didn't know what to do. I had to think fast.

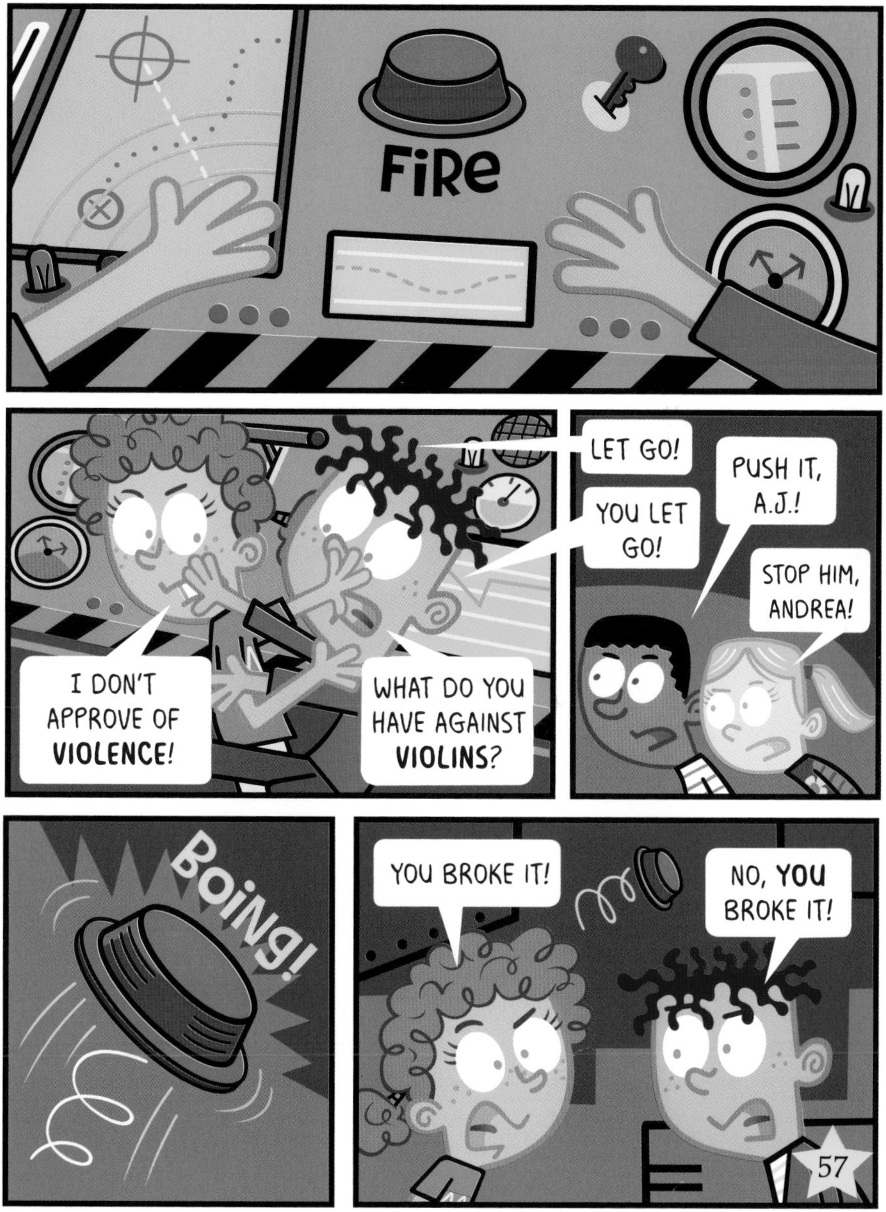

FiRe
LET GO!
YOU LET GO!
I DON'T APPROVE OF **VIOLENCE**!
WHAT DO YOU HAVE AGAINST **VIOLINS**?
PUSH IT, A.J.!
STOP HIM, ANDREA!
BoiNg!
YOU BROKE IT!
NO, **YOU** BROKE IT!

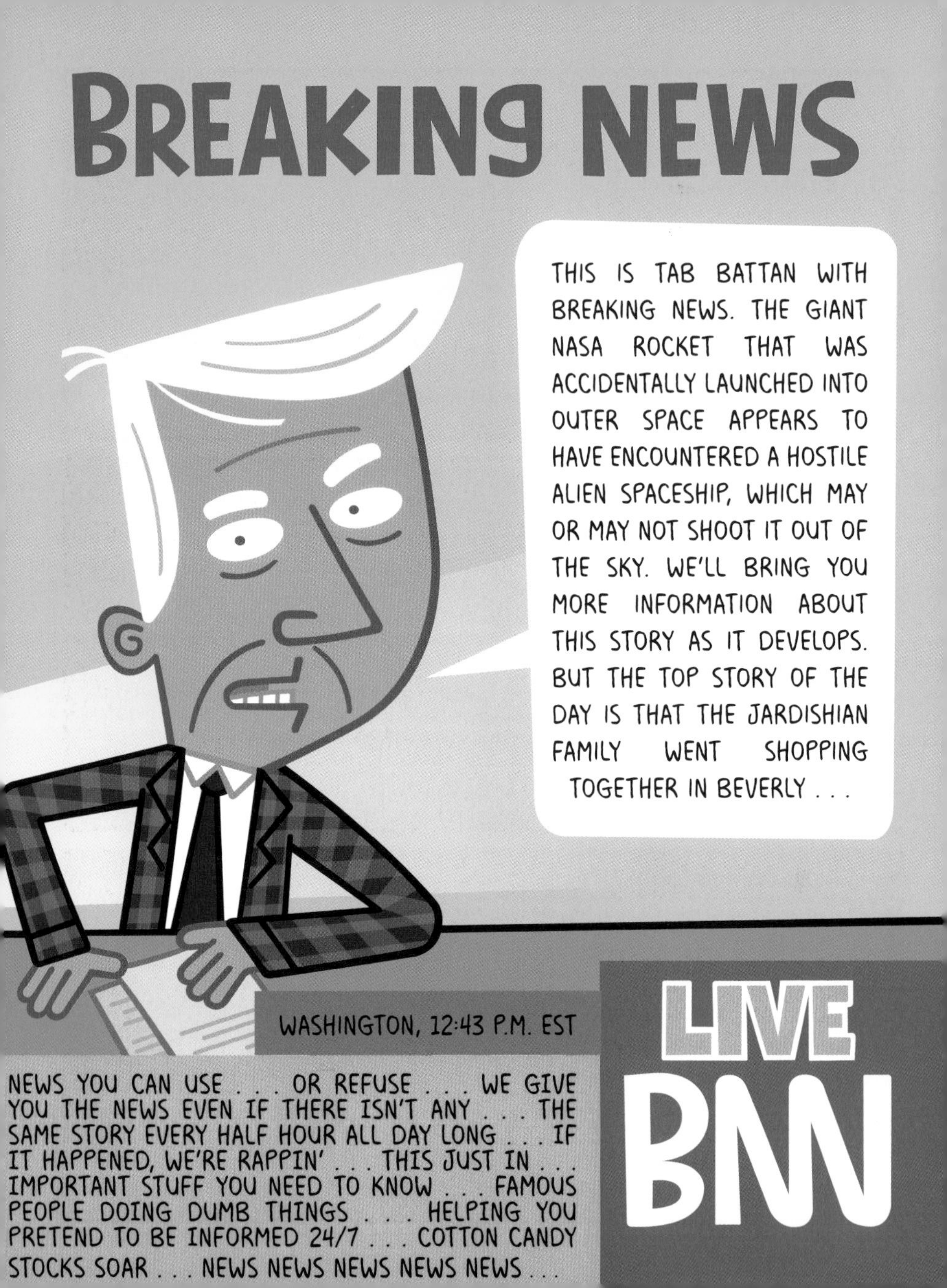
BREAKING NEWS
THIS IS TAB BATTAN WITH BREAKING NEWS. THE GIANT NASA ROCKET THAT WAS ACCIDENTALLY LAUNCHED INTO OUTER SPACE APPEARS TO HAVE ENCOUNTERED A HOSTILE ALIEN SPACESHIP, WHICH MAY OR MAY NOT SHOOT IT OUT OF THE SKY. WE'LL BRING YOU MORE INFORMATION ABOUT THIS STORY AS IT DEVELOPS. BUT THE TOP STORY OF THE DAY IS THAT THE JARDISHIAN FAMILY WENT SHOPPING TOGETHER IN BEVERLY . . .
WASHINGTON, 12:43 P.M. EST
LIVE
BNN
NEWS YOU CAN USE . . . OR REFUSE . . . WE GIVE YOU THE NEWS EVEN IF THERE ISN'T ANY . . . THE SAME STORY EVERY HALF HOUR ALL DAY LONG . . . IF IT HAPPENED, WE'RE RAPPIN' . . . THIS JUST IN . . . IMPORTANT STUFF YOU NEED TO KNOW . . . FAMOUS PEOPLE DOING DUMB THINGS . . . HELPING YOU PRETEND TO BE INFORMED 24/7 . . . COTTON CANDY STOCKS SOAR . . . NEWS NEWS NEWS NEWS NEWS . . .

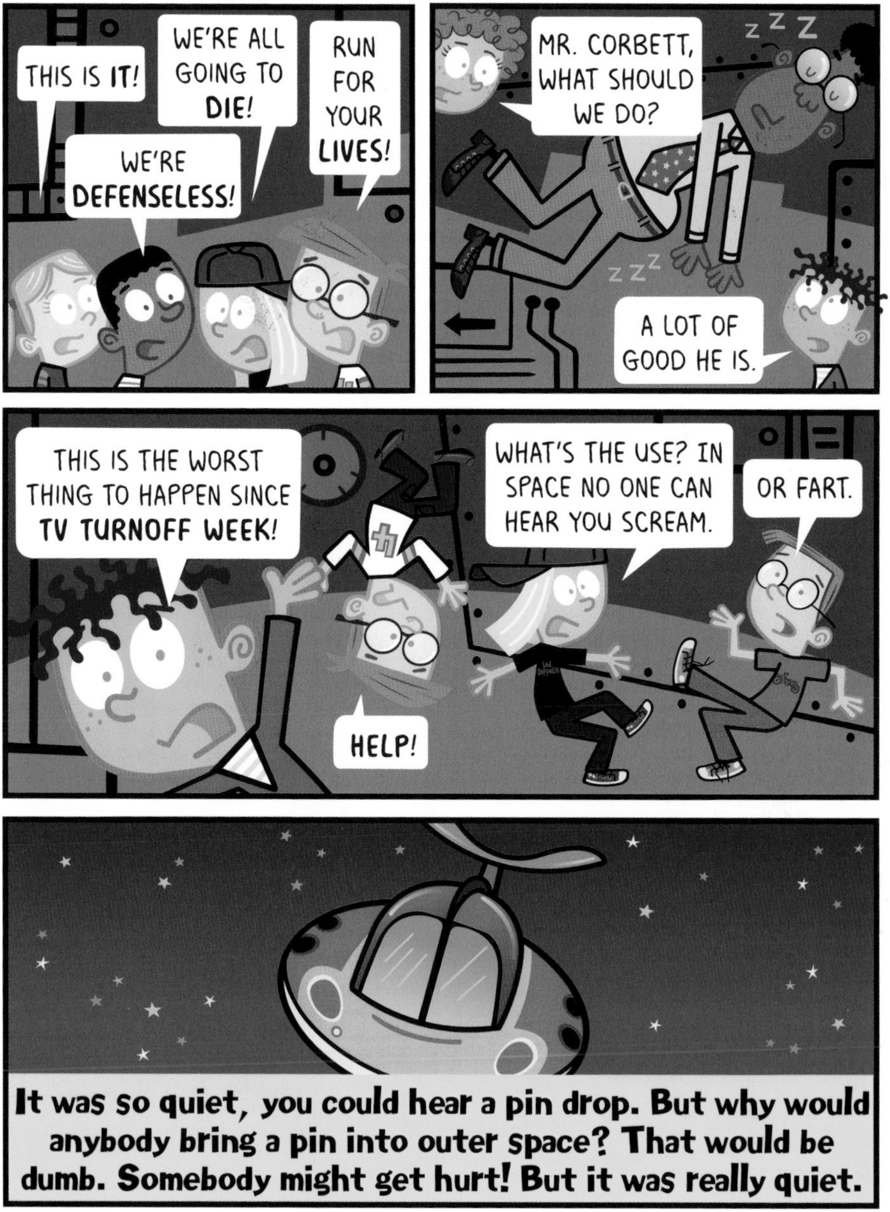
THIS IS IT!
WE'RE ALL GOING TO DIE!
RUN FOR YOUR LIVES!
WE'RE DEFENSELESS!
MR. CORBETT, WHAT SHOULD WE DO?
Z Z Z
Z Z Z
A LOT OF GOOD HE IS.
THIS IS THE WORST THING TO HAPPEN SINCE TV TURNOFF WEEK!
HELP!
WHAT'S THE USE? IN SPACE NO ONE CAN HEAR YOU SCREAM.
OR FART.

It was so quiet, you could hear a pin drop. But why would anybody bring a pin into outer space? That would be dumb. Somebody might get hurt! But it was really quiet.

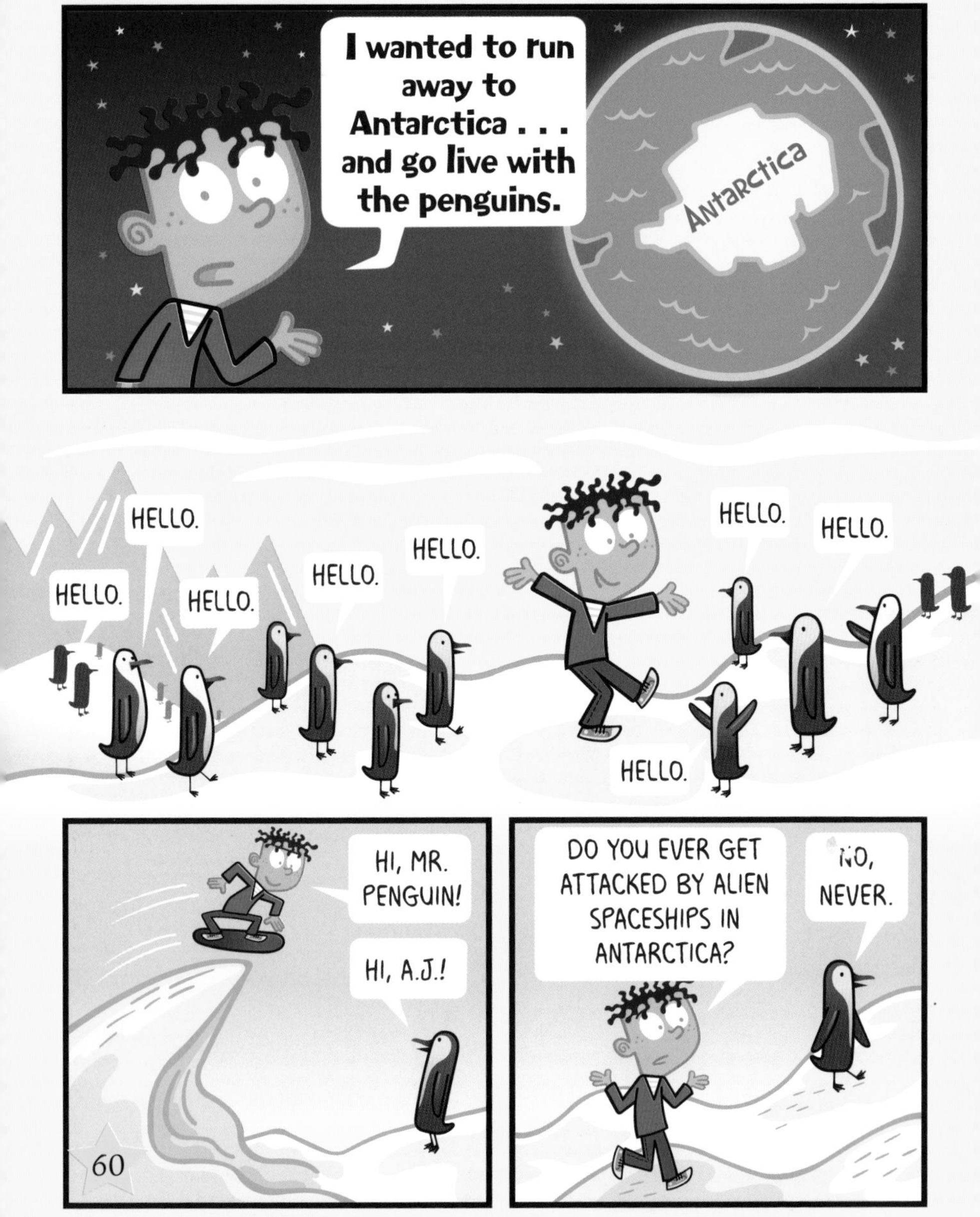
I wanted to run away to Antarctica . . . and go live with the penguins.
Antarctica
HELLO.
HELLO.
HELLO.
HELLO.
HELLO.
HELLO.
HELLO.
HELLO.
HI, MR. PENGUIN!
HI, A.J.!
DO YOU EVER GET ATTACKED BY ALIEN SPACESHIPS IN ANTARCTICA?
NO, NEVER.

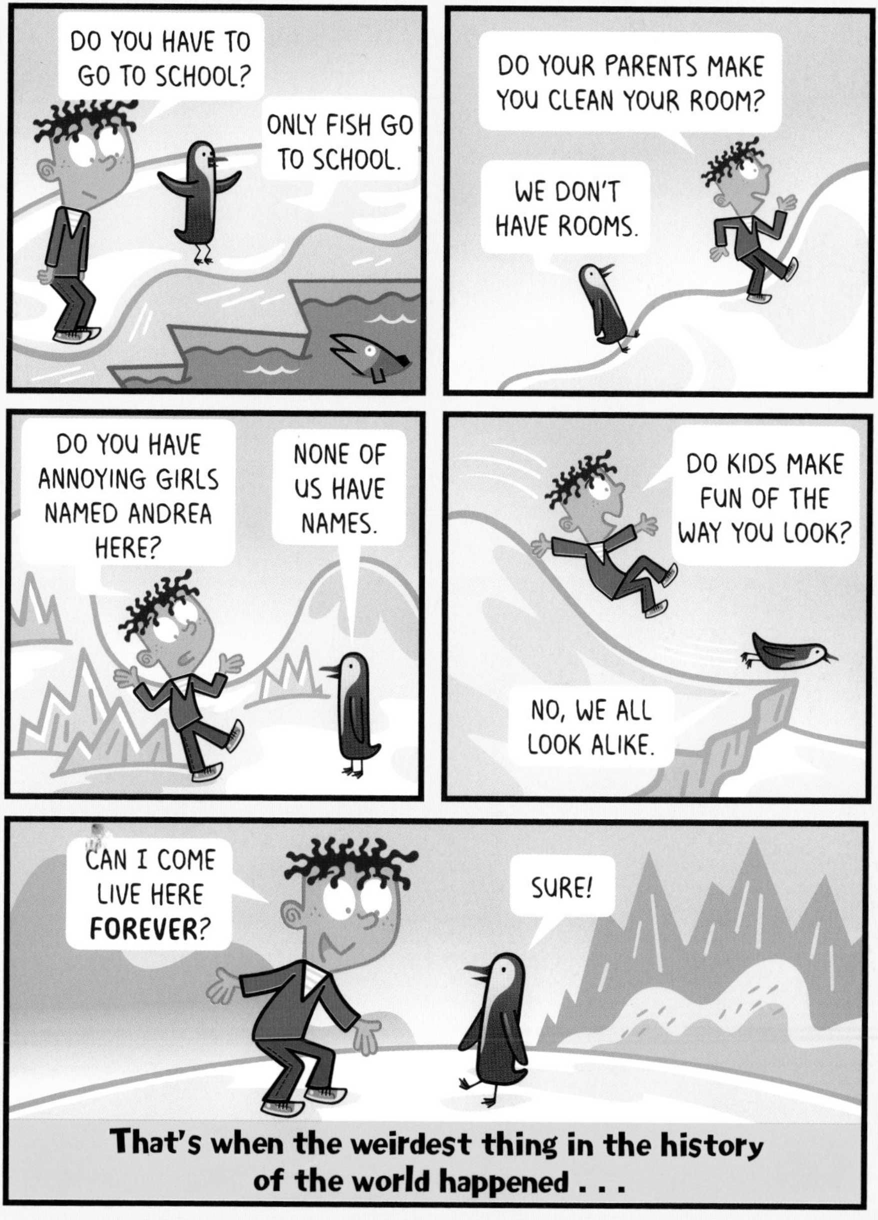
DO YOU HAVE TO GO TO SCHOOL?
ONLY FISH GO TO SCHOOL.
DO YOUR PARENTS MAKE YOU CLEAN YOUR ROOM?
WE DON'T HAVE ROOMS.
DO YOU HAVE ANNOYING GIRLS NAMED ANDREA HERE?
NONE OF US HAVE NAMES.
DO KIDS MAKE FUN OF THE WAY YOU LOOK?
NO, WE ALL LOOK ALIKE.
CAN I COME LIVE HERE **FOREVER**?
SURE!
That's when the weirdest thing in the history of the world happened . . .

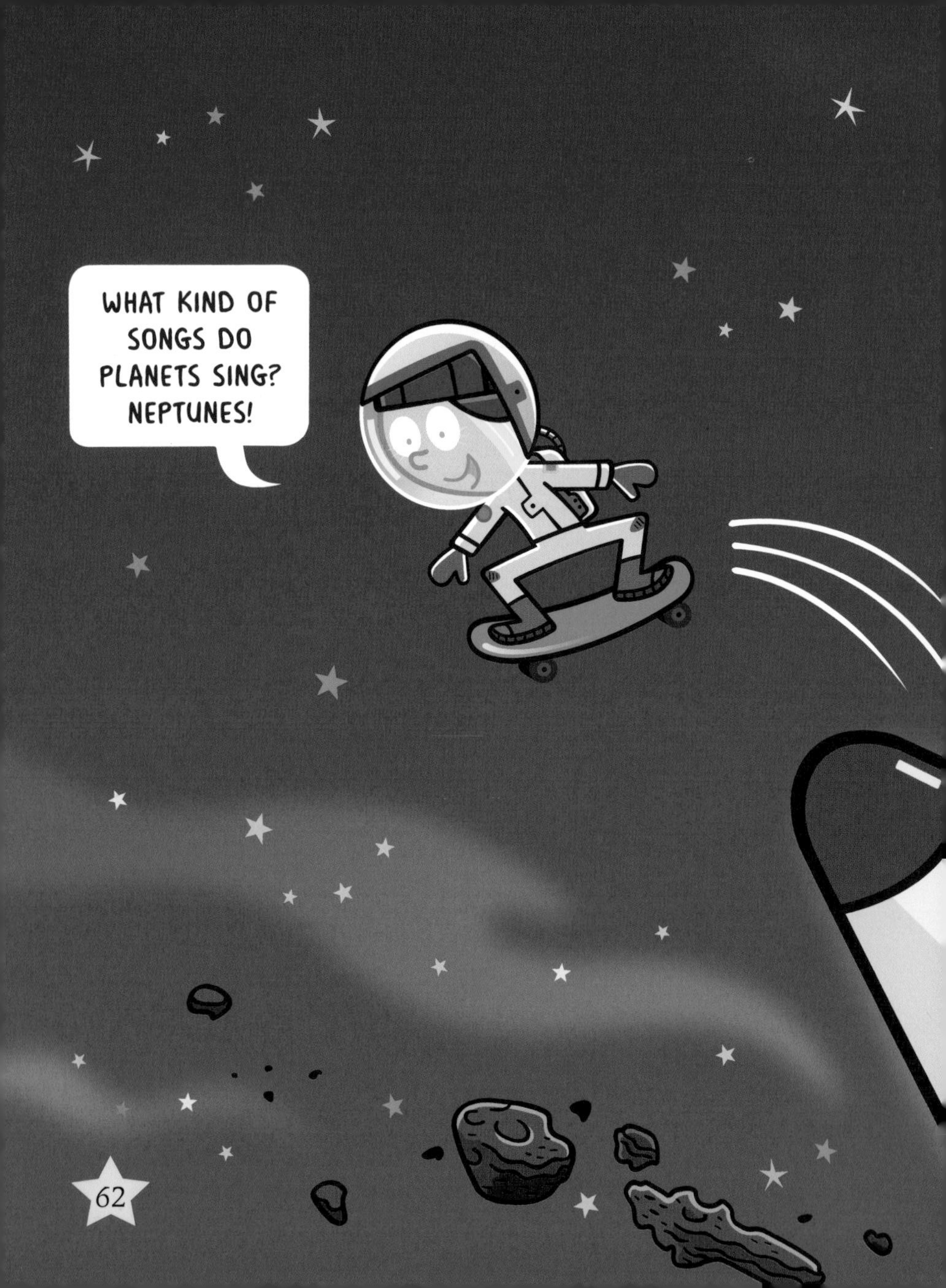
WHAT KIND OF SONGS DO PLANETS SING? NEPTUNES!

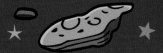

CHAPTER 7

Getting Exciting!

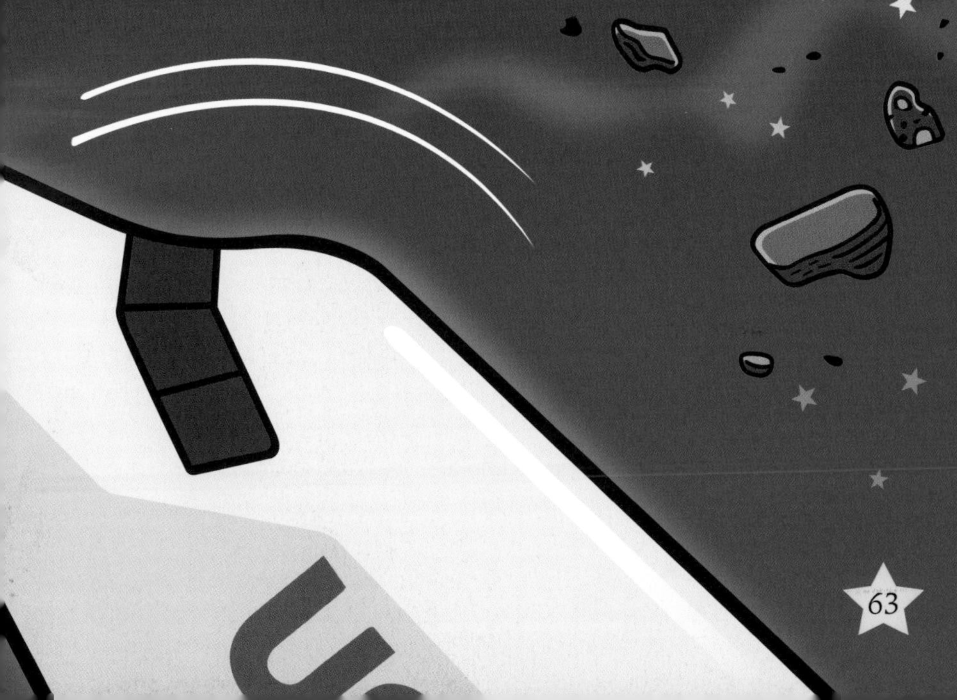

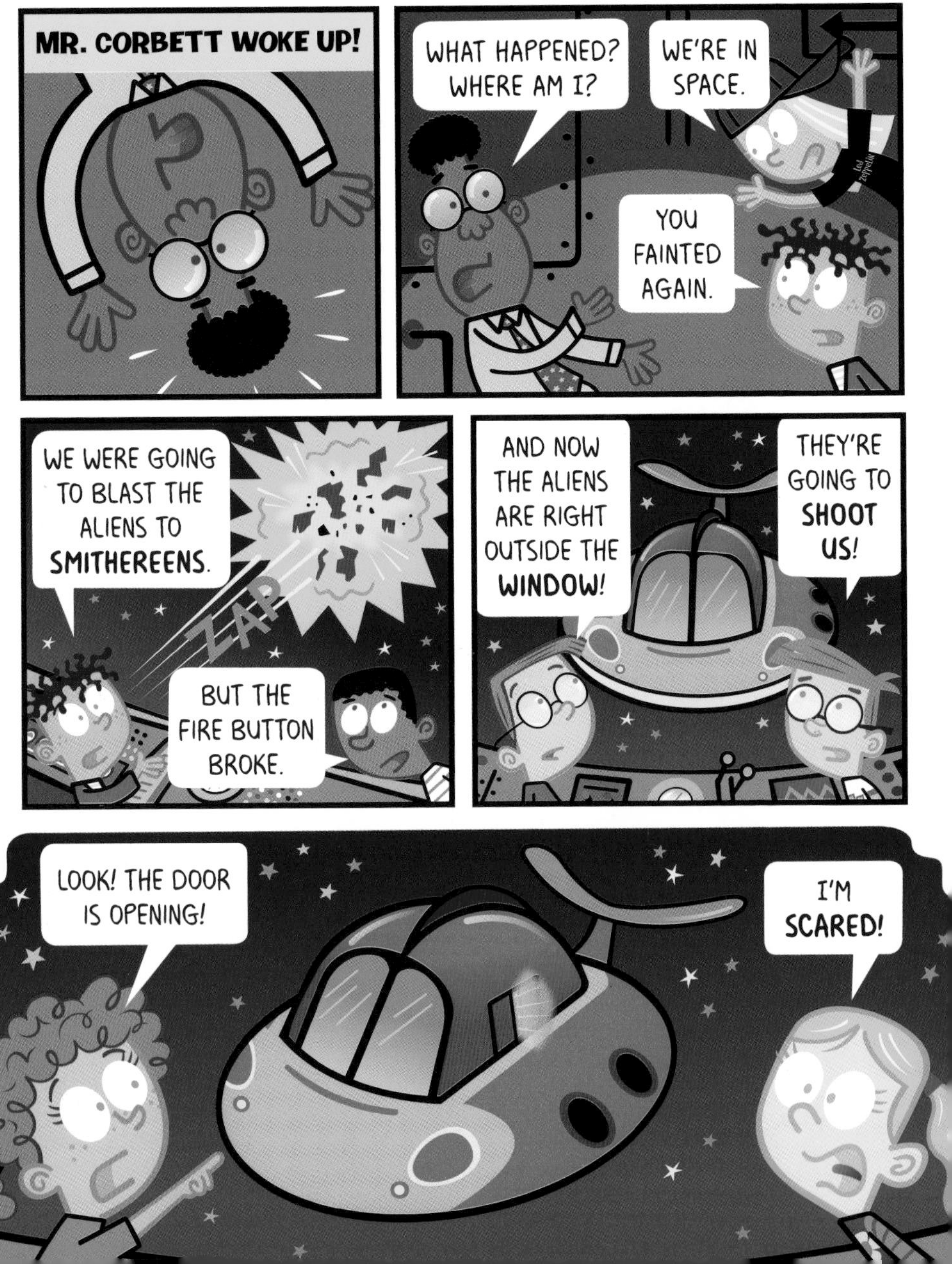
MR. CORBETT WOKE UP!
WHAT HAPPENED? WHERE AM I?
WE'RE IN SPACE.
YOU FAINTED AGAIN.
WE WERE GOING TO BLAST THE ALIENS TO SMITHEREENS.
ZAP
BUT THE FIRE BUTTON BROKE.
AND NOW THE ALIENS ARE RIGHT OUTSIDE THE WINDOW!
THEY'RE GOING TO SHOOT US!
LOOK! THE DOOR IS OPENING!
I'M SCARED!

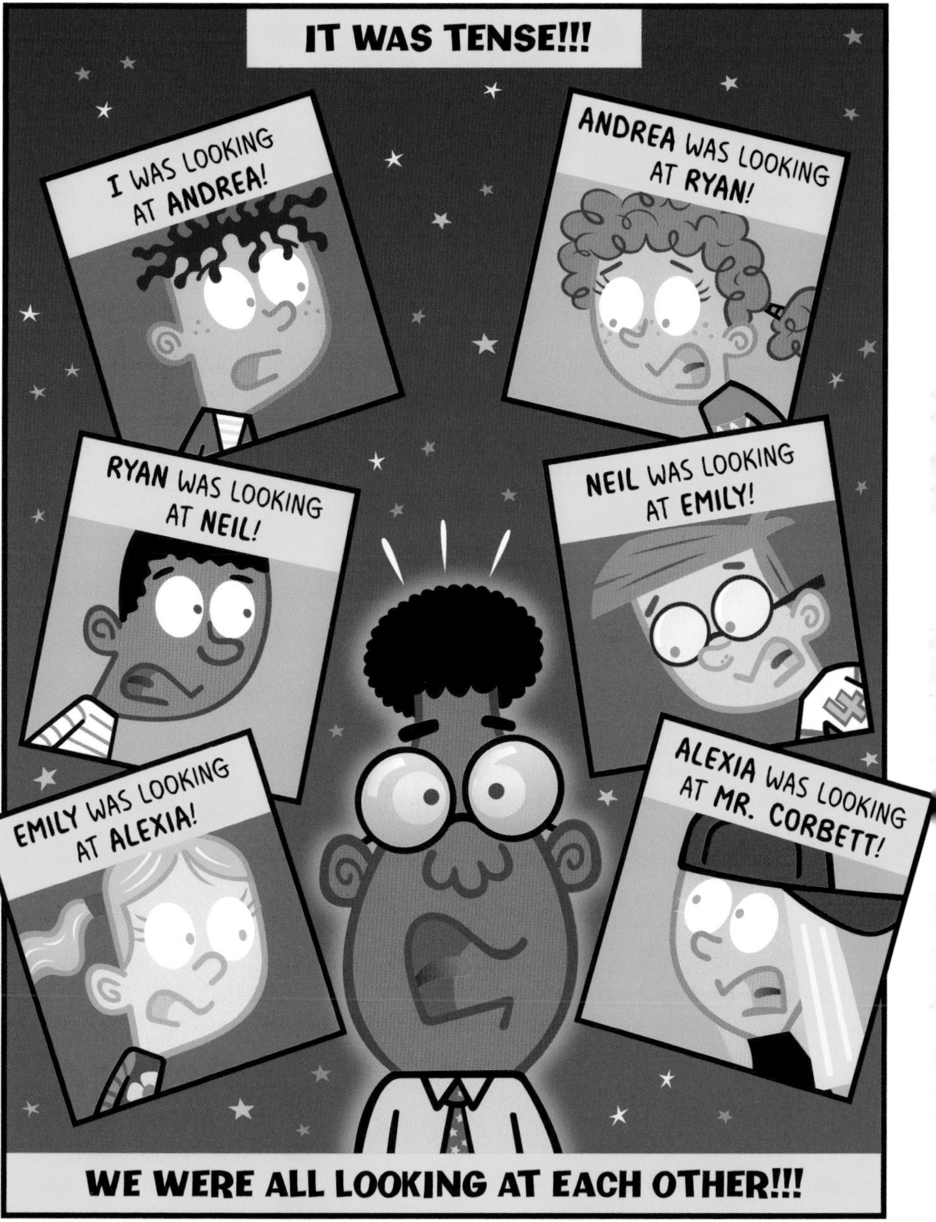
IT WAS TENSE!!!
I WAS LOOKING AT ANDREA!
ANDREA WAS LOOKING AT RYAN!
RYAN WAS LOOKING AT NEIL!
NEIL WAS LOOKING AT EMILY!
EMILY WAS LOOKING AT ALEXIA!
ALEXIA WAS LOOKING AT MR. CORBETT!
WE WERE ALL LOOKING AT EACH OTHER!!!

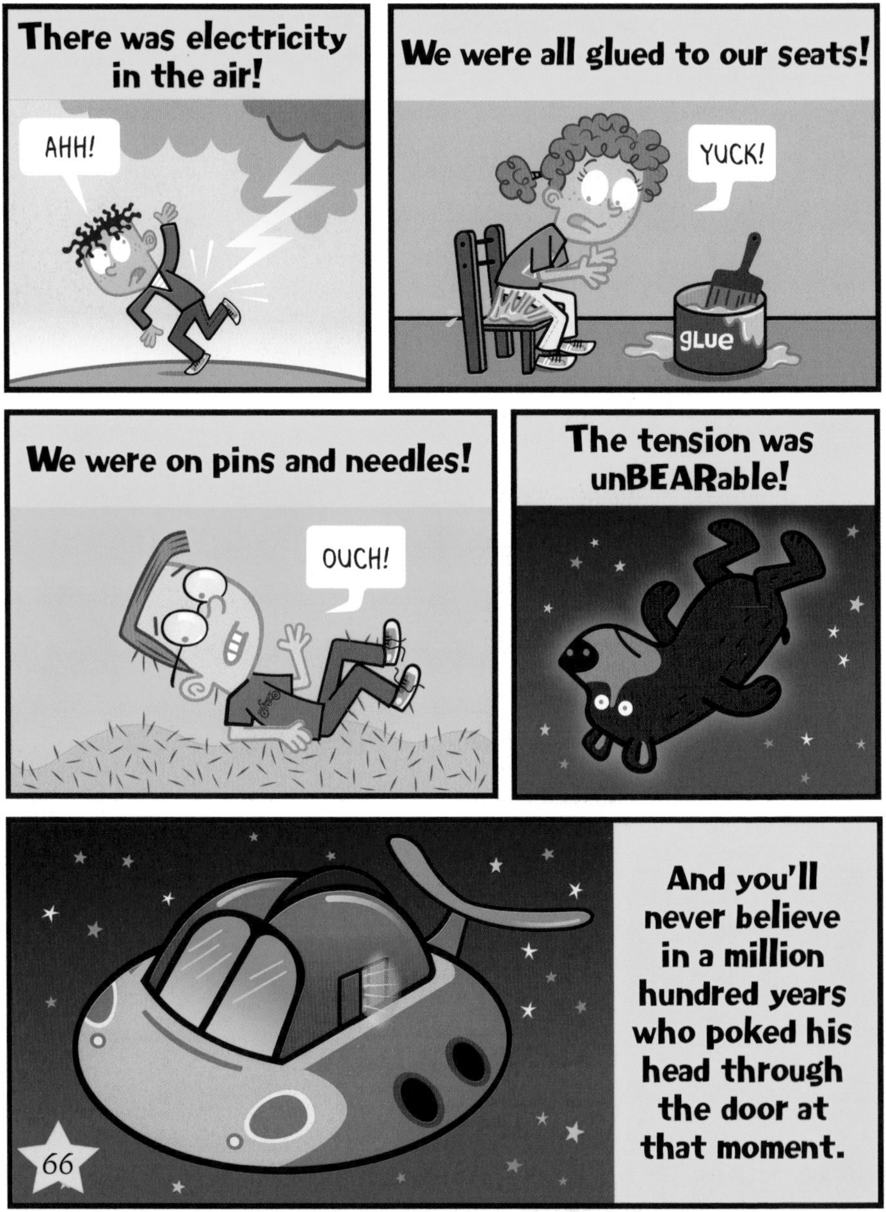
There was electricity in the air!
AHH!
We were all glued to our seats!
YUCK!
gLue
We were on pins and needles!
OUCH!
The tension was unBEARable!
And you'll never believe in a million hundred years who poked his head through the door at that moment.

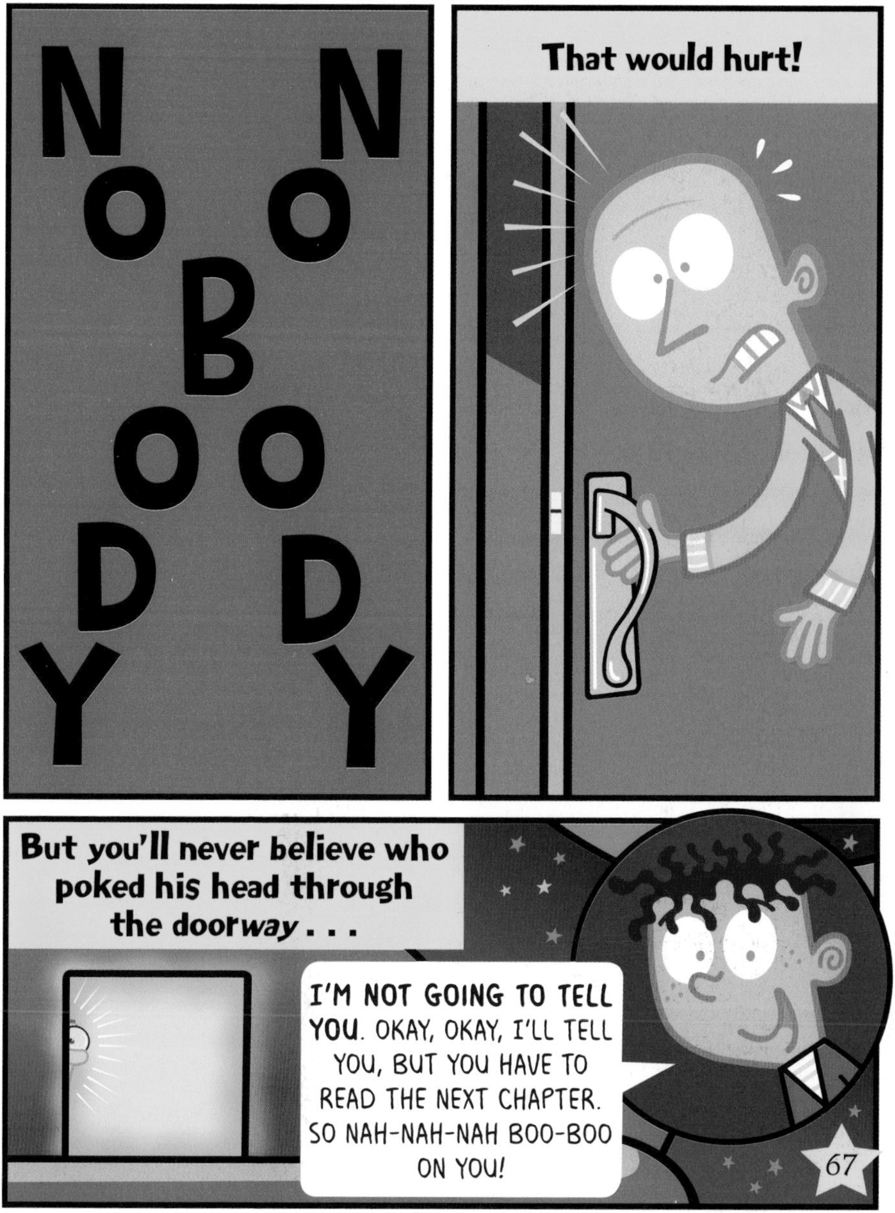
NOBODY
That would hurt!
But you'll never believe who poked his head through the doorway . . .
I'M NOT GOING TO TELL YOU. OKAY, OKAY, I'LL TELL YOU, BUT YOU HAVE TO READ THE NEXT CHAPTER. SO NAH-NAH-NAH BOO-BOO ON YOU!

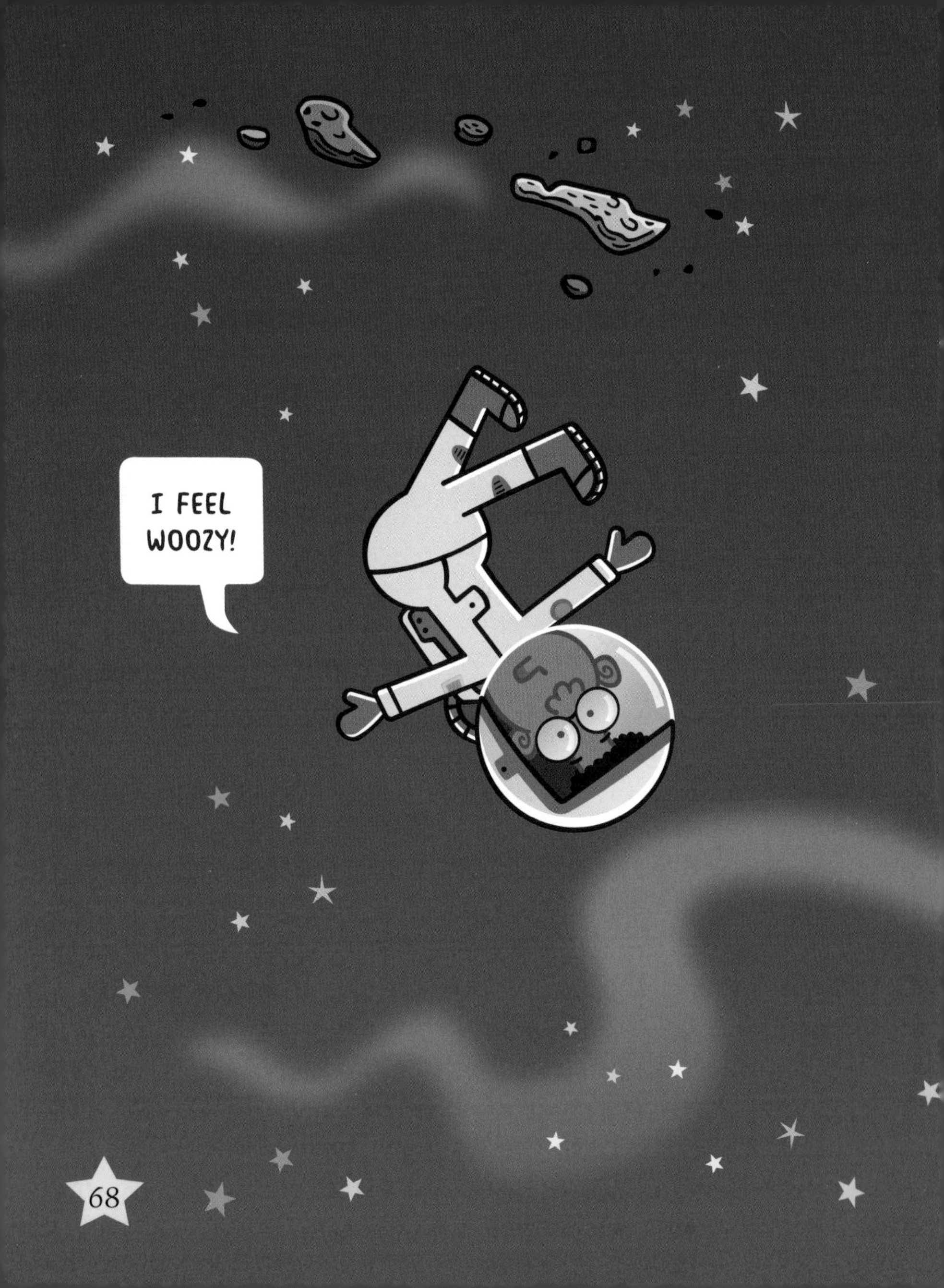
I FEEL WOOZY!

CHapteR 8

Almost the End

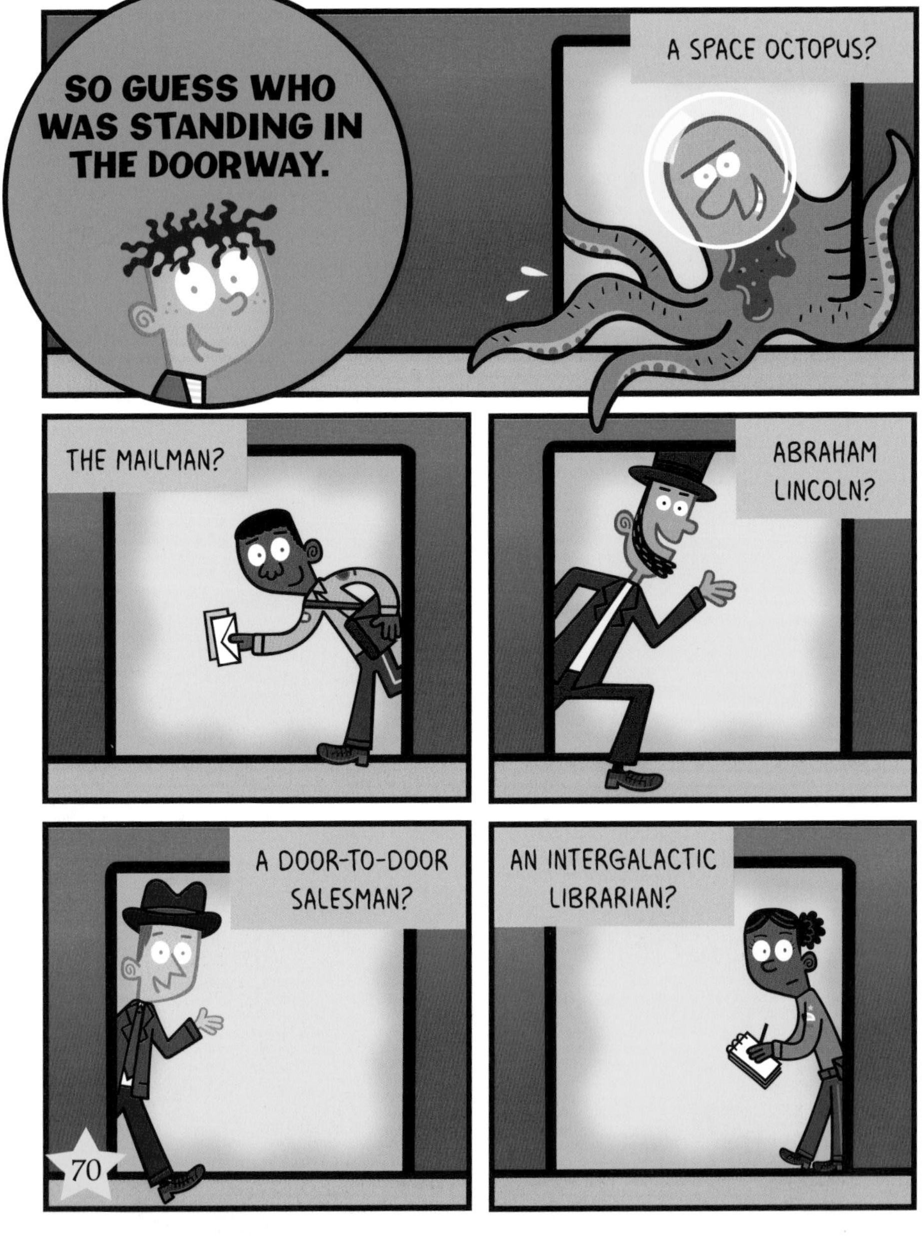
SO GUESS WHO WAS STANDING IN THE DOORWAY.
A SPACE OCTOPUS?
THE MAILMAN?
ABRAHAM LINCOLN?
A DOOR-TO-DOOR SALESMAN?
AN INTERGALACTIC LIBRARIAN?

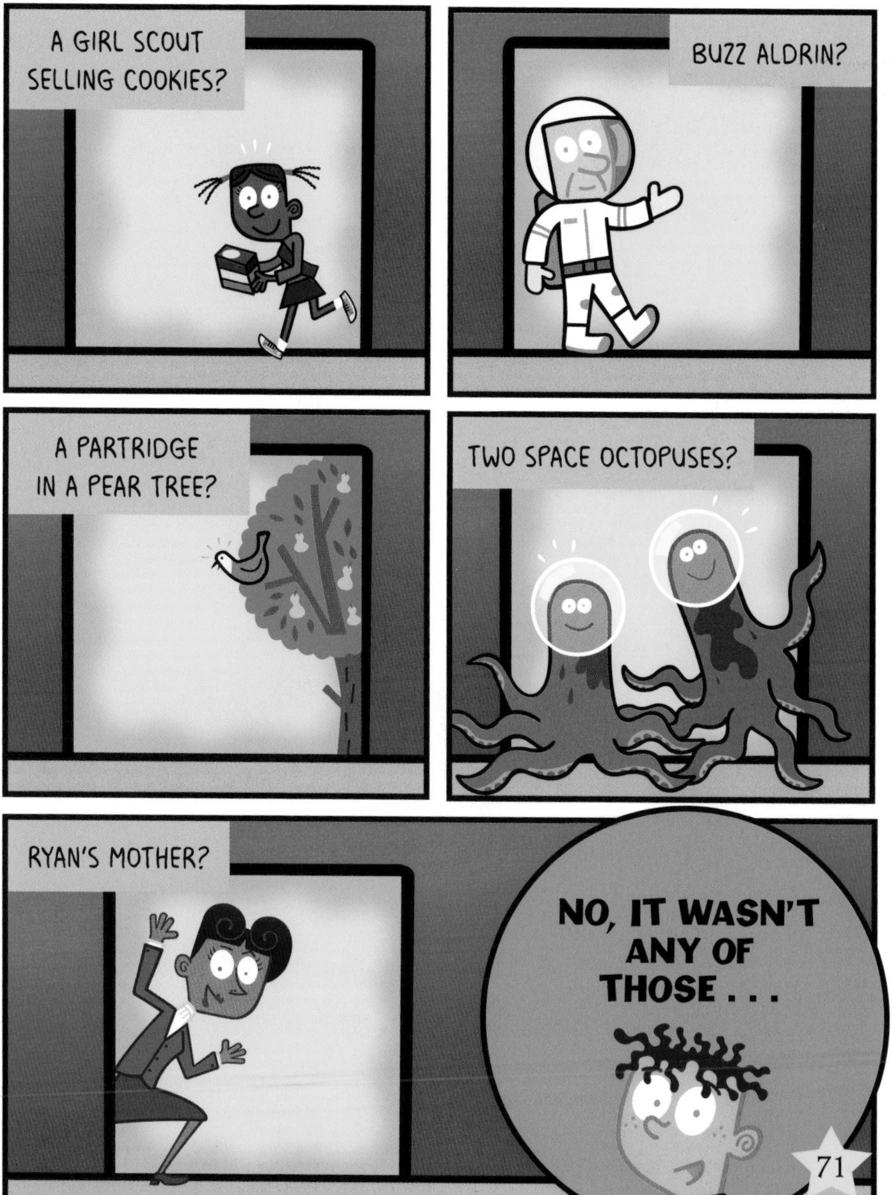
A GIRL SCOUT SELLING COOKIES?
BUZZ ALDRIN?
A PARTRIDGE IN A PEAR TREE?
TWO SPACE OCTOPUSES?
RYAN'S MOTHER?
NO, IT WASN'T ANY OF THOSE . . .

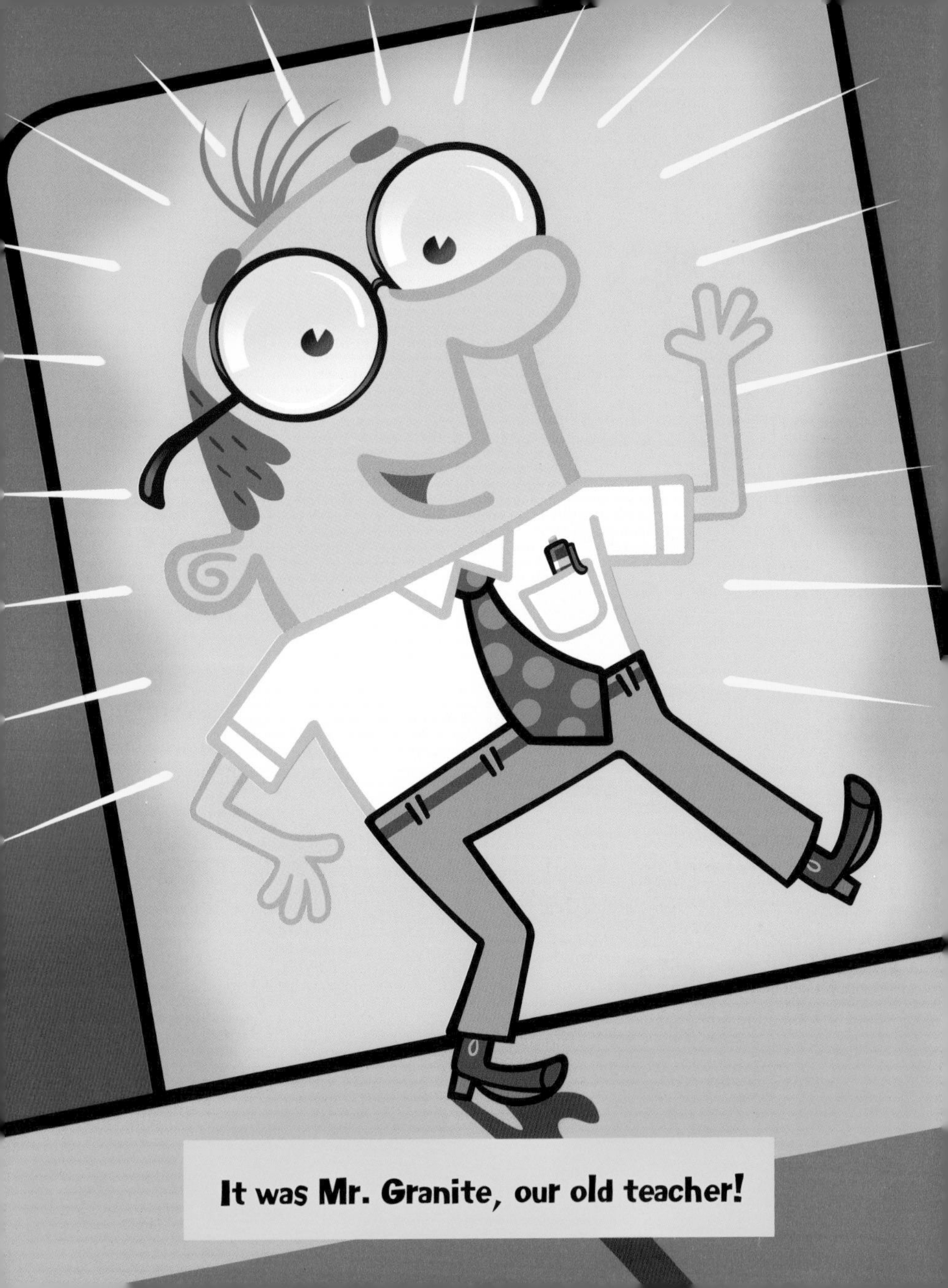

It was Mr. Granite, our old teacher!

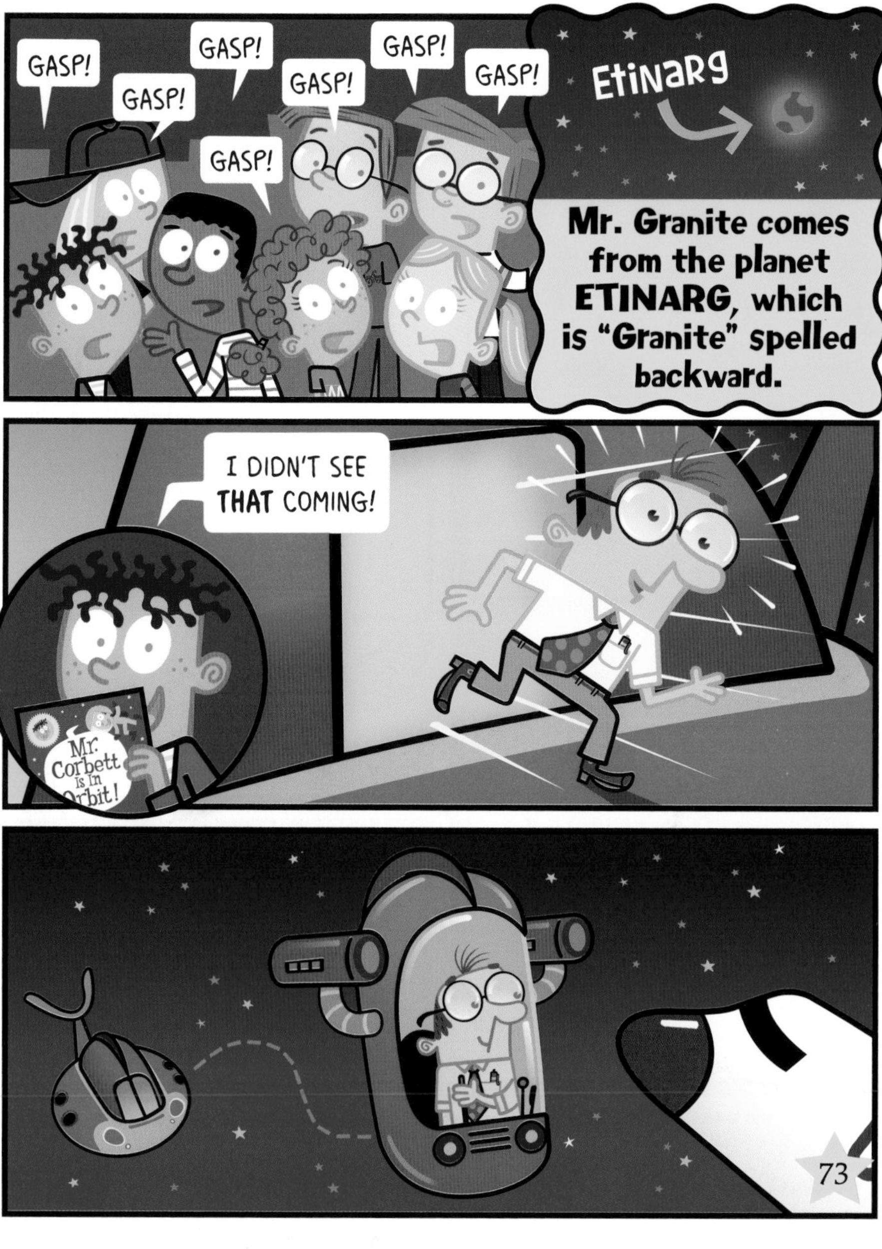
GASP!
GASP!
GASP!
GASP!
GASP!
GASP!
GASP!
Etinarg
Mr. Granite comes from the planet ETINARG, which is "Granite" spelled backward.
I DIDN'T SEE THAT COMING!
Mr. Corbett Is In Orbit!

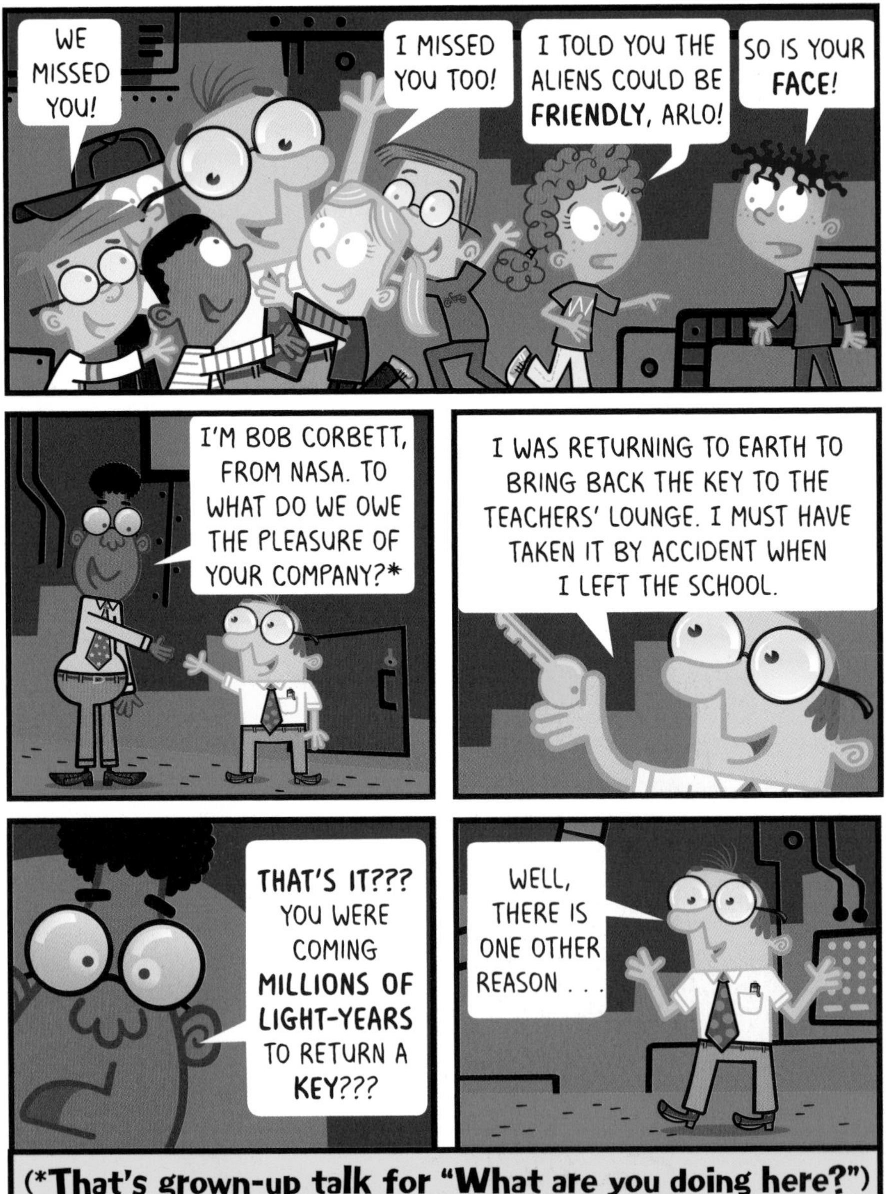
WE MISSED YOU!
I MISSED YOU TOO!
I TOLD YOU THE ALIENS COULD BE **FRIENDLY**, ARLO!
SO IS YOUR **FACE**!
I'M BOB CORBETT, FROM NASA. TO WHAT DO WE OWE THE PLEASURE OF YOUR COMPANY?*
I WAS RETURNING TO EARTH TO BRING BACK THE KEY TO THE TEACHERS' LOUNGE. I MUST HAVE TAKEN IT BY ACCIDENT WHEN I LEFT THE SCHOOL.
THAT'S IT??? YOU WERE COMING **MILLIONS OF LIGHT-YEARS** TO RETURN A **KEY**???
WELL, THERE IS ONE OTHER REASON . . .

(*That's grown-up talk for "What are you doing here?")

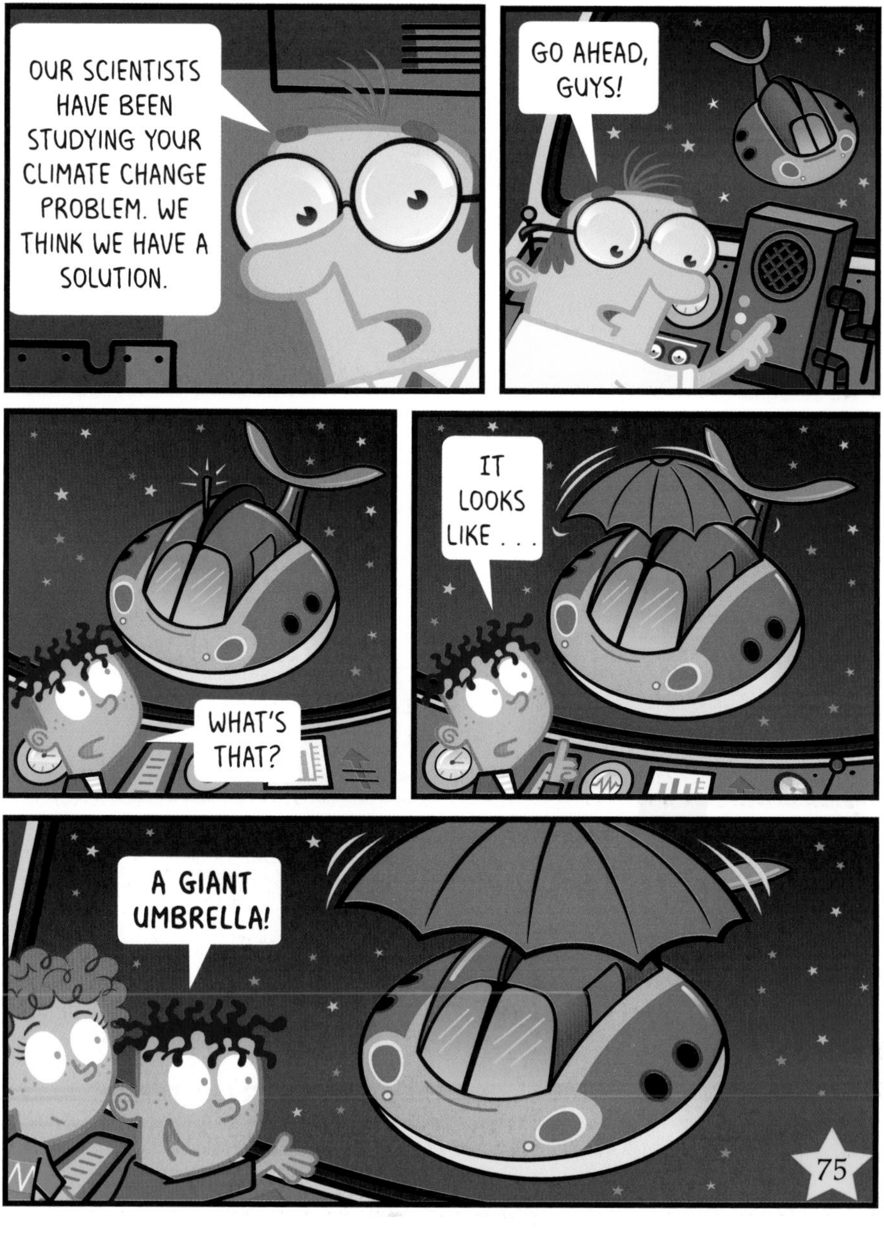
OUR SCIENTISTS HAVE BEEN STUDYING YOUR CLIMATE CHANGE PROBLEM. WE THINK WE HAVE A SOLUTION.
GO AHEAD, GUYS!
WHAT'S THAT?
IT LOOKS LIKE . . .
A GIANT UMBRELLA!

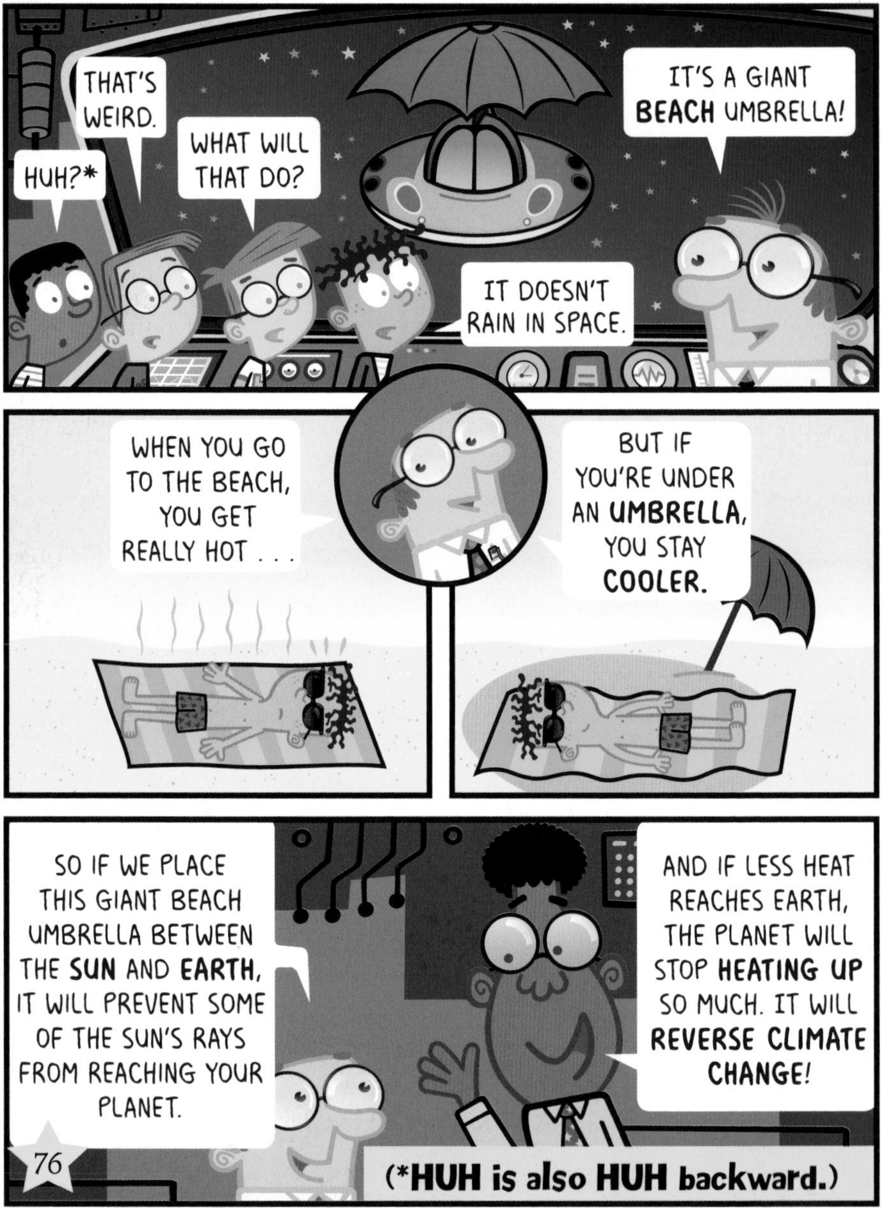

HUH?*
THAT'S WEIRD.
WHAT WILL THAT DO?
IT DOESN'T RAIN IN SPACE.
IT'S A GIANT BEACH UMBRELLA!
WHEN YOU GO TO THE BEACH, YOU GET REALLY HOT . . .
BUT IF YOU'RE UNDER AN UMBRELLA, YOU STAY COOLER.
SO IF WE PLACE THIS GIANT BEACH UMBRELLA BETWEEN THE SUN AND EARTH, IT WILL PREVENT SOME OF THE SUN'S RAYS FROM REACHING YOUR PLANET.
AND IF LESS HEAT REACHES EARTH, THE PLANET WILL STOP HEATING UP SO MUCH. IT WILL REVERSE CLIMATE CHANGE!
(*HUH is also HUH backward.)

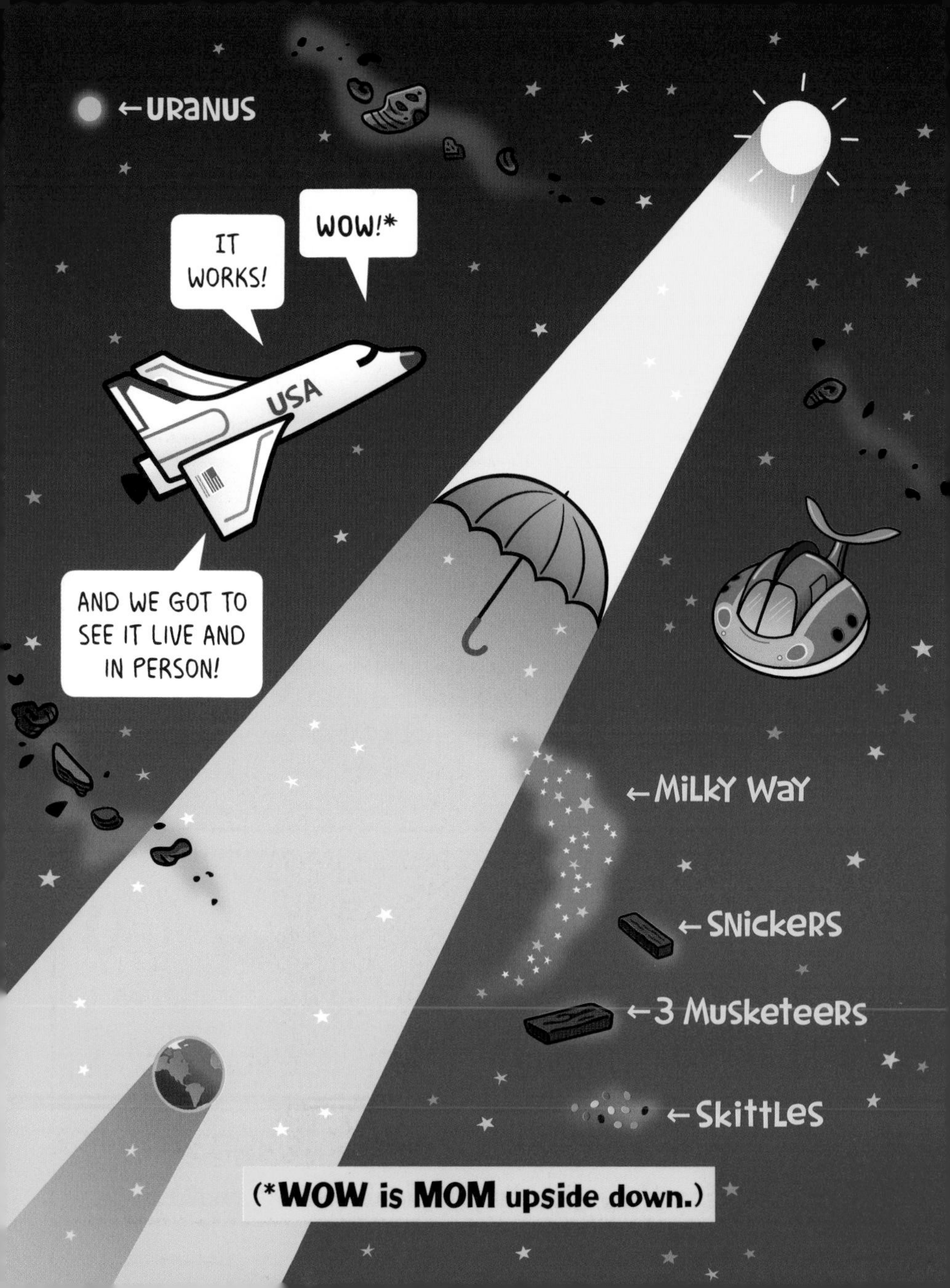
←URANUS
IT WORKS!
WOW!*
AND WE GOT TO SEE IT LIVE AND IN PERSON!
USA
←MILKY WAY
←SNICKERS
←3 MUSKETEERS
←SKITTLES

(***WOW** is **MOM** upside down.)

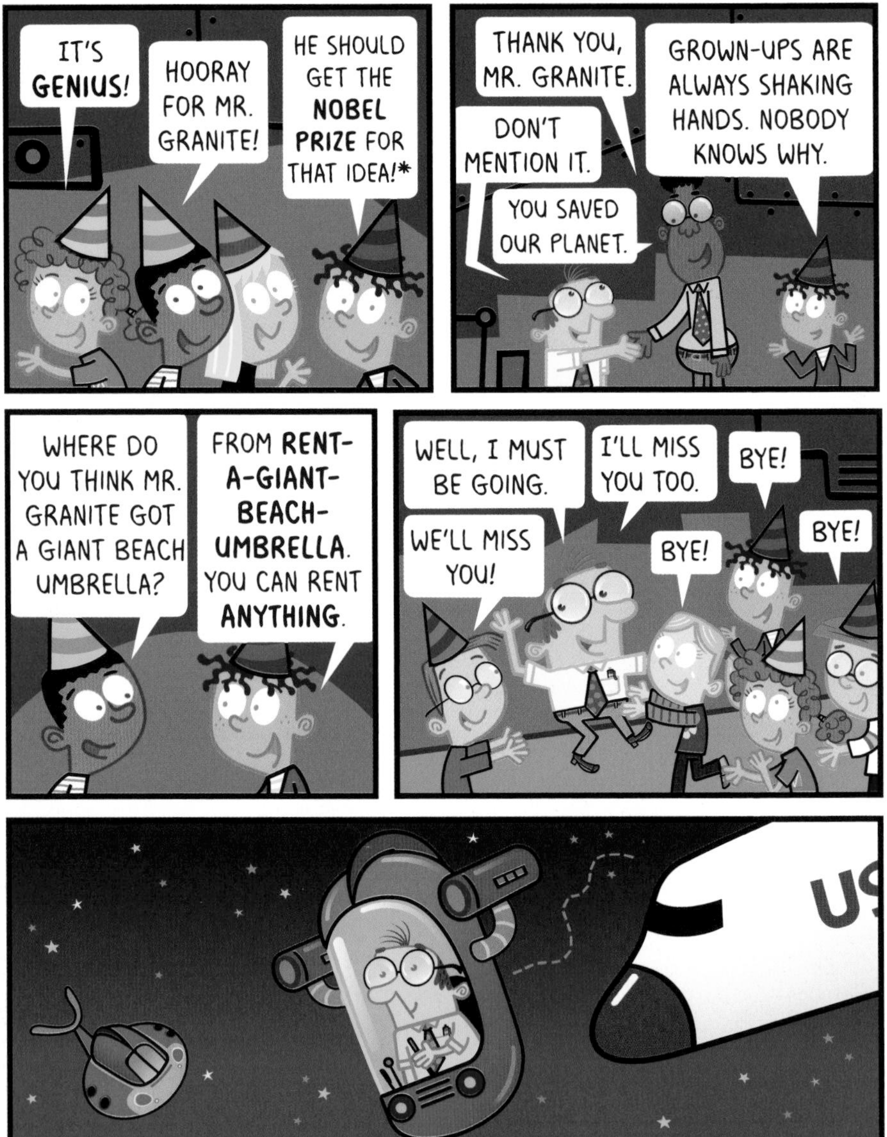
IT'S **GENIUS!**
HOORAY FOR MR. GRANITE!
HE SHOULD GET THE **NOBEL PRIZE** FOR THAT IDEA!*
THANK YOU, MR. GRANITE.
DON'T MENTION IT.
YOU SAVED OUR PLANET.
GROWN-UPS ARE ALWAYS SHAKING HANDS. NOBODY KNOWS WHY.
WHERE DO YOU THINK MR. GRANITE GOT A GIANT BEACH UMBRELLA?
FROM **RENT-A-GIANT-BEACH-UMBRELLA**. YOU CAN RENT **ANYTHING**.
WELL, I MUST BE GOING.
I'LL MISS YOU TOO.
BYE!
WE'LL MISS YOU!
BYE!
BYE!
(*That's a prize they give to people who don't have bells.)

BREAKING NEWS

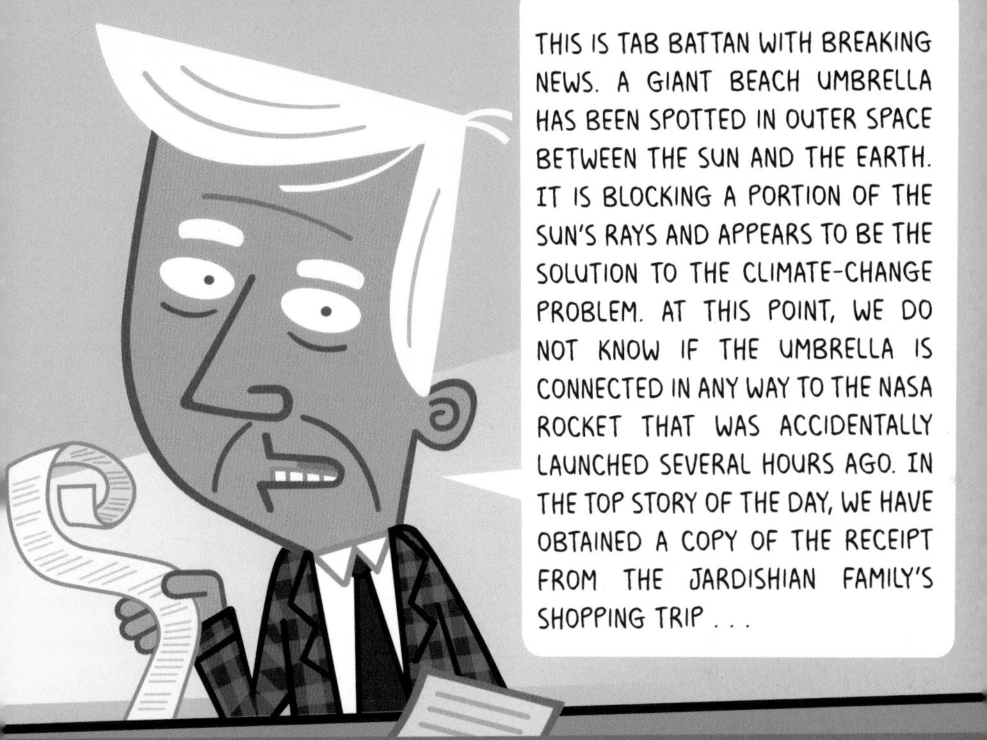
THIS IS TAB BATTAN WITH BREAKING NEWS. A GIANT BEACH UMBRELLA HAS BEEN SPOTTED IN OUTER SPACE BETWEEN THE SUN AND THE EARTH. IT IS BLOCKING A PORTION OF THE SUN'S RAYS AND APPEARS TO BE THE SOLUTION TO THE CLIMATE-CHANGE PROBLEM. AT THIS POINT, WE DO NOT KNOW IF THE UMBRELLA IS CONNECTED IN ANY WAY TO THE NASA ROCKET THAT WAS ACCIDENTALLY LAUNCHED SEVERAL HOURS AGO. IN THE TOP STORY OF THE DAY, WE HAVE OBTAINED A COPY OF THE RECEIPT FROM THE JARDISHIAN FAMILY'S SHOPPING TRIP . . .

WASHINGTON, 2:15 P.M. EST

A CORNUCOPIA OF NEWS . . . BAD STUFF HAPPENING 24/7 . . . COTTON CANDY STOCKS PLUMMET . . . THERE WAS A FIRE SOMEWHERE . . . CELEBRITIES WALKING DOWN THE STREET HOLDING COFFEE CUPS . . . WATCH US OR GET A LIFE . . . SOMEBODY GOT CAUGHT DOING BAD STUFF . . . MEANINGLESS INFO THAT DOESN'T CONCERN YOU . . . WHY ARE YOU STILL READING THIS? IF YOU TURN US OFF, YOU'LL BE SORRY . . .

LIVE

BNN

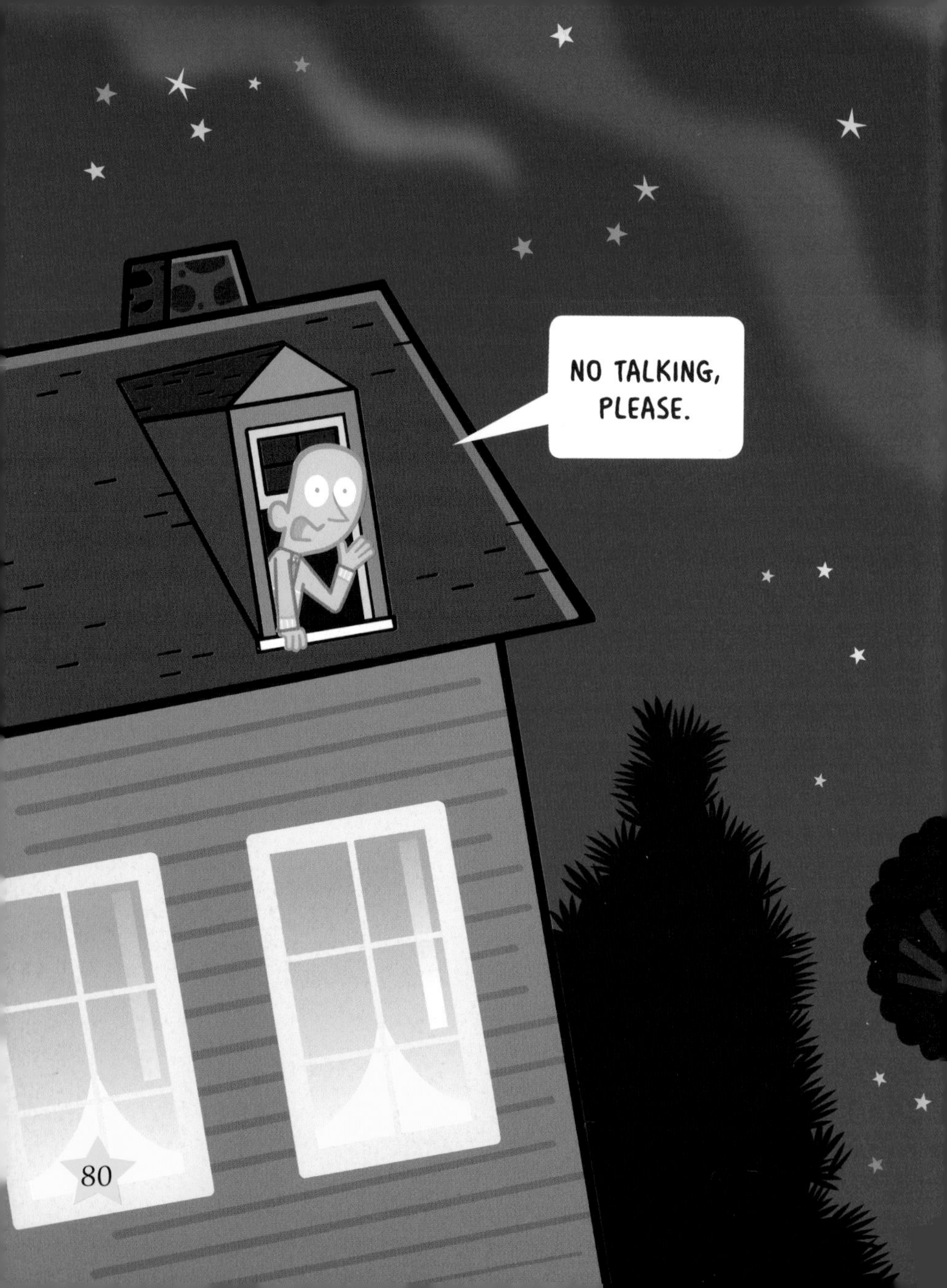
NO TALKING, PLEASE.

CHAPTER 9

The End

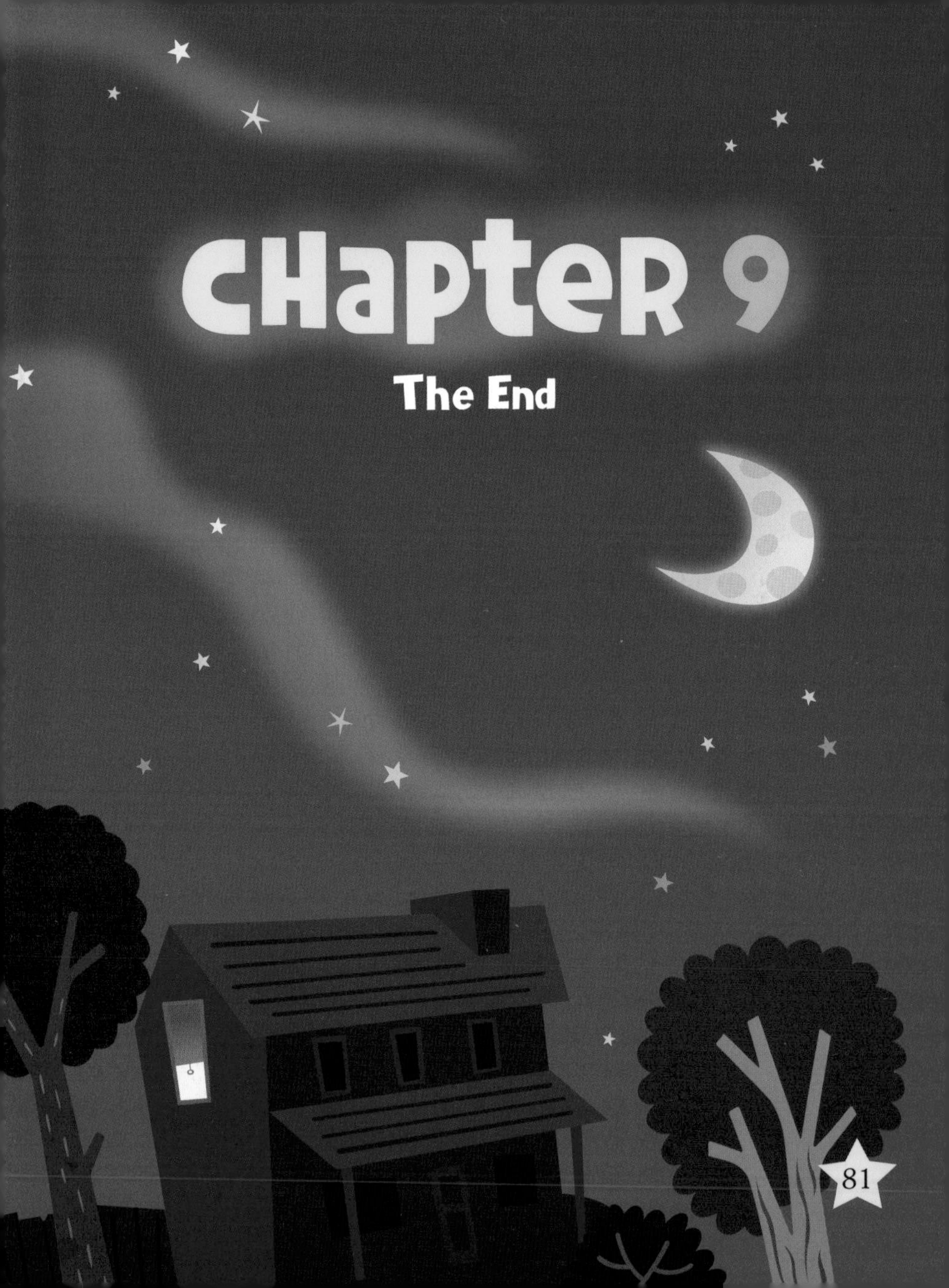

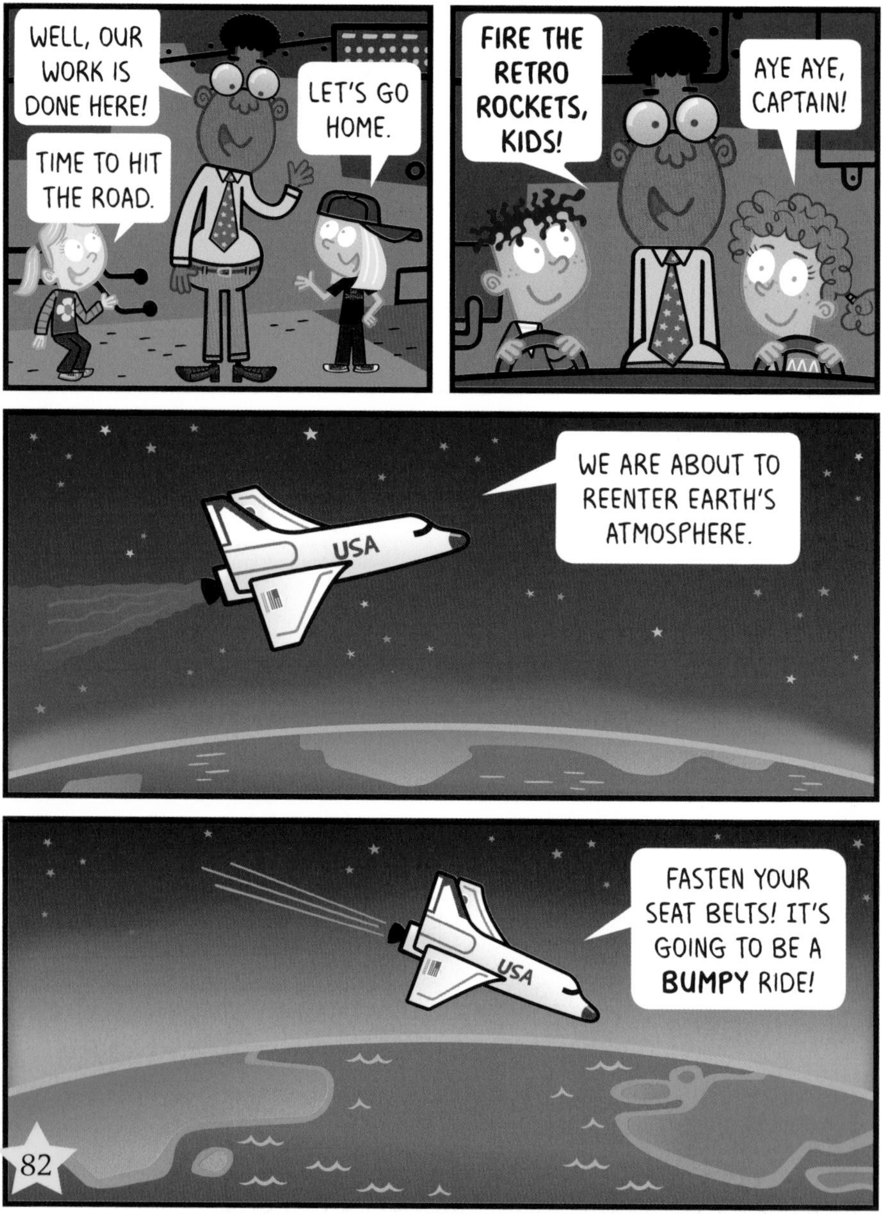
WELL, OUR WORK IS DONE HERE!
TIME TO HIT THE ROAD.
LET'S GO HOME.
FIRE THE RETRO ROCKETS, KIDS!
AYE AYE, CAPTAIN!
WE ARE ABOUT TO REENTER EARTH'S ATMOSPHERE.
USA
FASTEN YOUR SEAT BELTS! IT'S GOING TO BE A **BUMPY** RIDE!
USA

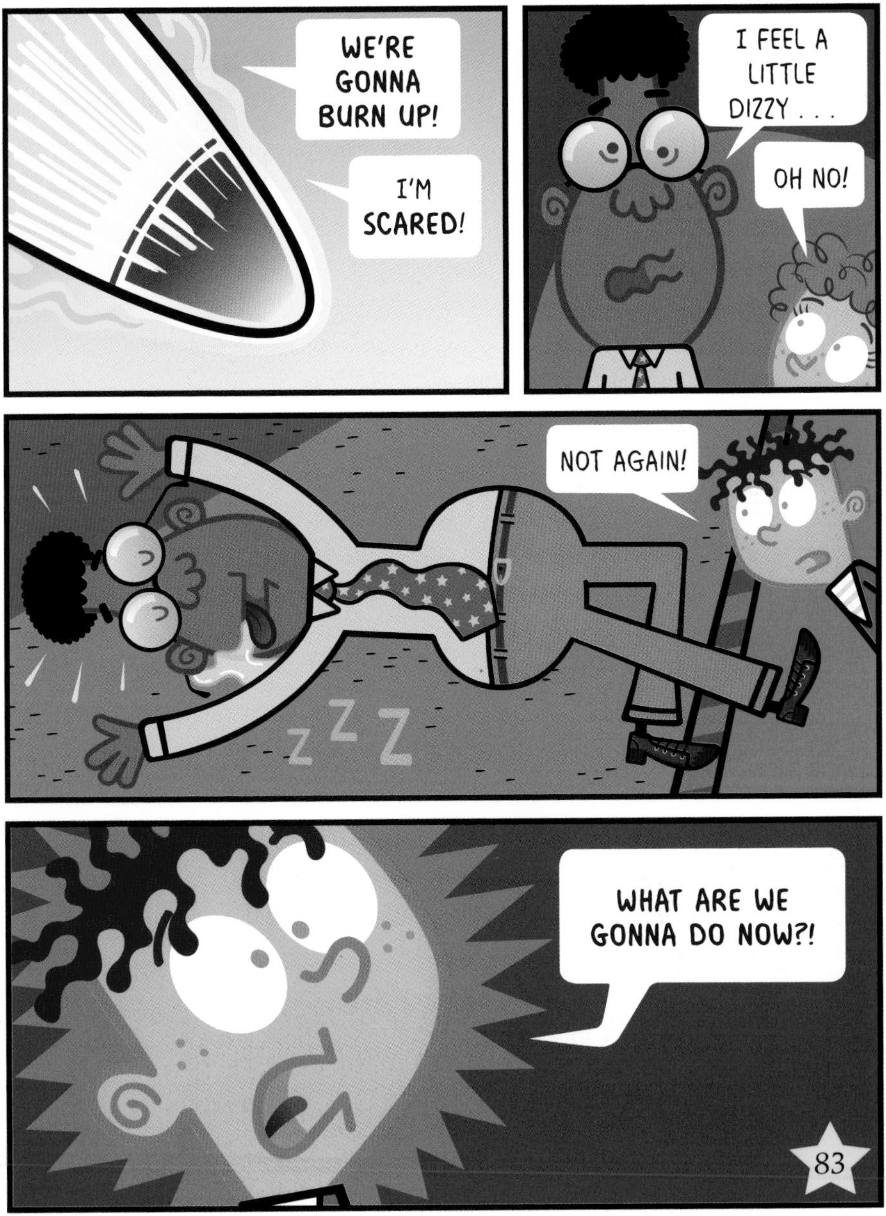
WE'RE GONNA BURN UP!
I'M SCARED!
I FEEL A LITTLE DIZZY . . .
OH NO!
NOT AGAIN!
zZZ
WHAT ARE WE GONNA DO NOW?!

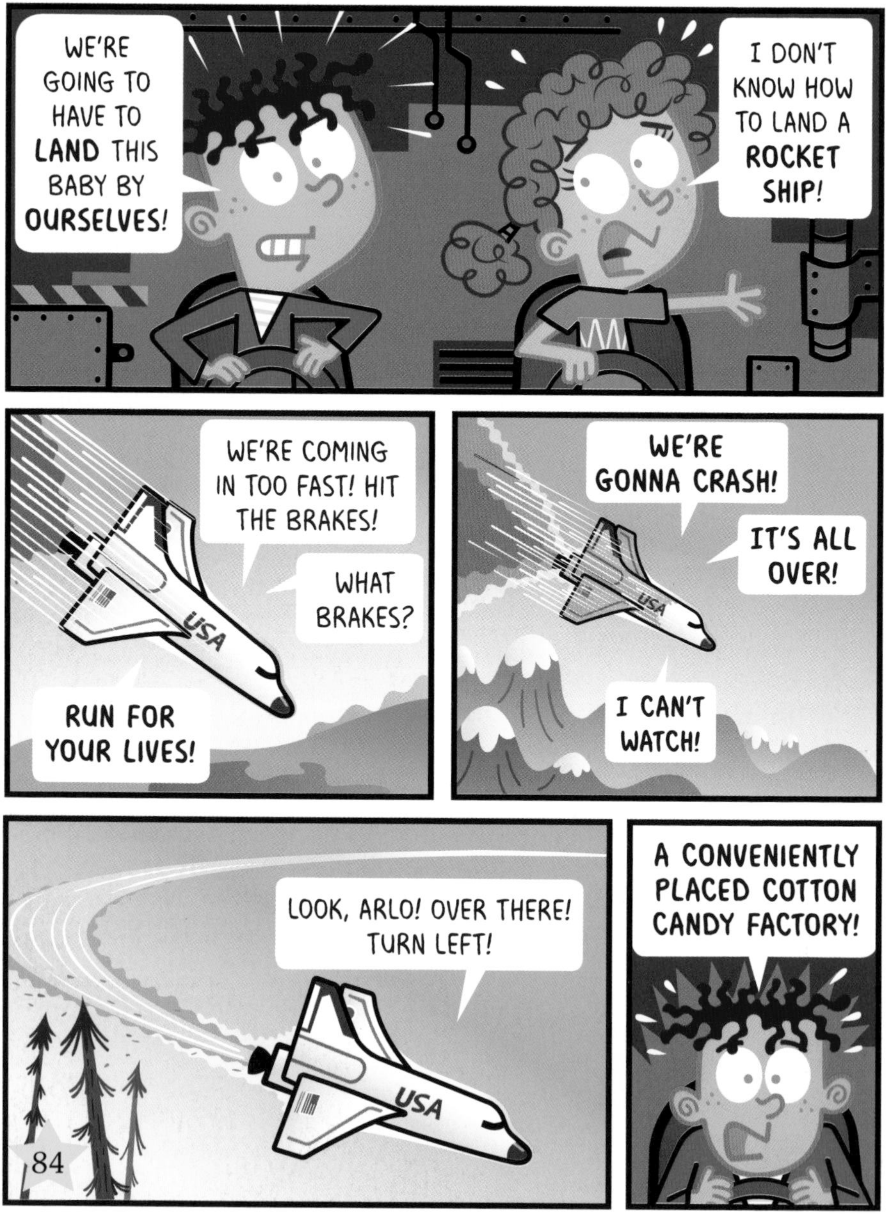
WE'RE GOING TO HAVE TO LAND THIS BABY BY OURSELVES!
I DON'T KNOW HOW TO LAND A ROCKET SHIP!
WE'RE COMING IN TOO FAST! HIT THE BRAKES!
WHAT BRAKES?
RUN FOR YOUR LIVES!
USA
WE'RE GONNA CRASH!
IT'S ALL OVER!
I CAN'T WATCH!
USA
LOOK, ARLO! OVER THERE! TURN LEFT!
USA
A CONVENIENTLY PLACED COTTON CANDY FACTORY!

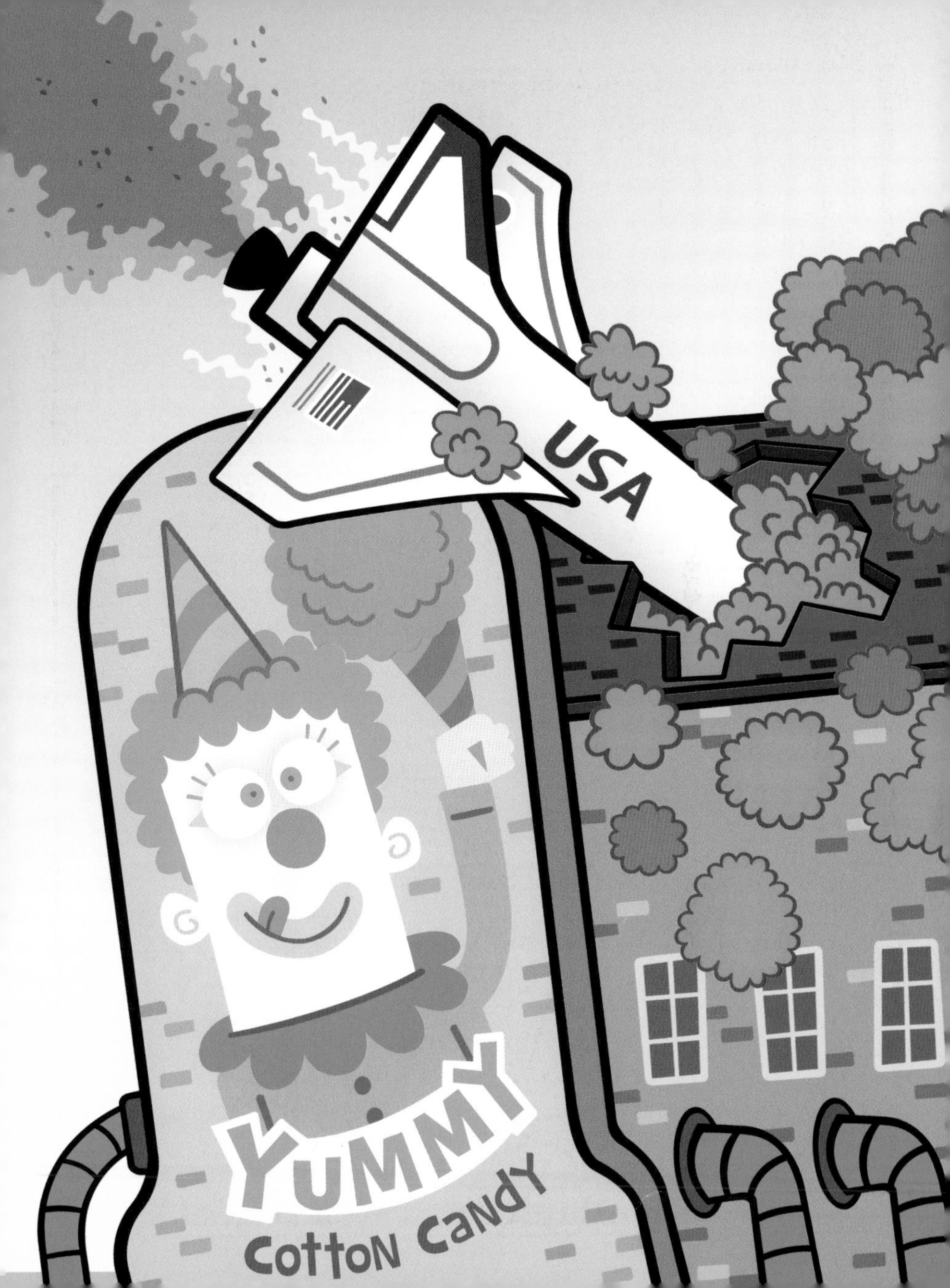
USA
YUMMY
Cotton Candy

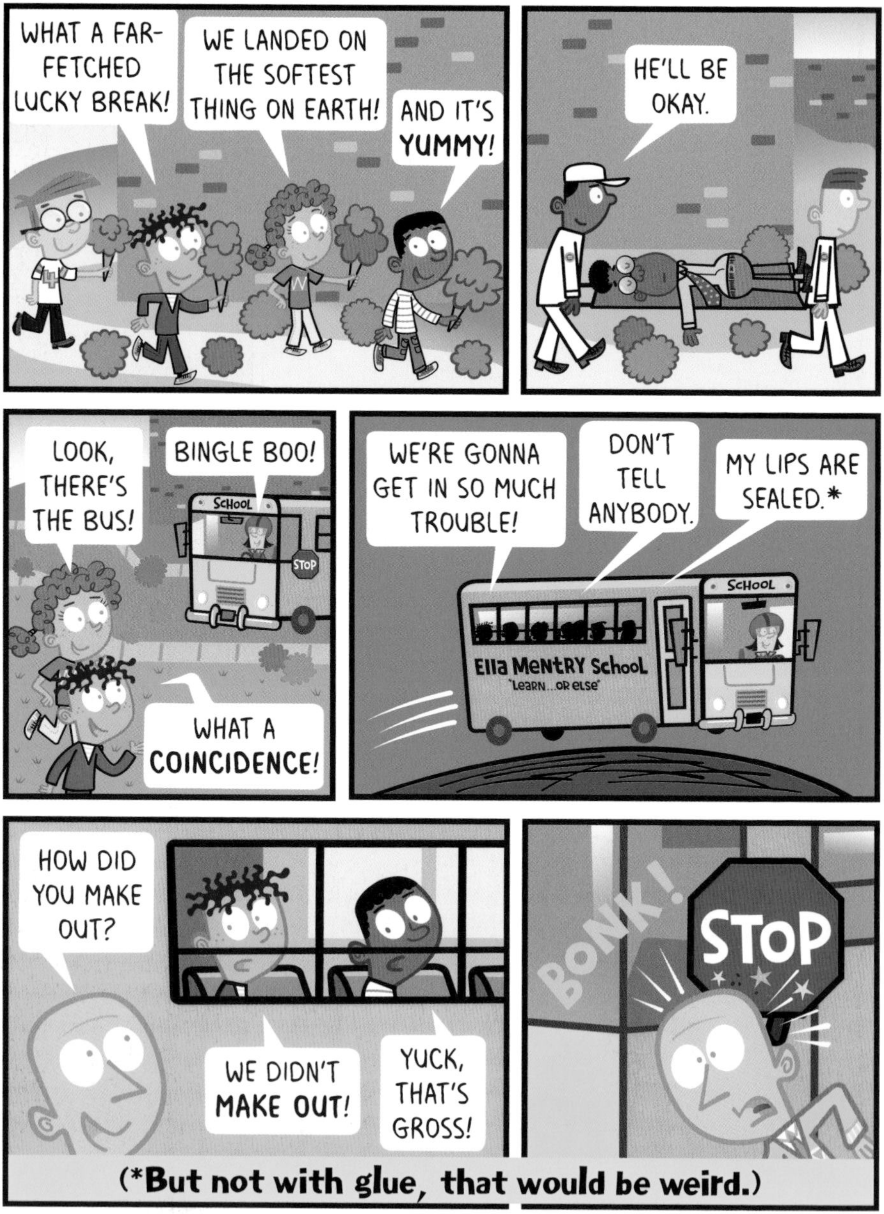
WHAT A FAR-FETCHED LUCKY BREAK!
WE LANDED ON THE SOFTEST THING ON EARTH!
AND IT'S YUMMY!
HE'LL BE OKAY.
LOOK, THERE'S THE BUS!
BINGLE BOO!
SCHOOL
STOP
WHAT A COINCIDENCE!
WE'RE GONNA GET IN SO MUCH TROUBLE!
DON'T TELL ANYBODY.
MY LIPS ARE SEALED.*
SCHOOL
Ella MentRY School
"Learn...or else"
HOW DID YOU MAKE OUT?
WE DIDN'T MAKE OUT!
YUCK, THAT'S GROSS!
BONK!
STOP
(*But not with glue, that would be weird.)

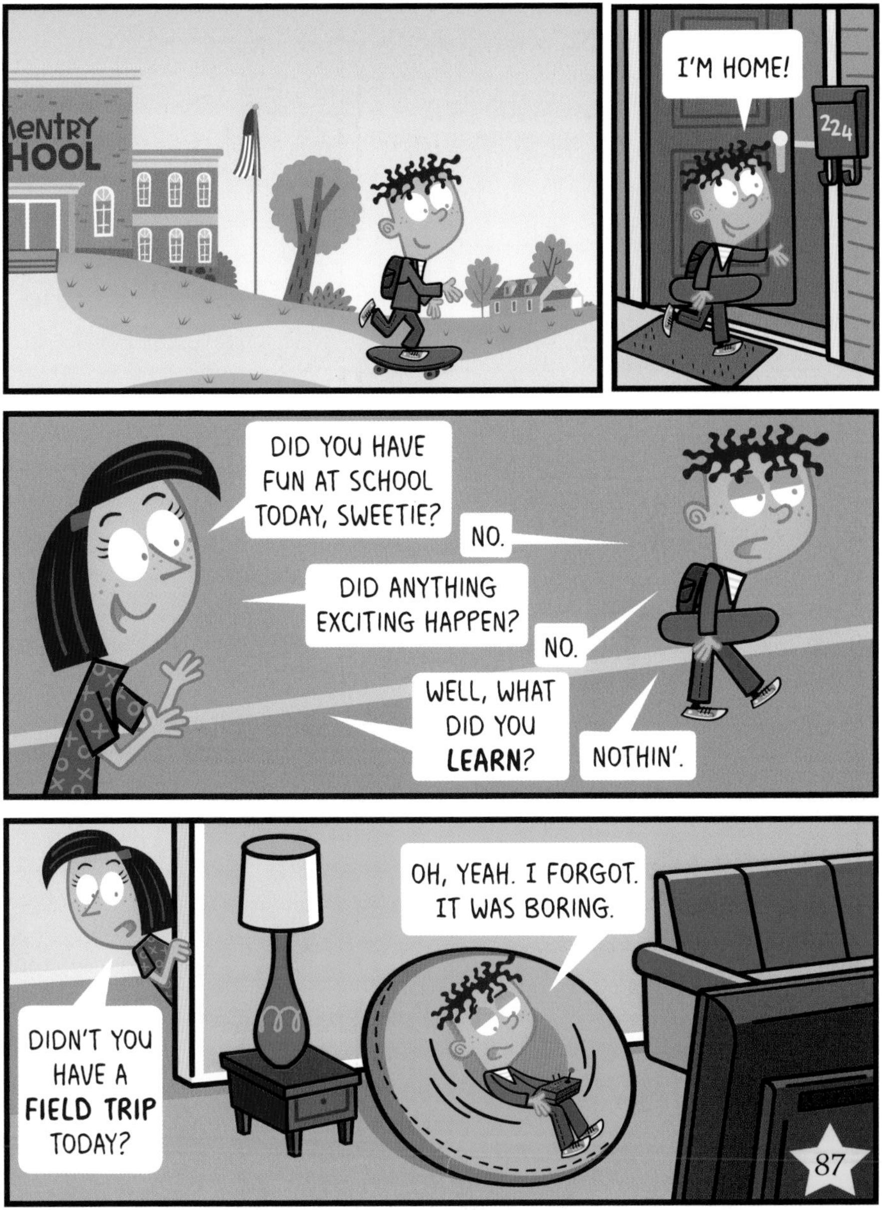

MENTRY
HOOL
I'M HOME!
224
DID YOU HAVE FUN AT SCHOOL TODAY, SWEETIE?
NO.
DID ANYTHING EXCITING HAPPEN?
NO.
WELL, WHAT DID YOU **LEARN**?
NOTHIN'.
DIDN'T YOU HAVE A **FIELD TRIP** TODAY?
OH, YEAH. I FORGOT. IT WAS BORING.

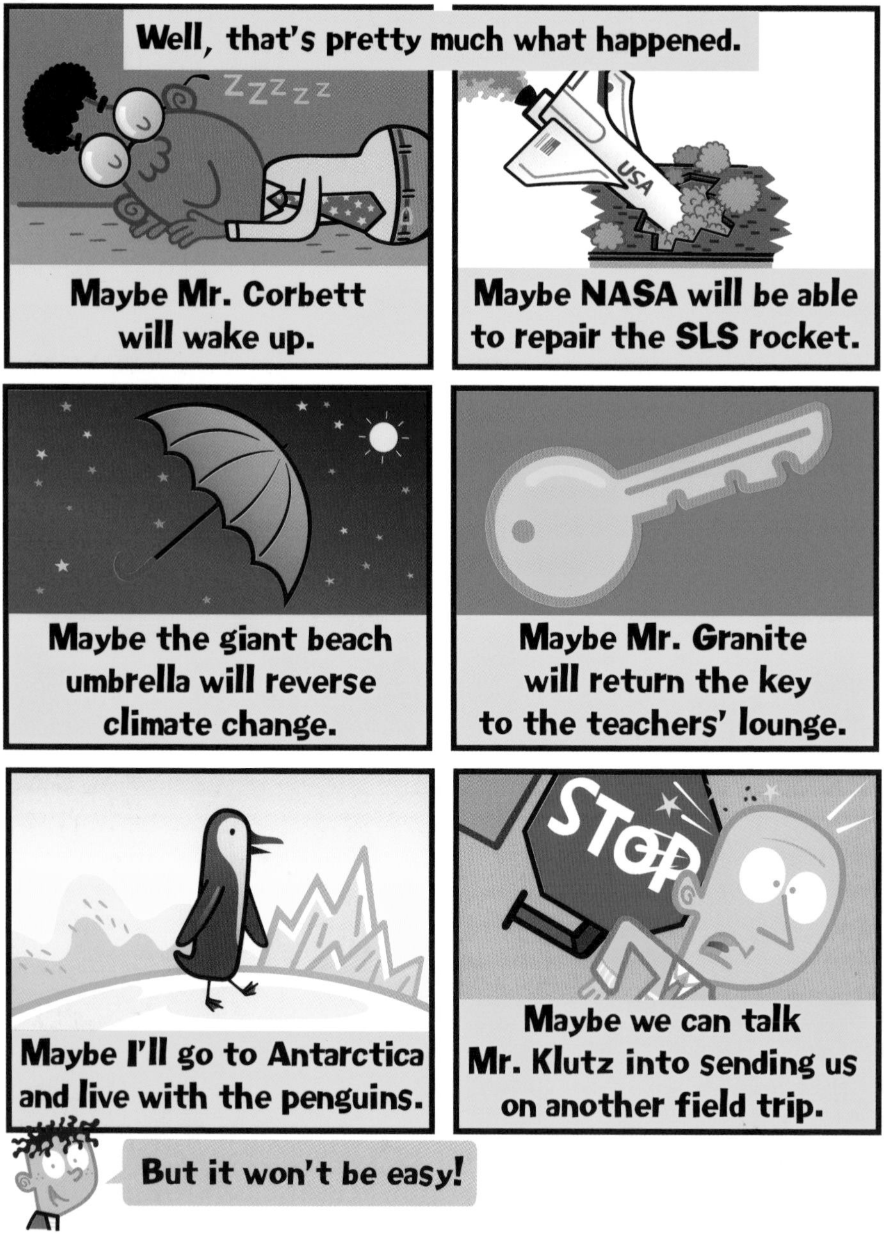
Well, that's pretty much what happened.
ZZZzzz
Maybe Mr. Corbett will wake up.
USA
Maybe NASA will be able to repair the SLS rocket.
Maybe the giant beach umbrella will reverse climate change.
Maybe Mr. Granite will return the key to the teachers' lounge.
Maybe I'll go to Antarctica and live with the penguins.
STOP
Maybe we can talk Mr. Klutz into sending us on another field trip.
But it won't be easy!

A NOTE FOR THE READER

IT'S EXTREMELY DOUBTFUL THAT ANYONE WILL DEPLOY A GIANT BEACH UMBRELLA IN OUTER SPACE, OR THAT THIS WOULD BE A SOLUTION TO CLIMATE CHANGE. IF YOU WANT TO HELP PROTECT THE PLANET, HERE ARE SOME REAL, PRACTICAL THINGS YOU CAN DO . . .

Educate Your Parents!

WHEN YOU WERE YOUNGER, YOUR PARENTS TAUGHT YOU HOW TO RIDE A BIKE, HOW TO TIE YOUR SHOES, AND HOW TO CATCH A BALL. NOW, IT'S UP TO **YOU** TO EDUCATE **THEM**. CONVINCE **THEM** TO VOTE FOR POLITICIANS WHO WILL PROTECT OUR ENVIRONMENT INSTEAD OF DESTROY IT. THIS IS NOT A REPUBLICAN OR DEMOCRATIC ISSUE. DOESN'T **EVERYONE** WANT TO LIVE IN A SAFE, CLEAN WORLD? FIND OUT WHICH CANDIDATES ARE ENDORSED BY ENVIRONMENTAL GROUPS SUCH AS THE SIERRA CLUB AND GREENPEACE. CONVINCE YOUR PARENTS TO SUPPORT THOSE CANDIDATES.

Contact Politicians!

REMIND THEM THAT **YOU** ARE THE FUTURE. TELL THEM HOW IMPORTANT IT IS TO PROTECT OUR PLANET. GET YOUR CLASS TO WRITE LETTERS. YOUR TEACHER CAN HELP YOU FIND THE ADDRESS OF YOUR LOCAL POLITICAL LEADERS.

GET YOUR SCHOOL INVOLVED!

FORM A CLUB OF KIDS WHO CARE ABOUT THE ENVIRONMENT.
START A PETITION. MAKE YOUR VOICE HEARD.

Get Started!
HERE ARE SOME WEBSITES WHERE YOU CAN GET MORE INFORMATION.

CLIMATE KIDS: CLIMATEKIDS.NASA.GOV/CLIMATE-CHANGE-MEANING

NATIONAL GEOGRAPHIC KIDS: WWW.NATGEOKIDS.COM/UK/DISCOVER
/GEOGRAPHY/GENERAL-GEOGRAPHY/WHAT-IS-CLIMATE-CHANGE

GREENPEACE: WWW.GREENPEACE.ORG/USA

SIERRA CLUB: WWW.SIERRACLUB.ORG/HOME

CENTER FOR CLIMATE CHANGE AND ENERGY SOLUTIONS:
WWW.C2ES.ORG/CONTENT/CLIMATE-BASICS-FOR-KIDS

NATURAL RESOURCES DEFENSE COUNCIL: WWW.NRDC.ORG

ENVIRONMENTAL DEFENSE FUND: WWW.EDF.ORG

EARTH DAY NETWORK: WWW.EARTHDAY.ORG